PRAISE FOR *THE NATURALIST*

"[A] smoothly written suspense novel from Thriller Award finalist Mayne . . . The action builds to [an] . . . exciting confrontation between Cray and his foe, and scientific detail lends verisimilitude."

—*Publishers Weekly*

"With a strong sense of place and palpable suspense that builds to a violent confrontation and resolution, Mayne's (*Angel Killer*) series debut will satisfy devotees of outdoors mysteries and intriguing characters."

—*Library Journal*

"*The Naturalist* is a suspenseful, tense, and wholly entertaining story . . . Compliments to Andrew Mayne for the brilliant first entry in a fascinating new series."

—*New York Journal of Books*

"An engrossing mix of science, speculation, and suspense, *The Naturalist* will suck you in."

—*Omnivoracious*

"A tour de force of a thriller."

—*Gumshoe Review*

MURDER THEORY

OTHER TITLES BY ANDREW MAYNE

Looking Glass
The Naturalist

JESSICA BLACKWOOD SERIES

Black Fall
Name of the Devil
Angel Killer

THE CHRONOLOGICAL MAN SERIES

The Monster in the Mist
The Martian Emperor
Station Breaker
Public Enemy Zero
Hollywood Pharaohs
Knight School
The Grendel's Shadow

NONFICTION

The Cure for Writer's Block
How to Write a Novella in 24 Hours

MURDER THEORY

ANDREW MAYNE

THOMAS & MERCER

Text copyright © 2019 by Andrew Mayne
All rights reserved.

Published by Thomas & Mercer, Seattle

www.apub.com

Amazon, the Amazon logo, and Thomas & Mercer are trademarks of Amazon.com, Inc., or its affiliates.

ISBN-13: 9781503904347
ISBN-10: 1503904342

Cover design by M. S. Corley

Printed in the United States of America

MURDER THEORY

PROLOGUE
#Fanboy

The helpless man in the wheelchair thrilled him. It wasn't a physical thrill or something he'd describe as deviant but the fact that it was *this* man who was unconscious and at his mercy that excited him.

He pushed the chair to the edge of the concrete patio and turned the man toward him, then sat on the bench. What thoughts, he wondered, were streaming through the man's unconscious mind at this moment? He had a thousand questions for him, the mystery of human consciousness only one of them. He was even more fascinated by what made this man's own thinking so unique.

And it was *unique.* He gazed at the stars overhead. Sirius stood out, a glimmering spark among a million suns that didn't shine nearly so bright because they were farther away. He scanned the sky until he found a distant, fuzzy cluster that was actually a galaxy. Yes. This man was like a luminous object from beyond—that's how special his mind was.

If only there were time to talk to him, time to interact with that intellect and see how he measured up.

At that moment, he felt sad. For he had seen how they'd measured up. This man had been clever, too clever by far, yet here he was, unconscious, utterly defenseless.

The left carotid artery stood out in the moonlight as his head lay slumped to the side, exposing the vulnerable blood vessel. It almost seemed like an accident of evolution to put such a fragile weak spot right there.

He could take the scalpel from his pocket and end the man's life in seconds, watch him bleed out, drifting further and further into his unconscious until he was gone.

It would be a painless way to die. In a sense, the man was already dead. The sentient part that asked questions, made conclusions, and took actions wasn't really there at this moment. One slice of an artery and it would never return.

He removed the scalpel and slid the plastic sheath off the end. As a test of his own will, he pressed the point to the curve of the artery—not enough pressure to puncture the skin, just enough to crater the flesh.

Yes. He could do it. It'd take only a pound or two of pressure—less than a firm handshake the two men might have exchanged. In one moment the diamond-shaped blade could slide into the skin, through the epidermis, and slice the carotid, severing it in two.

All that blood being pumped by the heart to sustain the brain—*that* brain—would gush out. It'd leave a terrible mess. Nothing short of arson would hide all of the man's DNA if they ever came looking for him.

But that didn't matter. If they came . . . when they came, it would be too late. Not just for this man. But for all of them.

Plans were already in motion. The deed had been done.

Finding this man was merely an unexpected twist. A delightful end to a . . . he'd never decided precisely what to call it. Although he was certain they'd have a name for it. They could put a name on any tragedy. They could put a face on it, too.

How long before they put his face on it?

He didn't expect them to take forever to find him, but he also assumed that something so peculiar as this could take longer than he expected.

When this man had shown up, he'd thought for a moment that they'd discovered him sooner. But no. *Only* this man showed up. His reasoning had made leaps where others had merely crawled. And that had led him here. Alone. Putting him in his current vulnerable position.

The man capped the scalpel and placed it back in his pocket. He removed the pistol from his waistband. It was an ugly weapon he'd used only a few times. It was as far removed from his preferred method of killing as he could imagine.

He cradled the gun in his hands like a prayer book, contemplated it for a moment, then looked back up at the man in the wheelchair as he began to stir.

He'd be alert soon. They say you should never meet your heroes. Killing them only makes things more awkward.

CHAPTER ONE
The Polonium Gambit

I'm in a basement below the United States embassy in Moscow, sitting across from an outwardly nervous man. His name is Constantine Konovalov. He's already been questioned by embassy officials and CIA operatives, but that's routine for foreign employees of a US embassy. I'm a mystery to him, and his eyes keep darting to the large black aluminum case sitting on the table in front of me. He knows the Americans would never use torture on a Russian citizen in a situation like this. Or rather, that's what he's been told by his Russian handlers, who prepared him for this job and routinely debrief him.

The United States has more than twelve hundred employees in the Russian embassy and related properties. The majority of them are Russian citizens. Hiring this many locals is a practical necessity and a security nightmare.

Konovalov is a spy. Technically, all the Russians working in the embassy are. While they may not be Russian Federal Security Service employees or professional intelligence gatherers, they're regularly grilled for information.

We do the same to US citizens working for the Russians in our country. The difference is that I've been brought in to find out if Konovalov is a killer.

Six days ago, another Russian, Timothy Artemiev, spoke to embassy officials about the possibility of defecting. Artemiev ran a small software firm whose primary contract was with the Russian government. He built bots for hacking other computer networks. After the third time Russian authorities turned down travel permission for him to go to a conference in another country, he realized they were never going to let him leave. He was too valuable.

Artemiev died four days ago while hiding out in one of our safe houses outside Moscow. He was poisoned with radioactive material, either thorium or polonium.

Intelligence officials have narrowed down the potential suspects to two dozen people. We've been holding them for several hours. In another two hours, we're going to have to let them go or risk a diplomatic crisis.

Catching the killer also means finding out who inside the embassy leaked Artemiev's location. We can put pressure on the person we think did it, but fingering the wrong individual will surely backfire.

I'm not an interrogator. I'm not even a spy. I'm a scientist. Specifically, I'm a computational biologist who uses computers to model living systems. I was asked to come here because of my so-called unorthodox methods.

"Mr. Konovalov, I'm going to need you to provide some samples," I tell him as I open the latches of the case.

"Are you a doctor?" he asks in mildly accented English.

"Just a technician." I remove some vials and swabs. "It'll only take a moment." I slide on a pair of thin gloves and get up from the table and walk around to him.

Konovalov is nervous but doesn't protest as I take an earwax sample. He's oblivious to the hair sample I collect as my hand braces his head.

"There we go," I say, returning to my seat. "Just spit in that vial and we're done."

He obliges, more confused than concerned. If he's our man, then he knows that none of the samples I collected will show traces of contact with polonium or thorium.

I'm actually performing a more indirect test. Three of them, in fact. The people in the other room watching on closed-circuit television are monitoring every single step of the process.

Right now, a thermal-imaging system is measuring his internal body heat. Another system, built into the table, is using millimeter radar to look for skin responses.

I take a swab of his saliva, put it into a vial, and give it a shake.

"Are you seeing if I'm part monkey?" he asks, making a joke.

"No, Mr. Konovalov. I'm just testing for iodine."

Iodine pills can help with some of the symptoms of radioactive exposure. People who know they'll be handling radioactive materials sometimes take the pills prophylactically in hopes of limiting their risk.

The vial turns blue, and I make a note of this, doing my best to ignore Konovalov's reaction. I think I catch a flicker in his eyes, but he's too well trained to react openly.

I put the vial away. "Thank you, Mr. Konovalov."

He starts to get up, but I stop him before he reaches the door. "One more thing."

Konovalov's hand is on the doorknob. Something is running through his head. If he's our guy, then right now he's trying to decide if he should make a run for it.

I pick the vial up. It's now bright red. "Could you sit down again?"

Our hit man is not going to fall for a bluff he knows isn't technically accurate. I have to be very careful.

I reach into the briefcase and pull out a pair of black gloves with a silver sheen to them.

Konovalov's eyes narrow.

Interesting.

These are radiation gloves lined with lead to limit exposure. They're actually Russian ones I purchased for this exact purpose.

I take out a small box from my case and set it on the table. There's a broken seal across the top that reads *Oak Ridge National Laboratory*.

"I just need to get a skin scraping," I explain as I remove a tiny needle.

Konovalov's face goes pale. This isn't needle response—this is a fear of death.

Whoever killed Artemiev used something similar and would know that Oak Ridge National Laboratory is where the United States government produces its own nuclear materials.

I stand and walk around the table to him again.

Konovalov shouts, "*Nyet!* This is bullshit!"

I keep a careful distance. Konovalov is probably our guy and more than likely an expert in hand-to-hand combat.

The door bursts open, and two marines enter, followed by Charles Kaman, head of embassy security.

"Constantine, why don't we talk in my office?" Kaman suggests in a conversational manner.

Konovalov is escorted out of the room and to some other place where he'll presumably be grilled, threatened, and then bribed.

I toss the vial into the garbage can and gather the props. Reed Stanworth, who I assume works directly for the CIA section chief, walks into the room and sits in Konovalov's seat.

"Great show, man. Great show."

Reed is a secret embed at the embassy who officially runs their social-media team. He spent two years at Snapchat and projects a Southern California bro vibe. I suspect all of it is an act.

"We'll see," I reply.

"Good to let the others go?"

I flip through a folder and stop on a name. "You should talk to Isolde Ershova, too," I reply. "She also had a strong response."

Reed shakes his head. "The redhead? She's clean. She lost her father in the *Kursk* submarine mishap and has no love for the politicians. In fact, out of everyone, she's the least likely candidate for a spy."

"Don't you think that makes her the most suspicious of all?"

He gives me a dismissive headshake. "That's not really how it works. We have profiles we look for. Things we check."

"Sure. Don't you think the Russians know that, too? If I was trying to sneak operatives in here, and not just informants, I'd send in people who fit the profile of least suspicious. I'd also want to know who the person who did the actual hiring thought was the most attractive."

Reed's carefree manner fades away, and his eyes narrow like Konovalov's. He glances down and realizes he's sitting in the hot seat— the chair they use to measure emotional responses.

Reed isn't a double agent, at least as far as I know. He's sloppy, which is just as bad. His carelessness is what led to the hiring of Konovalov and Ershova, which ultimately led to the death of a man we could have used in this post–Cold War conflict.

The door opens, and Charles Kaman enters for a second time. "Reed, I think we should talk."

Reed glares at me. "Who the fuck *are* you?"

"Just a scientist."

At least that's what I tell myself.

CHAPTER TWO

ARRIVAL

I step off the plane in Atlanta and head to the center of the terminal, trying to will my body into accepting this new time zone. It's never the traveling that gets me; it's adjusting afterward.

While away, I did my best to keep the lab in Austin going but leaned heavily on Sheila, the office manager, to provide parental supervision.

I spoke to her on the plane trip back and got the latest updates. Our lab is in the middle of a biome research project that will hopefully make it easier to track where somebody—*cough, terrorists*—has been by looking at their gut bacteria.

The only looming concern I have about the project is that our current patron, General Figueroa, a well-meaning but intense man, is pushing for me to deliver a technology that can determine "terrorist genes."

While I have noticed at least one such correlation between terrorists, it's about as conclusive as realizing that professional quarterbacks share some genetics. Far more people have those genes and don't play professional football . . . or blow up city markets.

In my nightmare scenario, my technology is used as an excuse to round up Middle Eastern men on the sole basis that they have a "suspicious" genetic profile.

"Tell Figueroa we're still doing feasibility studies," I told Sheila.

"Actually, I think Todd's handling it," she replied.

My lab manager handling it made me nervous, even though Todd Pogue knows my thoughts on the issue. The last thing we need is another harebrained scheme that uses science to kill instead of save lives.

In a staff meeting, I once belittled a research paper we'd received that proposed using aerial DNA scanners on drones to make sure that the incinerated people were actually the ones that had been targeted.

"And I guess these geniuses plan on using the DNA to bring back the person if they got it wrong?"

That caused nervous laughter from a few of my lab techs. When I scanned the list of researchers who'd written the paper, I realized that it included Dr. T. Pogue—my lab manager.

The only other news from Sheila was that the FBI was trying to get ahold of me. This was nothing new. I only treat such requests urgently if the word *subpoena* is mentioned.

"Hey, stranger," says a familiar voice as I enter the Ecco restaurant in the Atlanta airport. Sitting at a table in front of me is Jillian, my long-suffering girlfriend, the woman who literally saved my life.

We arranged this little rendezvous the moment I left the Moscow embassy. She'd been planning a trip to visit her late husband's parents in Montana when the embassy thing came up and I had to fly out in the dead of night.

Jillian is used to this kind of scheduling interference by now, and we do our best to accommodate it. I spend most of my time in my government-backed lab in Austin, but even that can be a twenty-four-hour job. To lighten the load, I hired Todd Pogue as lab manager—or rather, I was given him by the Pentagon—but he has turned out to be more of a clock puncher, and it feels like I spend more time settling disputes between him and others than actually doing research.

And I'm supposed to be the difficult one who needs managing . . .

I take a seat and have a sip of her wine. She reaches a hand across the table and caresses the back of mine. It's these moments that keep me grounded.

Jillian understands more than I ever will. She's a former soldier, a widow, and a survivor of a horrifying ordeal, in which one of the most notorious serial killers in history tried to kill her in order to lure me into a trap.

When other couples start to tell boring vacation stories, Jillian loves to say, "Theo, remember the time we were almost murdered by the Grizzly Killer?"

We both share a dark sense of humor. She's also learned to deal with what she calls "RoboTheo," her name for me when I go into analytical mode and miss obvious social cues.

I'm told I can be *almost* charming when I'm around her. "So, did things work out?" she asks.

"Affirmative." She knows that's all I can say on the matter. "You?"

"Pretty well. Things are going well at the Crust. We're hiring some college kids, and I think I've got another baker." She reaches into her bag and pulls out a small cardboard box. "Try this . . . but be warned, if you say 'diet,' I'll stab you to death with a butter knife."

The Crust is the bakery she just started. While I never expected it to break even, she's actually been turning a tidy little profit. Sometimes I fantasize about quitting the lab and working as her taste tester.

I remove a dark cupcake from the box. Reddish-brown frosting is generously piled on top. One bite later I'm grinning.

"Cinnamon, chocolate, and is that a little peppermint oil?"

"Yes. And it's Mexican chocolate," she replies.

"Another winner."

"I kept bringing cupcakes by the lab while you were away."

"Good girl. That'll make them hate me less."

"They don't hate you. Well, maybe Todd does. But Sheila is in love with you. She'd better watch it."

Although she's in her late forties, Sheila looks much younger and is in great shape. Most of the guys in the lab have a secret crush on her. Probably Todd the most.

I suspect that Jillian doesn't just drop by to bring baked goods, but to remind Sheila that my army-trained killer girlfriend is around and watching.

A waitress takes our order, and I let out a yawn. I try not to do the math of when I slept last.

I spent the flight to Moscow on a State Department jet, trying to come up with some kind of scheme to help the embassy lure out the spy. They were hoping for breakthrough science. The best I could do was offer up the iodine test and the earwax sample. The latter actually can tell us if someone has been in a faraway city during the last several days. We found a way to compare the pollution in earwax from different cities. The technology works particularly well in China. Next time you're in a foreign city and spot some free Q-tips in the bathroom, be warned: it might be an intelligence-gathering plot. While it's not as telling as certain other forms of tradecraft, the Q-Test, as we call it, can tell you if someone was lying when they said they were in Shanghai when the Q-tip says Beijing.

It's a marginally useful trick. My life these days seems to be about coming up with such gimmicks rather than more groundbreaking technologies.

"Is that man watching you?" Jillian says between bites of her salmon.

"Yep," I reply when I spot the clean-cut young man in a suit watching me from over by the host stand.

"I think he's trying to decide whether to come and talk to you."

Despite my best efforts not to be noticed, I developed a bit of a public reputation after I caught the Grizzly Killer. While I avoid interviews on the subject, I speak to law-enforcement agencies now and then, and crime documentaries on TV keep showing my face.

Jillian is watching him and not trying to hide her suspicion. This is her looking out for me. When you're a semifamous serial-killer hunter, you don't exactly have the most stable fan base.

"He's harmless," I explain while not looking in his direction.

"How do you figure?"

"Looks federal. Local. He might have been someone I spoke to here."

Jillian ponders the implication of the word *here*. That was the last case, the last killer.

"Dr. Cray?" the man calls out to me.

"Here we go," I tell Jillian and wave the man over.

He invites himself to a seat. "I'm Sean Nicolson. Special Agent Sean Nicolson. Atlanta FBI. You can call me Sean."

"Sean, this is Jillian."

"Ma'am. It's a pleasure to meet you. I know all about your involvement in the Vik case. You're quite brave."

Hopefully he doesn't know everything. Jillian is the one who actually killed Joe Vik. I took the fall because I knew the killer had a lot of friends in law enforcement in that part of Montana, and we didn't know what the repercussions might be for Jillian and her family.

"What can we do for you?" Jillian asks a little too curtly.

"I'm real sorry to interrupt, Dr. Cray. But I heard you'd be coming through here, and I was hoping to catch you."

"Theo. Just call me Theo. Catch me? I hope you don't mean in a legal sense."

"Oh, no, sir. I have questions about a case."

Jillian and I exchange looks. We were both afraid this was going to happen. I get a lot of calls about cases. People expect me to do some kind of science mumbo jumbo and solve what could have been uncovered with old-fashioned detective work. It didn't take a genius to find Joe Vik. The problem was the law-enforcement system there was broken and everyone was looking the other way.

I shrug. "I'm not really that useful in handling cases. I'm just a lab guy. I'm sure you're doing the best work possible. If you're looking for outside scientific opinion, I can refer you to the Computational Forensics Group at Bozeman. They're actually up to speed on my methods and have improved them considerably. I refer all new cases there."

"This isn't a new case, Dr. Cray. I'm talking about the Toy Man murders."

Jillian's hand slides across the table to touch mine. Her fingers are as cold as my own.

"The Toy Man?" I shrug again. "Oyo's dead, and I've already given my testimony." Testimony that I gave very carefully, because I was the one who killed him.

"Yes. I know. I'm talking about the new murders."

CHAPTER THREE

INCIDENT

"Did they find a new location where Oyo buried bodies?" I ask. In addition to Los Angeles and Atlanta, I strongly suspected that he had a third killing ground in the Northeast.

"No," Nicolson replies. "I'm talking about here in Atlanta. Haven't you seen the news?"

"No. I've been a little out of reach. Are you saying new murders? Like people killed after Oyo died?"

"Yes, but let me be clear: these aren't murders we think *he* did." Nicolson makes a nervous laugh. "That would be really weird. These happened at Oyo's property outside Atlanta. Where you tracked him to."

"The garden and church camp?"

He nods. "Right. We had a team of forensic techs doing an excavation there after we found a possible earlier layer of bodies."

"More children." Jillian sighs.

These things weigh on her as much as they do on me. I've shared with her some of what I feel when I wake up in the dead of night.

"So we're talking about older murders?"

Nicolson shakes his head. "Two of our techs were just killed, and another one's missing."

"Murdered? How?" I ask.

"One was stabbed to death. The other was struck on the side of the head repeatedly."

Nicolson is earnest and seems genuinely troubled by the incident. These were probably people he knew—maybe not socially, but they were faces familiar to him. This has to hit especially hard.

"And the third technician?"

"Daniel Marcus. We're afraid that he may have been abducted. Some of the blood at the crime scene belonged to him."

"Abducted?" I want to point out that in a case like this, the missing person is almost always the perpetrator. I'm not sure if Agent Nicolson is leaving something out or having a difficult time accepting the idea that the third person's the most likely suspect.

"That's the prevailing theory at the moment. Marcus didn't have a history of violence or any red flags, if that's what you're wondering. He's a real good guy."

"This is tragic, but why are you reaching out to me? Your forensics people are more than capable of dealing with something like this."

His eyes dart around the restaurant, then land on Jillian. "Could we talk somewhere else? Maybe at the FBI office?"

I have to be terse. "I'm getting on a plane in forty minutes. I'd like to spend that time with my girlfriend before she goes away for a week. If there's something you need to share with me, then now is the time."

"All right, but please, please keep this confidential. We've had other violent incidents relating to employees working that scene. One agent's wife is in a coma from a severe beating and there's no suspect."

"And you think these things are connected?"

"They all worked the Toy Man site when we uncovered the lower layer of bodies. About the same time when unusual things started showing up."

"Unusual things?" I ask.

"Clay figures, animal bones, other artifacts our cultural-studies people associate with black magic."

"Oyo practiced rituals. That's not unusual. I'd expect you'd find objects like that."

"Yes, but some of these have been left around the crime scene recently."

"Again, that should be no surprise. Famous crime scenes get all kinds of weird visitors."

"True, but FBI employees don't usually start getting killed like the people who uncovered King Tut's tomb."

"That's a myth. Statistically they lived as long as anyone else in that time period." I feel Jillian squeeze my hand. "But I understand where you're coming from. People are spooked."

"Exactly. And right now, I don't know if we're on our best mental footing to look into this. We already have agents from DC here, which hasn't gone over very well."

"What would you like me to do?"

"I'd like you to give us your perspective on things. Maybe there's something else about the case you're aware of that we're not. Right now, we're trying to find Marcus. That's the most important thing at the moment. If he's still alive . . ."

Nicolson has a decent poker face. There's a lot more going on behind his eyes than he's letting on. I can't tell if it's because he thinks Marcus is a suspect or because he has an entirely different theory that he hasn't shared.

I wanted to put the Toy Man in the past. So many aspects of the case were unsettling. His victims were primarily young African American boys with unusual features. He targeted kids in foster homes who were at risk. This made it hard even for locals to realize there was a serial killer on the loose.

He killed for years in South Central Los Angeles and Atlanta while working as a reverend. He even ran a church camp next to his killing room here.

The night I found him, he was about to kill another boy, but Oyo got away and almost managed to leave the country. He murdered two people and hid in their home while their children were tied up in the bathroom.

I shot him through a plate-glass window. I told the police he was reaching for his gun.

He wasn't. I wasn't going to give him the chance. I outright killed him.

Which, in a way, means I'm not all that different from Constantine Konovalov. He killed for the state because they told him that Artemiev was a threat to their security.

Someone who doesn't know me might think I killed Oyo in an act of blind rage over what he'd done. Actually, I killed him in a moment of serene calm. It was what had to be done. I made a calculated decision and pulled the trigger. The risk of him getting away or slipping through the system was too great.

I don't know what's going on in Atlanta, but Nicolson has lured me in. Oyo worked with an accomplice before. That man died in custody overseas. The thought that he or someone else could still be out there getting revenge chills my bones.

From the way Jillian is looking at me, I can tell she's probably thinking what I'm thinking: if this is related to Oyo, then I'm a target as well.

Nicolson knows this but hasn't said anything. There's another agenda there. But I have no idea what that is.

The smart thing to do is to walk away.

Unfortunately, my curiosity doesn't always lead me to do the smart thing.

"Agent Nicolson, would you mind giving Theo and me a few moments?" asks Jillian.

"Of course. I'm sure you two need to discuss this." He gets up and leaves the table.

We don't need to discuss this. Jillian knows what's on my mind. She holds my hands between hers and gives me a lopsided smile. "Poor Theo. They just won't leave you alone."

"Poor Jillian. Stuck with the maddest professor of them all."

"I don't know that I'm *stuck* . . ." She gives me a playful wink.

I'm not the same man who went into the woods to find Joe Vik. The experience changed me. I became something different.

What disturbed me the most when I looked at Joe Vik's DNA, trying to find out what makes a killer, was that we shared more traits than I cared to realize.

I have the need to hunt as well.

CHAPTER FOUR
THE EDGE

I pull up in my rental car across from Oyo's property and the adjacent church camp on the outskirts of Atlanta. An involuntary shiver goes down my back as the animal part of my brain recognizes where I am.

A metal fence wraps around the perimeter of Oyo's lot. No-trespassing signs and police tape cover the gate, warning citizens away. But that hasn't stopped people from leaving flowers and pictures of the victims. Overhead, moonlight casts a bluish halo on the trees and overgrown shrubbery that were once part of the nursery that was there before Oyo bought the land. While it was connected physically to the church camp he operated next door, he'd cleverly hidden the ownership so that the two places were never legally connected.

The wealthy donors who helped him purchase the land were his last victims. It chills me to think that he bought the church camp because it was located next to the overgrown garden and shed where he could conduct his murders in secrecy.

Disadvantaged children getting their first summer camp experience slept no more than a hundred yards away from the room where Oyo molested and terrorized his young victims before killing them in the most savage ways imaginable.

The man the world has come to know as the Toy Man has haunted me in a way that Joe Vik never did. Vik was a powerful force of nature. I'm convinced that he was born to kill. His actions were his own and he went to great efforts to conceal them, but he never tried to stop himself. On the night he attempted to kill me, he also murdered his entire family—mere props to be thrown aside when no longer needed.

Oyo also had a compulsion to kill—and consume—his victims. But his murders were wrapped in religious rites based upon a hybrid mix of West and East African beliefs and Christianity. There are hundreds of shamans who have committed similar acts. In parts of Africa even today, "witch children," boys and girls born with albinism or other uncommon features, are treated as outcasts and killed for their supposed magical powers.

When I mention this to colleagues, they demonstrate the appropriate amount of horror at such barbarism. Then I ask them how many people they know who crack jokes about the disabled or mentally handicapped.

To be sure, it's one thing to murder a child for having different genes and another to make a joke at the expense of someone who is dealing with a handicap, but they're both acts of cruelty and dehumanization. While legal lines sharply define what can and cannot be done, our personal sense of right and wrong doesn't necessarily hew so closely to them.

I killed Oyo. If I'd been brought to trial, some courts might have decided that I committed murder. That doesn't weigh heavily on me. I believe I made the morally correct choice.

But so did Oyo.

I think he believed he was morally correct when he killed those children. While he may have gained personal enjoyment from the murders, they followed the same ritualistic patterns of certain sanctioned forms of killing. Does it matter that the executioner likes his job?

I had a philosophy teacher who gave me one of the greatest gifts I've ever received. It was a mental toolbox. While the concept wasn't uniquely his, the way he used it stayed with me, and it still shapes how I think about things today.

Professor Rickman—Rick, as we called him—asked us to imagine a toolbox and inside it pairs of glasses that affect what you see and what you think. With each one comes a certain knowledge set.

It was his way of putting Theory of Mind to practical use—understanding how others see the world. There are glasses for trying to understand minority points of view, glasses for thinking like a Neolithic caveman, a Bronze Age farmer, and so on. Each one helps us understand that our points of view are shaped by what we see, what we've been told, and, lastly, how we process it all.

My favorite pair is the alien spectacles. These are the ones you wear when you want to see things from the point of view of someone from a different planet, a place where mammals never evolved into people and life took a totally different path.

How would an alien look at Oyo compared to the doctors and people present at the execution of a serial killer? How would an alien compare Oyo to the medieval Catholic Church torturing and killing heretics? Would an alien even perceive much difference between what Oyo did versus a doctor helping to euthanize a suffering patient?

You can extend this on and on to birth control, animal cruelty, and even the use of antibiotics to kill bacteria.

I don't subscribe to the idea that just because two things are on a moral gradient they're equal. That's irrational. However, I do believe it's important to take a look at something from different points of view.

When Europeans came to the Americas and witnessed Aztec sacrificial rituals, they were coming from a continent with practices that in many ways were equally barbaric, but because they understood the justifications of their own practices, they viewed them differently.

I've been in tactical-operations centers where terms like *collateral human casualties* are thrown around with the same cavalier attitude that the Aztec and allied leaders of Mesoamerican cultures must have had when they planned the Flower Wars, in which thousands of people were killed in ritual combat.

When I share these thoughts, I'm often labeled a peacenik or pacifist. I have to assert that I'm not against premeditated strikes or taking lives, I'm simply uncomfortable when everyone in the room gets uptight if they're even asked to think about the morality of what's being considered.

I glance across the road to the church camp Oyo ran and back to Oyo's shed in the derelict tree nursery. Two different lives, one serving the other.

Oyo deeply believed that his deeds were part of a religious ritual. Joe Vik simply wanted to kill.

Both men are evil because they were depriving other people of their lives through their direct actions. But Oyo had a strange justification.

How different was he from one of my Nordic ancestors who thought it appropriate to throw the living wives of a dead chieftain onto a burning pyre?

The part of Africa that Oyo was from was as steeped in superstition as my ancestors' European homeland. Somewhere in my family tree, there may be an Oyo. And because his culture shared his beliefs, he didn't have to do it in secrecy.

This is what's so scary about Oyo to me. With Joe Vik I can imagine that a gene controlling compulsion got switched off and he was raised in a hostile environment that pushed him over the edge.

While Oyo, too, might have had some genetic predisposition in play, he never dropped the religious veil. Joe Vik killed and buried his prey like a cunning animal. Oyo maintained his magical beliefs through every stage of his crimes, yet he killed for decades without being detected.

Oyo was extremely intelligent and charismatic. He was also batshit crazy. Any one of his ideas about killing or cannibalism giving him magical powers could easily have been tested and disproven. But he didn't test them. Trying to test them would have run counter to his belief system.

Joe Vik knew what he was. He saw that he was a monster in human skin and maintained that facade for as long as he could.

Oyo saw himself as a normal man who practiced a religion that others didn't understand. He didn't see himself as a monster. Neither did the Aztec chieftains, the priests of the Inquisition, or the Third Reich doctors who made a moral justification that led from stemming the spread of tuberculosis to genocide.

This is what scares me—the idea of becoming a monster without ever realizing it.

How does a man find himself naked on a blood-soaked floor with the dead body of a child at his feet with bite marks all over its skin and say to himself, "I'm not *that* fucked-up"?

Oyo managed to do it.

And every time I tell myself I'm totally cool with the fact that I killed him in cold blood, I could be taking one step closer to being him.

I flinch as I realize I'm being watched from the opposite side of my vehicle. A dark figure walks closer and taps on the window.

I regret not stopping to get a gun until I recognize the outline of Nicolson's head.

How long was he watching me?

CHAPTER FIVE

GATEWAY

As he unlocks the gate in front of Oyo's house, Nicolson asks a question that alarms me. It's not the question as much as the situation and the person asking it. It's almost as if he's been reading my mind.

"Do you believe in evil?"

"In a moral or supernatural sense? Yes to the former, and the latter is beyond my point of view."

Nicolson points to a small pool of melted black wax near the entrance. There's also a line of white powder—possibly salt—that runs along the fence. "What about that?"

I kneel for a closer look. The black candle is associated with dark magic rituals, while the salt is designed to hold back evil.

"I guess some people take this seriously."

"And how does that make you feel?" asks a gravelly voice from behind me.

I turn to find another man standing there. He appears to be in his fifties, smoking a cigar while dressed in a well-tailored, dark suit.

"Dr. Cray, this is Joe Gallard. He's helping us from DC."

"I'm just here to observe," says Gallard.

Uh-huh. Like US troops in Vietnam.

"What do you do for the bureau?" I ask.

"Help out on the occasional case from time to time. Mostly teach." He stubs out his cigar next to the little shrine.

Nicolson opens up the gate to the front yard. "This way, gentlemen."

"What do you teach?" I ask as we step into the old nursery.

"Mainly procedure."

Okay. This asshole is being intentionally vague with me. I can either ignore that or call him out on it. Old Theo would be blunt. New Theo would use this as an opportunity to observe him.

I decide to drop the matter.

Nicolson leads us around the house and into the backyard. All of the trees have been pulled out and the nursery is a series of pits with plywood boards tracing out paths. It resembles an archaeological dig at a sacrificial site—which technically it is. Only the sacrifices were uncomfortably recent.

"When I was here," I tell the men, "it was all trees and shrubs. I got lost while Oyo was chasing me. It seemed so much bigger."

"We found human remains in the soil, just like at the site in Los Angeles," Nicolson tells me. "When we started digging, we found an even deeper layer. The way Oyo butchered his victims, the parts were all spread out." He points to a sifting grate. "Our techs have had to use that on every square inch."

None of the work lights is on. We're looking at the yard under moonlight. Despite the lack of trees, it does remind me of the night I was last here. When I look to the back of the property, I stifle an involuntary gasp when I see the large shed covered in plastic.

That's where he killed them.

"You okay, Doctor?" asks Gallard.

"Fine. And it's Theo." I nod to the shed. "That place. I still see it in my nightmares."

"You have nightmares?" asks Nicolson.

"Of course. How could you not after seeing this?"

"Watch your step," says Nicolson as he takes out a small flashlight to light our way.

We walk out on the plywood to the middle of the excavation. Ladders and scaffolds rest in pits covered by canopies. It looks as if they were abandoned, which I guess they were.

Close to the end of the yard, police tape blocks off a section covered by clear plastic. It must encompass a quarter of the yard. I assume this is the crime scene within the crime scene.

Nicolson uses his light to illuminate the area, confirming my guess. "This is where it happened."

I realize his *it* and my *it* are two different events. Oyo was preparing to kill another child when I stopped him, but Nicolson's referring to the murder of the FBI technicians. I nod.

"We found Novak in the pit over here and Shea on the ground just above," Nicolson explains.

"Where was Marcus working?" I ask.

"Same pit. They'd uncovered a small finger bone and were searching for the rest of the body. Just the three of them were here that night. We had a police cruiser on the outside."

"Who was the last to speak to them?"

"We had a supervisor here earlier in the day, but other than texts and calls to family, it was just the three of them until the next shift showed up in the morning. Novak and Shea had been dead for hours." He pauses for a long moment. "Shea bled out. We think it took an hour for her to die."

"And there was no animosity between them and the missing tech?"

"Did Marcus do it?" Nicolson says bluntly. "We don't know. That's why we want to find him. It's just that . . ." He glances at Gallard, unsure what to say.

"What?" I prod him.

"All the weird shit."

"The candles? The salt?"

"The whole place. I was here some nights, pulling late shifts, and there was a strange vibe. This place isn't right." Nicolson stares at the ground. "The people in the neighborhood started telling stories about seeing a man in black wandering around the crime scene. Some people . . . some of them say it's the Toy Man. Especially after what happened to his body."

"What?" My heart just skipped a beat. "What happened to his body?"

Nicolson glances at Gallard. The older man nods for him to continue.

"It went missing. I mean, they couldn't find it for a couple days in the morgue. Then it showed up again. It was a clerical thing because of his other name. We still kept it under wraps, though." His voice falters as he says it, telling me something else.

"Let me guess, his body went missing the same time that the murders happened here?"

"Right," says Gallard. "Normally an unclaimed body is cremated after a certain amount of time. The coroner was holding on to Oyo's because there was some dispute with family overseas."

"Well, I can assure you that Oyo did not kill your technicians. He was very dead the last time I saw him."

"You mean when you killed him," says Gallard.

"Yes." I don't bother to offer my official explanation that Oyo drew on me first.

"That's quite an accomplishment. You've killed two of the most prolific serial killers ever." Gallard doesn't say this as a compliment. It comes across as suspicious.

"I'm sure if law enforcement had been able to respond more quickly, then the outcome would have been different. But this is the world we live in."

"Two serial killers," says Gallard. "You're a scientist. What are the odds?"

I've encountered his kind of professional skepticism before. "The odds of what? It wasn't a random event. I sought out both men. The first because he killed my student and the second because a grieving father asked for my help."

"I've worked at the bureau for years and I don't think I know anyone with the track record you have."

"I guess my methods are just more efficient. But as a profiler, you know there are always more data and better tools to be found."

There's a long pause in which the only sounds are the Georgia frogs and crickets. From the look on Nicolson's face, I can tell that I've said something he wasn't expecting.

"Too true, Theo. Too true. Maybe if I had you on my team, we could get things done a lot more efficiently—but there are always bureaucracies and legal hurdles to navigate."

"So let's cut to the chase. Why am I standing in the middle of a crime scene with an FBI profiler and an agent who clearly had some personal connection to the murdered technicians?"

"I pushed for it," says Nicolson. "Do you think Oyo could have had an accomplice?"

"Another one? It's possible, but you'd know better than I. I'm sure you've already explored this."

"We have," says Nicolson. "It just doesn't add up."

"You mean Oyo's body going missing and the weird artifacts? I can't speak to that, but I think Occam's razor provides a fairly obvious answer to what happened that night."

"And what is that?" asks Gallard.

"Marcus. Your missing technician killed them. What I can't understand is why you're having so much trouble accepting that."

"You don't know Marcus," Nicolson replies.

"No. And maybe that's an advantage. Unless there's something else I'm missing."

"There is," says Gallard. "But unfortunately we can't reveal that to you right now. Let's go back to the office and talk about this in a slightly more comfortable environment."

CHAPTER SIX

SWAB

Nicolson sets a bottle of water in front of me and takes a seat across the table in the small conference room while Gallard types away on his laptop computer. I followed them to the downtown FBI office and found the building still pretty active despite the late hour.

"So, you think Marcus did it?" asks Nicolson.

"I have no idea," I reply. "I don't even know if there is such a person as Marcus. All I know is what you told me, and my response was based upon prior situations—which is another way of describing a bias."

"Would you like to see the case file?" asks Gallard.

"Sure. But I expect you guys were more thorough than I would be."

He slides a thin folder over to me. I'm reminded of the time in Montana when Detective Glenn slipped in an image of a brutal murder to gauge my reaction. I used a similar technique in Moscow. While I was upset at Glenn at the time, I came to respect the man. He died trying to save my life when Vik went on his rampage.

This folder has diagrams and photos of the FBI techs' bodies where they were found. There are photos of the victims and some other information, but the bulk of it is pages of genetic sequence from blood found on the scene. Not the whole genome, only the markers that scientists look for that differ from individual to individual. I scan the lines of ATGC sequences.

"Can you read that?" asks Nicolson.

"Only a little." I point to the numbers next to each sequence. "That tells you where on the genome each sequence is located. Otherwise it's just like having a bunch of random ones and zeroes."

"You ever work with anybody else?" asks Gallard.

"I have a team back in Austin."

"Right. What's your company do?"

"We're a consulting group. We work with other institutions to develop laboratory procedures." That's the official description I give people.

"Yeah. I couldn't find anything on LinkedIn or Google. Are you in stealth mode or something?"

"We work with a limited client base and don't need to advertise, if that's what you're asking."

"Who funds you?"

"The institutions I just mentioned."

"Well, Theo, you didn't actually name any. You were just in Russia? What were you doing there?"

"Consulting." How would he respond if I told him I was in Moscow trying to find a Russian spy? It certainly sounds more intriguing than it actually was.

"For whom?" asks Gallard.

"A client."

"Did you enter the country with a work visa?"

He's pressing hard, and I don't think he realizes what the real truth is. While I could tell him more than I have, I don't feel he's entitled to that. Instead, I'll just shut him down as quickly as possible.

"I didn't need one."

"Because of the nature of the work?"

"Because I entered the country under diplomatic protection onboard a State Department jet."

Gallard's mouth hangs open for a moment. I think he'd been expecting to find out that I'd been consulting for some Russian biotech firm or selling unhackable phones to mobsters or something sinister. The implications of how I got to Russia and whom I work for are starting to sink in.

"So, you do a lot of overseas travel?" he finally asks.

"Some. Unfortunately, I can't talk about most of my work."

"I think I see," says Gallard. "In your other job—as a serial-killer hunter—do you ever work with anyone?"

"I don't really think of it as a job. And, yes, I've had help from people."

"You certainly treat it as one. Anyone specific?"

"Specific? How?"

"A partner. Like your girlfriend?"

"Jillian helped me with Joe Vik but wasn't with me when I looked into Oyo's case. The father of one of the victims provided some assistance there. He was the one that asked for my help."

"Do you think the father might have come to Atlanta after Oyo was killed?" asks Nicolson.

"Was William asked to give statements here? I don't know."

"What Nicolson means is, do you think he may have visited this crime scene?"

"I have no idea. It would seem odd."

There's a knock on the door, and a petite woman in a lab coat enters, pushing a metal cart. "Pardon me, gentlemen. You were just at the Oyo scene?"

"Yes?" replies Gallard.

"We need to get some postfield forensics. We're trying to avoid cross-contamination," she politely explains.

"This is new," Gallard groans. "Fine. What do you need?"

"Just some swabs and prints. Sorry to be a pain."

Gallard rolls his eyes. "Whatever."

She slips on a pair of blue gloves and takes samples from his fingernails, has him swab a cheek, then uses a digital scanner to copy his fingerprints.

"My turn," says Nicolson.

She takes out a new set of vials and swabs and starts to collect from him.

"I'm going to use the bathroom." I get up and walk out of the room and head to the men's room down the hall.

When I return, she's putting Nicolson's samples away.

Gallard glances at me and replies, "You know this isn't a drug test. If you were trying to flush it out, don't bother."

"Now you tell me," I reply as I sit down.

The technician takes off her gloves and throws them away, then replaces them with a new pair. I let her scrape under my fingernails and print me. When she raises the cotton swab, I take it from her and wipe the inside of my cheek, then hand it back to her.

She puts all the samples back onto her tray, then pushes the cart away. Gallard picks up the conversation where he'd left off.

"So, you don't think William would linger around a crime scene like this?"

"No. But little surprises me about people." I weigh the pros and cons of calling them out on the two big lies that are right in front of me. But then something else clicks into place and I feel the hair rise on the back of my neck. I turn to Gallard. "How is the profile coming?"

"Which one?"

"Mine. That's really why you asked me here."

Nicolson has no reaction. Gallard chuckles. "I don't want to hurt your feelings, Theo, but I'm not profiling you. You're not a suspect."

"Then tell your lab tech that she should have changed her gloves before getting Nicolson's sample and not just for mine. It looks kind of suspicious to someone like me."

Gallard raises a hand, but I push back the file and point at it. "This is bullshit."

"That's all we have so far," says Nicolson, defensively.

I flip open to the page of genetic sequences with the name Marcus written in pen across the top. "Then you should really look into why an Irish American has the same East African haploid groups as Oyo. It's like you just grabbed stuff from his file and shoved them in here to make it look thicker."

There's an awkward pause as Nicolson exchanges a quick glance with Gallard. That's exactly what they did. Something tells me that Nicolson wasn't so sure about the idea and Gallard pushed for it.

"I think your spy work has you a little paranoid," Gallard finally responds.

"Actually, it's made me impatient with bullshit like this." I get up and head for the door. Before leaving, I stop. "If you think I'm your guy on this, good luck."

"I'm sure you have a government-backed alibi," says Gallard.

"Actually, I was referring to the samples you took from me. Tell the lab they're going to need to use a larger database."

"What does that mean?" asks Nicolson.

I shut the door and leave them to figure out what I was telling them. It was a petty move on my part, but the moment they pushed the cart into the room and Gallard put on his little show about being frustrated, I knew something was up.

The sad part was all they had to do was ask.

CHAPTER SEVEN
PHANTOMS

"Dr. Cray!" Nicolson shouts at me as I'm about to climb into my rental car. I'm angry at being jerked around, but I'm also sympathetic that he is in over his head and probably being given bad advice by Gallard.

"What is it, Sean?" I say, key fob in hand.

"I'm sorry. I'm real sorry. We're at our wits' end here. Gallard was brought in and I mentioned you and . . . Well, I can't blame him. This is on me. It's . . . There's a lot going on here."

I unlock my car. "You're not convincing me."

"I can show you the file . . ."

"I have a lot of files waiting for me."

"Okay, then I can tell you why Gallard was interested in you."

I turn to face him. "Go on."

Nicolson glances over his shoulder, afraid that he might be overheard. "It's a case he's been following. Not really a case as much as . . . well, a suspicion."

"Me?"

"No. Not directly. He wanted to meet you because he was curious about you, but I genuinely wanted you to look into what happened here. Well, one thing led to another . . ."

"And you end up lying to me and clumsily trying to get forensic samples I would have gladly given you. Instead of fake ones."

"Fake ones?"

"The cheek swab. I keep preserved samples on me. That was chimpanzee DNA."

Nicolson stares at me, momentarily speechless. "Again, I apologize. There's a lot of weird stuff going on with this case. Gallard came down to see if it was connected to his thing."

"And what is his 'thing'?" I ask.

"He calls him the Phantom."

"Not exactly an original name for a serial killer," I reply.

"He's not a serial killer—at least as far as we know. It's hard to describe. Basically, the forensics lab at Quantico has noticed something peculiar in a handful of cases—many of them open-and-shut cases with airtight evidence," Nicolson explains.

"All right. You have my attention. What's so peculiar?"

"It might be a hair follicle in one case that we find in two others. Or a shoe print that matches multiple locations. Hair follicle A and shoe print B might be in one scene, and then shoe print B and a different hair follicle in another. And then that follicle with shoe print A. Do you get what I'm saying?"

"Like someone took three boxes of puzzle pieces and planted them in crime scenes?"

"Yes. Of course, we get tons of extraneous prints and follicles in crime scenes. It was an accident that the lab even noticed it. They were trying some AI matching software and it came up with connections to cases that were already closed."

"Are they reconsidering those cases?" I ask.

"They're looking into them, but the weird part is that a lot of these bits of evidence could have been left behind during various investigations. It could have come from someone who visited the crime scene after the fact. Or something else."

"You're worried about another Woman Without a Face?" I ask.

European detectives spent fifteen years searching for a killer whose DNA they found at more than fifty crime scenes and whom they believed guilty of six murders. Things took a weird turn when French police tried to ID the body of a burned male corpse and the DNA popped up again.

The DNA belonged to a woman, all right. A German woman who worked for the laboratory company that prepared the cotton swabs they used to collect DNA samples. She'd inadvertently been contaminating them with her own DNA.

"Yeah, but we've ruled that out, I think. Too many different samples. This would be someone closer to the investigation. Maybe."

"Like a lab tech?"

"Yes, except we don't have any who were at all the locations, or even nearby. It's like someone else has been visiting the crime scenes."

"A reporter? A serial-killer junkie?"

Nicolson shrugs. "Maybe. When the techs were killed and Marcus disappeared . . . Well, we found more samples from the Phantom."

"Oh," I say as it dawns on me. "Gallard thought I was the Phantom?"

"In his defense, if you search the FBI database for known individuals with a propensity toward visiting crime scenes, your name's at the top."

And all my government trips shrouded in secrecy make me hard for investigators to track down. "Rest easy, I'm not your phantom. It could be noise or a sampling problem."

I could also mention the fact that the FBI doesn't exactly have the most sterling reputation when it comes to hair samples as forensic evidence. A review of their procedures found that FBI experts gave inaccurate testimony in hundreds of cases, overstating the confidence level in matches. Some people even went to death row based on the flawed testimony.

When they realized their errors, they notified prosecutors but otherwise kept the matter as quiet as possible, fearing that it could lead to scores of retrials and suspects being exonerated.

It's a morally tricky area. Groups like the Innocence Project have helped free a lot of wrongfully convicted people, although some law-enforcement experts will insist that not all of the freed suspects were "innocent." Just the same, it's up to law enforcement to make sure that suspects get a fair trial based on evidence and not gut feelings.

While I think the FBI felt it was within its legal bounds not to go out of its way to notify defendants about the evidence in question, I also suspect the ones in charge may have thought they were doing the *moral* thing by not telling them.

The truth of the matter is that every large lab has its share of problems and procedures that need to be questioned. The Centers for Disease Control is rife with horrifying examples that raise questions about its labs' competence. Because it's a prominent government research facility, its mistakes are more visible than most.

"Forensic stuff is above my level of understanding," says Nicolson. "The main reason we asked Gallard to look into this is because of Marcus. There's nothing, and I mean nothing, in his profile or history that suggests any propensity for violent behavior. Even Gallard said he'd never seen anyone so unlikely to commit a murder be implicated in one. It throws a lot of profiling out the window. Usually you see signs after the fact. But looking back at Marcus, there was nothing."

"Is there a connection between Marcus and the Phantom? Could he have been visiting crime scenes after hours?"

"We thought about that. There are too many points where he was on the wrong side of the country. We're not even really seriously considering the Phantom hypothesis. Although I'd like to believe that Marcus was framed."

Nicolson's phone buzzes, and he checks it.

"Well, damn."

"What is it?"

"They found him."

"Marcus?"

He nods.

"Where are they bringing him?"

"Here. He's inbound in about twenty minutes." He glances at my car. "Are you sure you want to leave us just yet?"

CHAPTER EIGHT

FUGUE

The face of Daniel Marcus almost fills the screen on the wall of the dark conference room. Gallard is watching closely, occasionally asking the agent handling the video feed to switch to a wide view. Presumably so he can read Marcus's body language.

The main conference room where they're monitoring the interview is upstairs. From here, the agents leading the investigation are watching and sending their questions to the agent in the room with Marcus. I'm sitting quietly in the corner with my visitor badge clipped to my jacket pocket. When Nicolson ushered me in, he referred to me as Dr. Cray to the special agent in charge.

The interviewer, Agent Howe, a tall, dark-haired woman with a powerful presence, has a clinical approach to her questioning, not appearing too condescending or skeptical. I'm not sure how well I'd do if she were to grill me. There's a measured patience in her demeanor. She's quite comfortable letting unsettling silence make Marcus go into greater detail.

"How much do you recall about Thursday the eighteenth?" she asks.

Marcus gives a quick shake of his head. "Not much."

Nicolson leans in to whisper to me, "He volunteered to be interviewed. State police found him at a rest stop near the border."

"Do you recall getting up that morning?" Howe asks.

Marcus thinks this over. "It would have been the afternoon. We had the night shift. Yes. I remember getting dressed and going to the location."

"Okay. What do you remember about that night?"

"Nothing."

"Nothing?" A pause as she's probably getting questions sent to her. "Do you remember making any logs about the site?"

"Yes. I remember that. I filled out some forms, then went back into the pit. I was there for a while. I was getting hungry, but I was afraid I might be coming down with something. Some of the other people on the site got the flu that was going around. It made things stressful."

His words are almost monotone, like he's reciting a script.

I look over at Nicolson to see how he's reacting. His body language is easier to decipher than Marcus's. He's confused.

"What's the last thing you remember in the pit?" asks Howe.

Marcus exhales. "I'm not sure. I . . . I remember a shadow . . . then . . . nothing. The next thing I know, the police found me."

"Has he been examined by a doctor?" I ask Nicolson.

"There was a paramedic on the scene, and one of our people checked on him here. We wanted to talk to him before sending him to get examined at the hospital."

Marcus appears to be in shock, but it's hard to tell whether he's really just a bad actor. Gallard is stroking his chin and checking his computer from time to time. Something about Marcus isn't sitting right with him.

I'm not a behavioral psychologist. Arguably, I'm not even good at interpreting normal human behavior, let alone knowing if someone is lying. Some people have an intuition for this. It's not magical; they're simply more attuned to the changes in voice and mannerisms that indicate someone is being untruthful.

People can be quite effective lie detectors. Subjects listening to voice recordings can predict whether someone cheats on their spouse more often than chance would dictate. Women are apparently even better at this than men.

With the advent of thermal imaging like the kind used back in Moscow—millimeter radar and fMRI—we can measure thousands of data points to tell whether they're being truthful.

New research using AI has increased the accuracy to frightening levels. Double-blind studies have shown that machines are much better than humans at detecting deception, with far fewer false positives.

The old adage that lie detection can only tell you whether someone *believes* something is true doesn't really apply to the new forms of detection. We can see which parts of the brain are triggered when a subject is asked certain questions.

If I asked you where you were last Thursday, and you've convinced yourself you were at home, when I ask what you ate that night, your brain would be forced to create an answer if you didn't have a memory. While you may not be aware that your subconscious is inventing this on the fly, we can see a different section of your brain firing up, attempting to fill in the blank.

We're even at the point where we can ask you to remember to whom you talked and a computer can create a fuzzy image of their face, distinct from if you were asked to make up an image.

It's both incredibly promising and equally terrifying. My friends involved in this area of research are cautious about their technology because of its potential for abuse by well-intentioned people. Something I deal with on a daily basis.

That said, I'd love to be able to look into Daniel Marcus's head and see what's going on. I'm sure I could build some machine-learning models that would tell me much more than what we're getting right now—which isn't much.

Nicolson's and Gallard's reactions are telling me much more.

"You have no memory of the blackout period?" asks Howe.

"Correct," says Marcus.

"Do you know where your car is?"

Marcus contemplates this, then shakes his head.

"You're wearing a different set of clothes than what you wore to work. Do you know where you got these?"

He shakes his head again.

"Do you remember any physical pain? Like a headache?"

A hospital examination will tell us whether he suffered a concussion, but if he'd been injected with anything, traces of the substance would likely be gone in twenty-four hours. There's a chance they could find an injection point, but if his food or water had been drugged, we'd have no proof if we couldn't find the original source.

Marcus doesn't take as long to respond to the last question. He nods. "I had a headache."

"After the blackout?" asks Howe.

"Maybe . . . but I know I had one before. There was the flu thing going around."

Gallard squints as if he's trying to process this bit of information. Clearly, Marcus had him following a certain train of thought. I'm dying to ask him what he's thinking.

To my mind, Marcus's responses are hesitant and incomplete. It's hard for me to tell whether this is intentional omission or because he really doesn't recall what happened.

"I think I'd like to go to the hospital now," Marcus says.

"Okay. We have an ambulance coming. Is there anything else you can remember?"

"No. What do the others say?"

"The others?" asks Howe.

"Novak," he replies. "Novak and Shea?"

"They're dead," says Howe.

"Dead?" Marcus acts like he's trying to make sense of the word. "How?"

"We're still trying to determine that. Is there anything else you'd like to add?"

Marcus shakes his head and draws back into his chair. He stares down at his hands and refuses to answer any more questions. A few minutes later, he's escorted out of the room by a paramedic.

When the video feed ends, Gallard turns to me. "What's your analysis?"

"You mean my layperson analysis? Flipping a coin would yield a better response than my gut reaction."

"I'm glad you know your limits. What's your gut reaction anyway?"

"I use tools to make my observations. No offense, but the two best tools were watching how you and Nicolson reacted. That told me more than Marcus did. Nicolson seemed surprised by the way Marcus was talking, almost as if he didn't recognize him. You . . . it was like you did recognize him, or at least there was something familiar to you."

"You're more perceptive than you admit, Theo. I'll share with you my thoughts in a moment, but I really want to hear your gut reaction. Not as a scientist, but as a human being observing another."

"I want to say he's delusional, but my instincts tell me that he's lying through his teeth. What I can't understand is why he'd even bother talking to you without an attorney."

"I have a theory on that, too. But let's ask Nicolson what he thought." Gallard turns to the agent. "You knew the man."

Nicolson appears shaken. His voice falters as he speaks. "That . . . that wasn't Daniel."

CHAPTER NINE
REVENANT

"A different man?" asks Agent Van Owen. She's been sitting on the opposite side of the room, taking notes. An athletic woman with short blonde hair, she reminds me of an air force pilot and a little of Jillian.

"I have to think about it for a moment," says Nicolson, clearly uncomfortable. "Let me just think about it. Gallard? What was your opinion?"

Gallard sits back in his chair and crosses his arms. "I have Marcus's files in front of me. I've also been watching depositions he's given. While I don't know him, the portrait I have is very different from the man we just saw."

I raise my hand. "Dumb question. Are we talking literally different or he just acts differently than your expectation?"

"Sorry, Theo," says Gallard. "Acting different. Extremely different. The two things that are the most peculiar to me are that nothing I've seen in Marcus's file suggests he even has the capacity for that kind of manipulation." He turns his laptop around. It shows an image of Marcus in a suit speaking in a conference room. Gallard presses "Play."

Marcus is making a point about some forensic data and seems a little uneasy, almost threatened by the questions, which are technical. His hands are also animated.

"This is a very different person under pressure than the man we just saw."

"Marcus was always a little antsy," says Nicolson. "But I've seen him handle himself really well in depositions."

"Correct," says Gallard. He plays a different video. "You mean like this?"

Marcus is more competent. His sentences are complete and he's very calm as he speaks, his demeanor closer to what we just saw.

"Two different depositions," says Gallard. "Two different versions of the same man. Agent Nicolson, do you recall what the second deposition was about?"

"The Kingston case? A retrial, I think. They'd challenged some of his data and he was testifying to support them. He did a great job. We got a conviction."

"From the case notes, it appears that Marcus spent a week preparing for that. He also worked with our attorneys to make sure that he kept exactly on script. So now we've seen two versions of Marcus under pressure. One where he's caught off guard, the other where he's had a chance to prepare. He's an intelligent person, and it seems that when his back is against the wall, he's perfectly capable of keeping his story straight."

"But that doesn't mean he killed them," Nicolson protests.

"No. It doesn't. But there's something else you may not be aware of. Do you know the Egg Griddle case?" asks Gallard.

"That was before I got here. The owner of the restaurant was found murdered. Right? They thought the partner did it."

"Correct. Marcus did some of the forensics on that. The partner had the case thrown out. In part because the only testimony he gave without his attorney described blacking out before the murder long enough to introduce the element of doubt. Maybe he'd been drugged and someone else committed the crime," Gallard explains.

"Are you saying that Marcus just gave us the same alibi?" I ask.

Gallard points at his laptop. "I have the transcripts in front of me. Marcus gave us exactly the same alibi. Almost word for word. If it worked in that case, why not try it here?"

"So he did it," says Nicolson.

"My gut says yes, but something bothers me," says Gallard. "My professional instincts as a profiler say no. I've run his profile through our system, and it just doesn't get flagged. There's nothing violent about the man. There're no indicators that go with that kind of behavior. In fact, it's the opposite. He scores low on a number of aggression indicators. He's extremely nonconfrontational. That's probably why he went into forensics instead of becoming a field agent."

"Something switched? Like a trigger?" asks Nicolson.

"Yeah, except triggers leave clues. Instead, what we have here is a relatively passive individual whose empathy is at the high end of the spectrum. He'd feel horrible about killing someone. And if he did commit a crime like this, according to his profile, he'd confess."

"Dr. Cray? What's your take? Can people just change?"

I remember how a discussion of so-called were-frogs, cannibal tadpoles, led to me being a prime suspect in the Grizzly Killer case. I decide to choose my analogies carefully.

"People can certainly be conditioned to kill. That's what boot camp does. Adults can be led from one mental state to another until they reach the point where they'd do things they would have considered unspeakable. But unless Marcus was showing some questionable behavior before, it would seem unusual for there to be a purely psychological cause."

"Purely psychological?" asks Gallard.

"This isn't my area of expertise, but physical damage to the frontal lobe can theoretically cause behavioral changes. Phineas Gage and all that. Although there's a lot of skepticism on the degree of a behavioral change he experienced. Anatoli Bugorski had strikingly similar damage, but there was no personality shift."

"Bugorski?" asks Gallard.

"Oh, not really relevant. He was a Russian researcher who accidentally had a high-energy proton beam shoot a hole through his head. Almost like something out of a comic book. But he ended up with seizures and chronic fatigue instead of superpowers."

"Well, that's horrifying," replies Gallard. "Damage to the prefrontal lobe has been suggested numerous times as a cause for violent behavior. While I question the number of cases of violent behavior that are attributable to that, I don't reject the idea that in some situations it might be a cause. But you can understand why the FBI doesn't put much effort into investigating that as a trigger."

I nod. "Your job is to catch the man, not explain to a jury why it might not be his fault."

"What about Daniel's bike accident?" asks Nicolson.

"Bike accident?" asks Gallard.

"A year ago. He was on his bicycle and got hit by a car. He was out of work for weeks. Could that trigger something?"

"Were there MRIs?" I ask.

"Hold up," says Van Owen. "Like Dr. Cray just said, our job isn't to attribute a mental cause for Marcus. In fact, our job isn't even this case right now. We're just interested parties."

"Miranda," Nicolson replies, "he's one of ours. Any moment now they're going to transfer this over to another division, and they're going to treat him like a suspect off the street."

I don't point out that would be the ethical way to handle things. I'd do the same to help a colleague of mine. Another example of my personal ethics not hewing exactly to the letter of the law.

"Fine. But he might not want to release his medical records to us. In fact, I'm betting he's about to lawyer up real quick," she replies.

Nicolson turns to me. "What would we need?"

"MRIs if he had them taken. To look for possible damage. We'd also need someone who knows what they're looking for. This is way outside my field of expertise . . ." My voice drifts off as I think of something.

"What is it?" asks Gallard.

"You'll need an expert. But . . . hold on." I take out my phone and do a search through some of the medical databases I have access to. "Okay. We still want an expert, and they'll tell us why what I'm doing is dumb or has been done before and better, but I could collect a few thousand MRI images of brains that have no frontal-lobe damage and a few hundred that do and create a machine-learning model that would be able to give us a confidence score on an MRI."

"How long would that take?" asks Gallard.

"If the images are labeled properly, a few hours."

"A few hours?"

"I have a server back at the office that does this. I don't even have to write any original code. I can upload the images from here or use a Python script to get them in bulk."

"Of course," says Van Owen, mocking me.

I shrug. "The machines won, sister. We're just in denial. The problem is getting Marcus's MRIs."

Nicolson holds up his phone. "I have them. He asked for an attorney referral after the bike accident and forwarded them to me."

"Is using them even legal?" asks Van Owen.

Gallard raises his hands. "I don't think I want any part of this. I'm merely an observer at this point."

"As a mere observer, can you suggest a neuroscientist in the vicinity we might ask for an opinion?" I ask.

"Fine. But you need to get this wrapped up soon before the people upstairs find out. I'm sure they're going to ask my opinion any minute now. And if they don't like it, I'm on the first plane back to DC."

"What's the point?" asks Van Owen. "Marcus's attorneys can find all this out."

"If they charge him, this may be the only way to get him into a hospital instead of regular prison. Maybe there they can treat him," says Nicolson.

Hopefully. I'm more with Van Owen than I let on. This is a long shot and beyond my expertise. I'm only good at catching bad guys, not figuring out what to do after the fact.

My gut tells me I'm missing a big something that no machine-learning model is going to point out for me, and I get the distinct impression that Gallard feels the same way.

CHAPTER TEN

SCAN

Daniel Marcus's brains are projected all over Dr. Henrietta Leed's body as she stares at the zoomed image of his frontal lobe on the screen. From where I'm standing, it looks like a pixelated blob, but hopefully it means something more to her than me.

Dr. Leed is close to Gallard's age and has a no-nonsense demeanor. With spiked red hair and purple glasses, there's an eccentric streak about her, but she seems to know her stuff. She's a well-respected diagnostician, and the FBI uses her frequently on cases involving head trauma. She arrived less than an hour after Nicolson called her.

My computer model already gave me my result, but I haven't told Nicolson or the others. It could be complete nonsense. It's the first time I've attempted to do anything like this, and I don't want to change the course of an investigation on some haphazard scheme I came up with and probably screwed up by not filtering the images as thoroughly as I should have.

Leed asks Nicolson to click through several more MRI images. She takes out a ruler and measures parts of the screen. I have no idea whether this is actually an effective means to measure brain damage. I suspect that she may be putting on a bit of a show for us, like a witch doctor making a ceremony out of reading a splatter of bird entrails.

She studies the date at the edge of the screen. "This MRI was taken right after the accident?"

"Yes," Nicolson replies.

"And the next one? That was a follow-up done two months later?"

"Correct."

"Hmm." She says this loudly, pulling us all into her train of thought. "What do you think, Dr. . . . what was your name?"

"Theo," I reply.

"Dr. Theo, what do you think?"

"Actually, Theo is my first name."

She blinks at me in the light of the projection, as if I've just belched. "Okay. I'm glad we got that sorted out. What do you think?"

"I'm just a computational biologist."

"Huh? What are you here for, then? To count the microbes in his earwax?"

"Dr. Cray . . . um, Theo, has a wide area of expertise," offers Nicolson.

"Great, a generalist," she says. "What does the generalist have to say?"

"The generalist says this is your field."

"And you're sucking up all our oxygen in here for what reason?"

The woman is both amusing me and pissing me off at the same time. "I built a computer model to compare other cases of frontal-lobe damage to Daniel Marcus's MRIs."

"Is this the Johns Hopkins thing?" she asks.

"Uh, no. This is something I made in the last hour."

"Wonderful. And what does your model say?"

"Well, it only gives me a confidence level compared to the images that I gave it. I tested it with known samples, and those came back with point-eight-two and point-nine-four confidence. Known damage-free

MRIs had a significantly lower level of confidence. I'd need to test them more thoroughly to get a reliable P value."

"Are you trying to put me to sleep?" she asks.

"Ask me that question in a few minutes," I reply.

"Okay, wiseass, what did your little model say about Daniel?"

"It came back with a point-two-one confidence level," I explain.

"For us non–computer science types?"

"It doesn't think that Daniel Marcus showed any signs of frontal-lobe damage compared to other examples."

Nicolson swivels his head toward me. I can read the disappointment on his face. "It's just a model."

"And in this situation," says Leed, "one I'd have to agree with. Although I'd like to test it against some of my case files."

"I can give you server access so you can test the machine-learning model."

"Great. Whatever that means." She turns to Gallard and Nicolson. "If your guy did it, it wasn't because of any damage I can see here. To be honest, I think the whole frontal-lobe thing is a little wishy-washy to begin with."

She raises a hand to hold off any questions. "While prolonged damage can cause impulsive behavior, it's not like you bump your head and turn into Hannibal Lecter. There are lots of other associated symptoms. Was Marcus missing work? Were there incidents of workplace violence? Was he using profane language?"

"No," Nicolson replies. "None of that. He was a good guy."

"That's his problem. There are clinical examples of people demonstrating aberrant behavior after that kind of damage, from gambling addiction to an interest in child pornography, but those behaviors grow gradually—as if the damage caused them to slowly lose the ability to resist their urges. The id just creeps out over time."

"Could there be another cause?" asks Nicolson.

"Besides physical trauma? Certain kinds of drug use can affect that region. Again, over time. He'd be showing up at work with meth mouth or looking like a junkie. Small symptoms show up first."

"Okay. Could there be a drug that *made* him do this? Maybe he was slipped something and flipped out?"

Leed ponders this for a moment. "A blood and urine screening may show that. Two-oxo-three-hydroxy-LSD can show up for as long as five days after. A hair sample may show something if it was a high dose. The absence of any of that wouldn't prove that he wasn't dosed." She gestures to the screen. "All of that is out of my expertise. You asked me here to find out if there was any frontal-lobe damage visible on these scans. There's none that I can detect. That doesn't mean there isn't any, but nothing stands out. And it seems like your good Dr. Theo agrees with me. Are there any other questions?" She starts to gather her belongings.

Nicolson shrugs. Gallard shakes his head.

"Thank you," says Van Owen. "I'll show you to the elevator."

I raise my hand. "Hold up. A quick question. Have you ever personally seen any examples of frontal-lobe damage leading to aberrant behavior?"

"One time. One time that stands out, anyway. I was a resident working in the federal prison system. We had a patient come in. He was serving three life sentences for the murder of his wife and two children. Emerson, I think that was his name. He was the nastiest son of a bitch you'd ever want to meet. He's what people think of when they hear about Phineas Gage and all that crap. Only Emerson was the real deal. They had to have two guards escort him everywhere. I had to treat him while he was in cuffs and shackles.

"When I checked his charts, I was surprised to find out that he had no violent history prior to killing his family. He'd literally been a Boy Scout. Sometimes, all too often, to be honest, violent behavior gets swept under the carpet and people give too many second chances at a clean slate. Emerson didn't seem like that, from what I could tell. I'd been reading up on frontal- and temporal-lobe trauma and even tried checking eye movement for a saccade in certain directions. None of it was very helpful. But an odd thing happened. One of the lightbulbs blew out in the exam room. Now, that kind of thing happened all the time. It was an old building. But Emerson turned into a scared child for a moment. It wasn't like everything went dark, either. It was just the sound of the electrical pop that startled him. A moment later he was his asshole self.

"I checked his record and noticed that he'd worked as an electrician and his last job was as a handyman at an apartment complex. When I spoke to the superintendent of the building, he told me that the last day he saw Emerson before the murders, he'd found him slumped behind a washing machine where he'd been repairing the outlet.

"He said it looked like Emerson had electrocuted himself. Probably had a seizure. He asked Emerson what happened, but he had no memory and just wanted to go home. He refused an ambulance. Two weeks later, he killed his family.

"I know what you're all asking: Did that jolt of electricity turn him into a killer? I don't know. We could draw connections and speculate, but that's all we could do. Maybe he was a psychopath all along, waiting for the right moment. That happens.

"But the difference between Emerson and your guy is that if I looked at Emerson's brain, I'd bet anything I'd see the damage on the prefrontal or temporal lobe. Your guy? No dice. Not unless he was moonlighting as a clumsy electrician."

"Thank you, Dr. Leed," says Gallard as she leaves us with her observation. "I don't know what else there is to do."

"Fuck," Nicolson mutters as he looks up from his computer.

"Marcus got his attorney?" says Van Owen, looking up from hers.

"No. Not that. Did you see the last performance report?"

"How did you get a copy?" she asks.

"That's not important. Marcus got severely reprimanded by Novak. She came down hard on him for some mislabeling that could have cost a case."

"There's your motive," says Gallard. "The prosecutors will make a case that he was under a lot of stress and then snapped. They'll probably go for manslaughter. Going for the death penalty would be too tricky. Maybe over time they can get him into a mental hospital."

"Why not ask Marcus to do another MRI?" I suggest.

"Too risky," says Gallard. "If it comes back with nothing, like the others, he'll have a harder time claiming some kind of physical trauma, if that's the route they want to go. And without any incident to point to, there's no point. His best bet is to get some court psychologist to claim psychological issues—assuming they're not going to try to claim innocence."

"Thanks, Dr. Cray," says Nicolson. "Sorry I dragged you into this."

"I'm sorry I couldn't be more of a help." I check my phone. I might be able to catch a red-eye back to Austin. "Let me know if anything turns up."

"Will do."

I leave the conference room feeling as though there's something unfinished there. That we're still missing something.

I try to put it out of my head and worry about getting the office back on track and undoing any damage that Todd may have done in my absence.

Damn it . . . what is it about Leed's story that's sticking in the back of my mind?

CHAPTER ELEVEN

CATNIP

As I walk past the empty rows of seats in the airport terminal, I keep thinking about Marcus and Emerson. In particular how one freak event could have caused damage to Emerson's brain, turning an otherwise fine human being into a monster. This wasn't a gradual slide, but a sudden snap that made him into a different person entirely—or at least unleashed that part of all of us that wants to react violently to the slightest provocation.

That's not what made Joe Vik or Oyo Diallo. They both had excellent impulse control. That's what allowed them to function for so long. Emerson and now apparently Marcus acted impulsively and were apprehended soon after their first kills—as far as we know.

It's dangerous to give too much credence to simple pop-psychology answers. In the 1990s, as violent crime was hitting an uptick, we were warned by both conservatives and liberals about a new type of criminal. These so-called superpredators were the new generation of children that were joining gangs, selling drugs, and committing violence like never before. Or that's what the narrative said. It was also thinly veiled code for "black teenagers."

Despite the direst predictions of their elders, this so-called violent generation became the least violent since the 1960s. Our superpredators turned out to be less violent than the generation that was ready to criminalize them from birth. As a child of that generation, I'm still waiting for my apology.

Despite the failure of superpredators to prey properly and the zombie generation of crack babies we were told would soon follow, it doesn't mean that there aren't environmental and cultural trends that can influence violent behavior.

I've seen persuasive studies that show that the generation before the so-called superpredators was exposed to excessively high amounts of lead in the air, water, and their home environments, supposedly leading to higher incidences of violence in affected communities. Causation and correlation are not the same thing, but it's not something I'd discount immediately out of hand.

That's why I can't discount the idea that there could be an environmental factor affecting Marcus. But it's so hard to prove. Some factors are too subtle to detect.

Right now, my stomach is telling me that I'm hungry and that I'm craving a Reese's Peanut Butter Cup from the now-closed gift shop. I don't know if the craving is coming from my brain or the trillions of bacteria in my stomach that have learned to trip my nervous system by producing their own dopamine triggers.

They're really that clever. There's frightening research that some cases of obesity could be caused not by a fault in your genes, but by your gut microbes clamoring for the kinds of foods you shouldn't be eating.

I'm wary of too-convenient explanations or mental boogeymen that exonerate us from being lazy and making bad choices, but I can't deny that the evidence is growing that a number of behaviors and diseases may not be due to defects in our genes, but to the survival mechanisms of the biome within us.

That the human body or any other animal is a system comprised of millions of smaller systems, some of them completely separate from us genetically, shouldn't be an earthshaking revelation. We've suspected for more than a century that the mitochondria in our cells were originally a foreign organism that we developed a symbiotic relationship with. This eukaryote-mitochondrial matchup worked out pretty well and gave us everything from sponges to velociraptors, proving that evolution doesn't care where a good idea comes from, as long as it improves a species' odds of survival.

Further evidence of cross-species intermingling can be found in all the funky DNA that shouldn't be there if evolution followed clean and orderly rules. We humans have genes free-riding in our genome that were left behind by viruses that somehow managed to get their code written into the master program. That's why I don't worry too much about artificial intelligence wiping us out. We'll still survive somewhere—even if it's in a file marked "Delete when found."

I take a seat across from a girl wearing a University of Texas hoodie and playing with a kitten in her lap. The cat has a tortoiseshell coloring, and I watch and see if I can detect any of the so-called tortitude behavior that tortoiseshell owners insist is a real thing.

I give the girl a smile, trying not to look like a creep. She smiles back. The kitten, frustrated by the interruption in attention, swipes at her chin.

What does the cat make of her human? Is the girl a mama cat? A bigger playmate? Or some other thing that she's created her own mental model for?

We don't have to fit into ready classifications. While nature has helped us evolve these distinctions and they're hardwired into us, we can develop our own strange relationships with simple patterns—a washing machine that makes a child fall asleep or a song that energizes us. While we use words to describe these interactions, at some level certain things simply make a few of our neurons fire off in a particular pattern—like my gut bacteria telling me to break into the gift shop and snag a Peanut Butter Cup . . .

The cat pulls at the girl's hoodie with a claw, and the girl admonishes her pet. "Settle down, Elon."

This captures my attention. Male tortoiseshells are extremely rare. "Is your cat a boy?" I ask.

"No," says the girl. "I found her at South by Southwest after Elon Musk spoke. It seemed like a good name."

Watching the mischievous little Elon and trying to fight back the trillion-strong army of bacteria ordering me to smash down the glass window of the gift shop and consume every Peanut Butter Cup I can find, a thought strikes me.

It's a wild-card notion, but something in the back of my mind feels as if a piece of the upside-down puzzle I've been trying to solve got flipped over.

I call Nicolson.

"Dr. Cray? What's up?"

The words pour out of my mouth. "Can you give me the number for Marcus's attorney?"

"Yeah. Let me text someone. What's going on?"

"We need to get him another MRI as soon as possible," I reply.

"What's going on?" he asks again.

"It's a long shot. But if I'm right, we need to know now, not later. Other people could be in danger."

"But Marcus is in custody. He turned himself in."

"I know. It's not him I'm concerned about. I need to know everyone else who was at the Oyo property. Everyone who was sick with Marcus's flu."

I stand up so fast that Elon almost jumps out of the girl's lap. This could be bad. Real bad. I hope I'm wrong. I've never hoped I was more wrong in my life.

CHAPTER TWELVE

Membrane

Mike Jessup, Daniel Marcus's attorney, eyes me suspiciously from the chair next to me and across from Henrietta Leed's desk at Georgia Tech. He's an overweight man with a pink complexion who looks like he slept in his clothes, except the bloodshot look in his eyes tells me that he probably hasn't had any sleep since he got the call from his client's friends.

Outside the professor's window, students cross the quad toward their morning classes under a canopy of trees that have already lost their leaves.

"Can anyone tell me why I'm sitting here in the office of the physician the FBI may use in court against my client?" asks the lawyer.

"I've already told them I can't participate," says Leed. She gives me a subtle glance. "I've already been compromised, so to speak."

"Did you have the MRI done?" I ask.

"Do you know how hard it is to get an MRI done at that time of night?" Jessup shoots back. "Much less get the results back so quickly?"

"You're the legal adviser for the hospital. I thought you might be able to call in a favor."

"I did. I just want you to know that it wasn't something you just conjure up out of thin air. Now please tell me why I'm here. I showed up because I looked up your name. But why did you ask me in here when I should be getting ready to file a motion in the event the FBI decides to press charges against my client?"

"I have a theory."

"Ooh, a theory," he mocks. "I can rest easy. Let me tell the boys at the US attorney's office that they should stand down because you got a theory. Unless you're about to confess to the crime, your theory is a crock of nothing at this point and a waste of my time."

"Mr. Jessup, more lives than just your client's could be at stake right now. If I'm right, and I hope I'm not, it's way worse than I imagined."

"And how is this good for my client?" he replies.

"They're going to need his full cooperation. Possibly to stop other murders."

"By who?" he asks.

"I'll get to that. Like I said, chances are I'm wrong. But if I'm not, it'll be a bargaining chip to get your client help."

He turns to Professor Leed. "Does he ever get to the point?"

"Do you have the MRI scans?" I ask.

Jessup takes a thumb drive from his pocket. "I have MRI scans made under the name of John Doe. Does that satisfy you?"

That's a good trick on Jessup's behalf. If the records aren't under Marcus's name and they're inconclusive, the prosecution will have a hard time calling them in as exhibits if Jessup decides to plead insanity due to physical trauma.

Leed takes the thumb drive and plugs it into her computer. "Would you mind lowering the screen over my bookcase and turning down the lights?" she asks me.

I do as she requests, then sit again, turning my chair so I can see the projection. The wall fills with the image of her desktop, followed by an MRI scan similar to the ones we looked at last night.

The data points seem too chaotic for me to make sense of. I want to rip the thumb drive out and plug it in to my computer, but I wait for Leed to make her analysis.

She gets up from behind her desk and walks over to the screen. She could simply blow the image up on her own monitor, but I guess making it extralarge is part of the process. My mind wanders for a moment as I try to imagine what virtual reality will be like when we can step inside a 3-D human brain and examine each individual neuron.

She takes her ruler from her pocket and starts comparing areas. From my research, it appears she's measuring the thickness of a specific region in the frontal lobe. The red and white dots tell her about blood supply. More white than red is an indicator that the area isn't functioning.

"Does this mean anything to you?" Jessup asks me.

"Not at the macro level. I'd have to look at it on a mathematical level."

"Thanks for clearing that up."

I realize I gave him a confusing answer. "I'd have to compare it to a bunch of other brains to see how they're different. Dr. Leed's seen thousands, so she can spot the difference on sight."

"I wish it was that easy," she replies. "Mike, mind if I let computer boy have a look, using his whatever?"

"Fine. But you're now officially an unpaid adviser to the defense team."

"Uh, okay." I take the drive from Leed's desk and plug it in to my MacBook. After I drag the images over to my little application, it only takes a moment for it to give me an answer.

"Dr. Cray?" asks Leed. "What does it say?"

I close my computer. "You first. All I have is a number." Impulsively, I want to test her. She made me go first last time, and for all I know she could be conning me.

"Fine. I'll show you mine." She points to a portion of the image toward the front of the skull. "See this? All that white? It's like there's no wall there. To create this kind of deterioration, you'd have to use surgery or some kind of particle beam." She turns to Jessup. "Hand it over."

"Hand what over?" he asks.

"Marcus's real MRIs. This little courtroom trick doesn't fly around here."

"Henrietta, as God is my witness, that's the drive the doctor gave me."

"No trick?" She seems genuinely surprised.

"No trick."

She sits on the edge of her desk between us. "Holy shit. Holy fucking shit. Pardon my language, gentlemen. But I wasn't kidding. The only way I know to get this kind of damage is like I said. Surgery or some kind of medical proton beam. No trick?"

"No, ma'am."

Leed turns to me. "All right, computer boy, what does your magic box say?"

I call out the confidence level to her. "A point-nine-two certainty. Again, my model isn't that well trained. But it's been dead-on so far."

"Holy shit," she says again.

"Could someone tell me what this means? Did my client do it or didn't he?" asks Jessup.

"Oh, he did it," she says. "According to what I'm seeing, if he didn't do it, it was only a matter of time before he snapped and did *something*. See that area? That's what stops you from hitting the guy that looked at you funny. When you're drunk or high, it doesn't function so well. On your client, it's like it got completely stripped away. He was a ticking time bomb."

Jessup nods, the defense's argument already forming in his mind.

"I'll testify he's no guiltier than someone who unknowingly infects someone else with a deadly cold," says Leed. "It was physically—structurally—impossible for him to restrain himself. He's like a man who gets pushed off a building and lands on a pedestrian."

Jessup ponders this. "But if we plead insanity, he'll be hospitalized for the rest of his life."

Leed stares at him. "Your client *needs* to be institutionalized. Now. He could go off again at any moment. I've seen this before," she says, no doubt thinking about Emerson. "We need to get him help."

"Is it reversible?"

"Not presently. But who knows? I don't know if they've tried stem-cell therapy for this kind of thing. It'd make a great candidate." She shakes her head. "Still, how the hell did this happen?"

"I think I know," I reply, "and it terrifies me."

CHAPTER THIRTEEN
Toxic

"Bullshit," says Special Agent Weltz, who's in charge of the current investigation. "Save this prime-time crime-show bullshit for the courtroom and the dumb-ass jury willing to go for this crap."

I'm in yet another FBI conference room, making me wonder if there's an endless number of them in this building, each appearing like some kind of magical Harry Potter chamber whenever summoned.

Gallard, Nicolson, Van Owen, and a handful of others are seated around the table. My reputation was enough to get a thirty-minute meeting with them.

Ten minutes in, it appears the meeting may not make it another five. Weltz is prepared to formally announce charges against Marcus and declare the case closed. He's not too happy about me jumping up and saying that his suspect is crazy before he even gets the chance to point the finger. Unfortunately, there's so much more at stake here.

"Hear me out," I implore. "The deterioration in his prefrontal lobe is unlike almost anything seen before."

"And that makes him all the guiltier. What's your point? His lawyer can argue this in court. We have our man. Why are you still here?"

"Just bear with me, please. Because there was no evidence of overt physical trauma, I tried to find another potential cause that naturally occurred. That got me thinking of toxoplasmosis . . ."

"The thing in cat crap?" asks Van Owen.

"Yes," I reply. "It's in the soil, us, everywhere. In high concentrations, it may cause schizophrenia. Maybe. But we know it affects the behavior of mice, making them lose their fear of cats. Which leads them to getting eaten and the cats spreading the protist in the feces across a wider range. It may also affect humans, making them collect more cats."

"Great. The 'cat-litter' defense," says Weltz. "I'm sure Marcus's lawyer will love you for that. Can I go now?"

"I didn't say it was toxoplasmosis or anything related to *Toxoplasma gondii*. I think the carrier cycle's too short for that."

"Thank goodness. And I appreciate the fact that you're keeping the talk nontechnical," Weltz mugs to the room.

I take a deep breath and try to control myself . . . and fail. "Would you shut the fuck up for a moment? Seriously. Where was your sharp wit when I was hunting Joe Vik? What were you doing when Oyo Diallo was murdering children in your own backyard? Right. Here. Conner Brown, one of his first victims, was picked up off a street corner five blocks from here. His mom called this office eighty times. Eighty fucking times! Did you pick up the phone? Did you bother stopping by the church camp he was at a week before?" My voice starts to falter. "When they found his skull, it was fractured—fractured because I goddamn stepped on it when I was crawling through that nightmare of a backyard. His skull! I found a sliver of bone in my shoes days later." I take a deep breath. "Just give me a moment to finish what I'm saying."

The room has fallen deathly silent. I see aghast faces and realize that I'm on the verge of tears.

"My apologies." Weltz sounds contrite, although I suspect he's only humoring me until I leave.

Fine. Whatever.

"My point is that we have numerous examples of parasites that can influence behavior. Our own gut microbes do this all the time. Besides *Toxoplasma gondii*, there's *Ophiocordyceps unilateralis*. That's the fungus that turns ants into zombies, making them wander away from their colony until they find a more suitable place for the fungus to grow, then latch on to a stalk and slowly rot while they're still alive.

"And *Ophiocordyceps unilateralis* is far from a unique pathogen. There are scores of entomopathogenic organisms, from fungi to nematodes. We've only discovered the ones we have because they cause such visibly bizarre behavior. Who knows how many of them cause more subtle ones like shifting the migration patterns of birds or even apex predators like sharks . . . or people."

"Are you suggesting that some kind of parasite caused Marcus to lose his inhibition against violence?" asks Gallard.

"It's worse than that. He reported headaches, correct? Other people on the team also were affected by something. But nobody missed work for as long as someone suffering from the flu. This sounds different. Marcus's description is consistent with something fungal. But that's just a guess. We should get a respiratory analysis done and see if there are still spores present. We also need to test the point of infection."

"The point of infection?" asks Weltz. "Was this something growing under his fridge?"

"We should check there, but no. Aren't you following along?" I look around the room. "Aren't you getting it? There was another violent incident associated with the team working the Oyo property. They *all* might've been infected."

"Infected with what?" asks Gallard. "This spore? Why there?"

"I don't know. But you have a half acre of decomposing bodies and brain tissue. Although the techs used normal precautions, they might not be enough for an airborne spore. Especially one in high quantity."

"Are you saying this came from Oyo?" asks Van Owen. "That he was a carrier?"

"I don't know. I can't reconcile his restraint with Marcus's complete lack of it. Maybe it affects people differently. Maybe he had a kind of resistance. Maybe he had nothing to do with this."

"Dr. Cray, with all due respect. This is quite a lot to handle," says Weltz. "We'll ask that Marcus get some lab tests done. We'll also have the other team members do it if they volunteer. That's the best we can do."

I stare at him. "Are you kidding me? You don't find this with a routine blood test."

"Our hospital is pretty good here."

"Do they know how to screen for things they don't even have tests for? How does that work? You need to go down the road and call in the Centers for Disease Control. You need to quarantine the entire Oyo property. You need to decontaminate everyone who's been there. Me, you. Everyone."

I've lost them. I've seen this look in people's eyes before. This was how they looked at me when I said a man killed Juniper Parsons, not a bear. This was the look they gave me when I said the Toy Man was real.

Ironically, my track record doesn't give me the benefit of the doubt. It only makes them more skeptical. I was lucky twice, and now I'm believing my own press. That's what they're thinking. In a moment, one of them is going to suggest something proactive and then I'm going to be ushered from the room. They'll agree to look into it and then delegate it to someone without the ability to see it through.

"You know what?" I tell the group. "I'm done. I've lived this movie too many times. I can't go chasing down every monster." I head for the door and leave them with a parting comment. "Good luck."

I wish Marcus were the only one, but sooner or later they're going to realize that the agent's wife in the coma was beaten by her own husband. All the other acts of aggression will start to add up. More lives may be lost, but I did what I could.

CHAPTER FOURTEEN
WHIRLPOOL

Gallard stares at the ripples in his coffee. I reluctantly agreed to meet with him at this doughnut shop off Peachtree Street in downtown Atlanta after he frantically called me. I only agreed because nothing about the man struck me as frantic.

He's been staring at his cup since I sat down, either trying to find the right words or using this as some kind of manipulation tactic. Possibly both.

"For a seemingly coldhearted son of a bitch, you can be a passionate man," he finally says.

"Well, this was worth the detour from my trip to the airport."

"Hold on. I'm going somewhere with this." Gallard reaches into his jacket pocket and pulls out a wallet. He slides a small white rectangle out and stares at it for a moment. "Have a look."

It's a photograph of a woman. Her hair has a 1990s teased look to it, and the background reminds me of the kind you find in a mall photo studio. She has a pleasant smile, but there's something sad in her eyes.

"Who is this?" I ask, handing him back the photograph.

"Colleen Vincelli. In my case file, she's victim number six. She was murdered March 12, 1999, by Kevin C. Downes. I was looking for Downes. We didn't have a name. Just a series of victims in the Pennsylvania area. All female. All roughly Colleen's age.

"Witness who saw a man leaving the scene of the crime gave us a rough sketch. It seemed pretty generic, but we ran it in a few newspapers.

"My partner, who had been working the case with me, had some medical problems and was going through a divorce, so everything kind of fell upon me. We were getting leads, but our real focus was on the forensic data. We were pretty sure he'd slip up and we'd get some blood or semen that we could match to a database." He pauses, then adds, "That was my first problem."

"He didn't slip up?"

"Counting on him to. Now, whenever I hear that phrase, 'slip up,' in a serial-killer case, I wince. That means that what we're really waiting for is someone else to die. It doesn't mean we don't lack urgency, but it does mean that resourcefulness is often in short supply."

I nod my understanding.

"Downes slipped up. One of his victims bit him on the hand and drew some blood. This gave us DNA and an injury to look for when we started rounding up the usual sexual predators. This was two murders after Colleen. Victim number eight.

"We patted ourselves on the back and congratulated each other for stopping the next murder and the one after. The case was pretty solid, and the prosecution was able to get a quick conviction." Gallard makes a little shake of his head, his face a range of emotions. "The reason I carry Colleen's photo . . . the reason I have it with me . . ." He trails off and sighs. "When I was going back through the case files and the notes, I found a stack of messages—calls I needed to return. There were three or four of them from people who saw the artist's sketch in the paper.

"One of the callers was Colleen. Downes worked for a moving company. He'd done a move for a young woman in the apartment next door to Colleen and tried to strike up a conversation with her. She thought he was creepy. She saw the sketch in the newspaper and managed to get ahold of my office. She had his name. The company he worked for. Everything. She tried to tell me. I'd like to say I was too overworked to return the call, but the truth was I was confident that he'd 'slip up' and we'd get that forensic data. He did and we got it. But Colleen would be alive if I hadn't been so full of myself and stuck to basics.

"Nobody knows this. That memo was pulled from the files. But I can't tell you how often that kind of thing happens." He pauses for a long moment. "Anyway, what you said to Weltz back there struck home. I just wanted to say that."

I sit quietly for a moment, trying to tease out the message to his story. "I don't get it," I say after some thought.

"There's nothing to get."

"Am I your confessor?" I ask.

"No, asshole. I'm just trying to explain to you the state of the world. What I'm saying is that they'll look into your claim. They'll even call in the CDC to cover their ass. Maybe they'll find something, but don't expect a herculean effort."

"I wasn't."

"But as far as this murder virus or whatever, how serious do you expect the CDC to take it?"

I ponder this for a moment. The best infectious-disease researchers in the world work there. But they also wait for "slipups" in their own way. For them it's more data points. Nobody is going to comprehensively test the FBI team without clear evidence of an infection. Their toxicology panels aren't going to show signs of the infection. At best, they'll do some MRIs. If Marcus is the only one with the thinning of the region, which he may well be, then it'll end there.

"Damn," I reply after thinking about it.

"You're like a time traveler trying to explain forensics to a bunch of medieval monks who still think in terms of humors and vital essences."

It's nowhere near that extreme, but I get the point.

There's also been so much abuse of statistics and science in the courtroom that cops are distrustful of anyone with a PhD telling them they have a better way to do things.

"Okay. Suppose you're me. What would you do?"

"I don't know," says Gallard. "You have a lab? You work for the government? Maybe you can get them interested in this?"

"That could be complicated." I'm also not so sure I want to turn over to the government a pathogen that can make people into killing machines—assuming that it exists.

"I can get you access to the crime scene. Let you get samples. If that helps. Logs. Whatever."

I cross my arms and stare at the ceiling. How should I proceed—assuming I'm going to?

Who am I kidding? Of course I'm not going to let this go.

But what next?

"If there is a pathogen, then why haven't we seen it before?"

"You mean people killing people?" asks Gallard.

"No. It's not like that. I mean, this may be attributable to a tiny portion of violent behavior, but in no way is it causing an epidemic . . . or is it?" I think for a moment more. "What we need is some kind of filter—a way to narrow down the several thousand murders to ones that may be attributable to this pathogen. And then maybe I can look for a vector. It's what you'd call a big-data problem. But solvable. I think. The filter."

I start to think about how I can take all the murders in the last several years and compare them to similar environmental conditions, suspect behavior, times of year, and a few other factors, and keep on going until I get some kind of match. It'll be something that looks like statistical noise but isn't.

"Dr. Cray . . . ?" says Gallard.

"Yes. It's doable. Not a quick thing, but I might be able to find a pattern and then proceed from there. Maybe I can create some kind of environmental assay that lets me compare soil and other factors to a control group."

"Theo . . . ," Gallard tries again.

"Sorry. Just trying to figure out how to approach the problem."

"I have your test group," he replies.

"Pardon me?"

"You're looking for a small group of murders that share some statistical connection, correct?"

"Yes. That's how I can start looking."

"I have them. Nine of them. Nine cases that have a connection we can see but can't quite understand."

"Wait? You do?"

"Yes. I think Nicolson already mentioned them to you. The Phantom?"

"The cross-contamination of crime scenes?" To be honest, I'd dismissed that as . . . well, statistical noise.

"What if there's a connection? Listening to you has me thinking. Some of our equipment is sent from office to office when we have a major investigation. We have a handful of people who visit the crimes. None of them have been to all of them. But they're from the same center. Is it possible . . . ?" He hesitates as he considers the implications of what he's about to say. "Is it possible we've actually spread this?"

We both sit there in silence. While I can discount a number of things about that scenario, I can't eliminate it entirely.

"Bats and frogs," I reply.

"Pardon me?"

"If you visit certain bat sanctuaries, they ask that you make sure your shoes have been decontaminated and haven't been in other caverns. This is because there's a parasite that can be spread on the bottom of your shoes."

He raises his eyebrows. *So?*

"The more disturbing implication, and one that doesn't get as much attention because the people who may be aware of this problem could be the partial cause of the problem, is amphibian die-off. While there's ample evidence that pollution has been killing frogs and other amphibians in some locations, the rate at which some of these populations collapse doesn't track with gradual environmental damage. It's more like what you see when there's a viral outbreak like Ebola.

"When a particular group of frogs suddenly dies off from what appears to be a pathogen in a remote section of the Appalachians, you have to ask what introduced the pathogen to the area. Unfortunately, the answer in some cases may be the researchers investigating the frogs. There's reason to believe that their shoes and equipment act as delivery mechanisms when they go from one location to another. Basically, they take a parasite that one group of frogs has adapted to and introduce it into a different region where there is no resistance."

Gallard nods that he understands.

"It's a controversial theory, because it implicates the scientists investigating the very problem they're trying to solve. This could be the same situation."

"We can't tell anyone," says Gallard.

"What do you mean?"

"I mean, tell your lawyer or anyone you need to. But if we go back to the bureau with this, it'll cause problems."

"Problems are unavoidable," I reply.

"Okay, genius, think this through. Let's say we take this directly to the director. What's he going to do? He's going to call the head of the field lab and ask what the hell we're talking about.

"The lab chief will tell him it's bullshit, while quietly making sure all their equipment gets sterilized—if they take it that far. But what they'll definitely do is tell him that *you're* the pathogen. While the lab chief denies there's any problem that he helped create, you'll have the FBI after you for assailing their reputation. It has to be you."

"Me?"

"Yep." He touches the photograph of Colleen on the table. "Assuming that you're right, then this will happen again. If it isn't happening right now." He stirs his coffee with his spoon. "Crazy thing, the idea of that pathogen getting spread around."

I watch the whirlpool and get an unsettled feeling. "Fuck."

"What."

"Fungi. Viruses. Bacteria. They don't stay the same. Fungi and bacteria in particular, they exchange DNA haphazardly. This could be something *made* by cross-contaminating crime scenes."

"Damn. That's even worse."

"No. *Way* worse. The others may have been gradual. Marcus was affected pretty quickly." I find it hard to breathe. "This thing may have mutated. It could be even more virulent. More dangerous. This could become a real epidemic."

"An epidemic of violent behavior? Like more spree killers?"

"Precisely."

Gallard pushes his coffee away, unable to finish it. I've lost all trace of appetite myself. There's no way I can drop this now.

CHAPTER FIFTEEN
KELP

The sky and the sea are all the shades of gray blending into a dark foreboding where the ocean curves into the horizon. In the distance, a black figure is walking toward me. He waves to me, and I wave back, then try to imagine my Viking ancestors looking into the hostile waves and telling themselves this was a good day to set sail for different shores.

To be sure, they saw the sea differently than I do. They could read the currents, the winds, perceiving many elements I'm oblivious to. They also had their own instruments, like the *sólarsteinn*, or sunstone, as we call it in the Anglo tongue.

While the sunstone was mentioned allegorically in medieval texts, historians and scientists weren't quite sure if this was a real thing. Supposedly it could tell you where in the sky the sun was on a heavily overcast day—a not-too-uncommon condition in the North Atlantic.

While the minerals cordierite and Icelandic spar have polarizing properties that could maybe sort of tell you where the sun was, people trying to use them came away with mixed results.

The breakthrough came courtesy of two scientists at a laser-research laboratory who decided not to discount the other parts of the legend. The sunstone wasn't only a piece of crystal you looked through to find the sun; it was also supposed to give the user the magical gift of being able to see the sun on an overcast day. That's a subtle distinction to a modern person, but not to an ancient who didn't have an understanding of the physiology of the eye to explain this phenomenon.

The scientists tried an interesting experiment. They noticed that in a certain position, Icelandic spar could act as a depolarizer, making all the photons given off by the diffuse light take on random orientations. When they had people look through the Icelandic spar at a cloudy horizon, then suddenly yank the crystal away, they saw with their own naked eye a yellowish line where the sun was located. In theory, because of a small defect of the eye, looking through the sunstone made it momentarily hypersensitive to polarized light.

At least that's the theory. I don't know if it's true, but I like the idea that the Vikings figured out something practical about quantum physics and neurology that we're only now beginning to grasp.

I especially like the idea of a magical crystal that could help me separate the signal from all the noise.

"This is the spot," says the man as he catches his breath, "where we found the first body. Skylar Steven. You're Dr. Cray? Right?"

I extend my hand. Sergeant Newell shakes mine in a cold grip. He was the New Jersey State Police officer who responded to the first report of the triple homicide as he came on duty. He's in his civvies: a thick wool jacket over blue jeans and tall black boots. A baseball cap shadows his face, which has a pale-parchment tone.

"There was a tide pool here. Steven's body was lying in it, still bleeding out. There were crabs all over him. What a sight. Something out of a movie. A woman and her dog found him. The paramedics got here first. They knew he was a goner. All that blood, it looked like he got run over by a boat propeller." He points into the distance down the beach. "And then we found the other one and the other. This way."

I follow him down the shoreline as he paints a vivid picture of the morning he found the bodies. "I'm in the middle of calling this in, and people are starting to gather. Some college kid asks me about the other one. I'm like, 'What other one?' and then he points me to here." Newell points to a small patch of kelp. "This is where I found Ernie Calder. He was lying faceup. Slashed like the others. His head was all tilted to the side. Ugh. What a mess. Yardley was over here. Just as bad."

Gallard's case file has photos of the bodies. It's not difficult to match the memory of those to Newell's firsthand account.

"Then what happened?" I ask.

"I was standing here with a couple of other officers, waiting to see if the coast guard had any reports of a missing boat. That's when I looked a little farther down the shore and thought to myself, *We need to call homicide.* I kind of had an idea, an image, of what happened. It all started to make sense."

Newell nods to a fishing pier jutting out into the ocean. Made from dark timber, the structure looks like something the Romans built and forgot about. It also looks ready to collapse into the ocean with the next pounding wave.

I follow Newell onto the pier, and we slip through the metal gate blocking the entrance.

"The thing was condemned, but some of the older guys still came here to fish. Local cops looked the other way."

The floorboards are covered in seagull crap and flaking paint. Some of the planks are missing, while others are rotting away in place.

At the end of the pier, speckles of blood, fish scales, and more seagull droppings are splattered all over the wood. Off to one side, a whole section has been removed; fencing now covers the hole that looks straight down into the frothing waves.

"The techs cut out the boards with the blood splatter. But I can show you pictures. When I got here and saw the puddles of blood and the seagulls walking in it, getting their goddamn feet wet, it wasn't hard to figure out what happened. Someone went berserk with their fish knife and carved up the others.

"It only took a few hours to figure out who that was. Carl Dunhill. He was a regular here, too. Nice guy. Quiet. But nice. He'd been friendly with the other guys—drinking and fishing buddies. We arrested him at work. He was a bridge tender."

I raise my eyebrows.

"Yeah, that made things difficult. We showed up at the bridge and had to ask him to call in his replacement."

"How was he?" I ask.

"Carl? He wasn't the same guy. He was distant. I don't know if that's because he realized what he'd done. Or if he was just in his own world. Either way, he came with us but didn't say much, other than muttering that it was a horrible dream."

"Where is he now?"

"Serving three life sentences. I heard he's in solitary confinement because he attacked some guards or something."

"Did he ever have any violent behavior before?"

The officer shrugs. "Some drunk-and-disorderlys. He'd get pretty wasted. People saw him stumbling home fairly often."

"What about when they arrested him?" I ask.

"He looked like he hadn't slept much. But not hungover. You'd think a guy like that would have got himself shit-faced after doing something like that. But nope."

Interesting.

I survey the pier and try to imagine how the FBI got any useful forensics out here other than the blood. With the salt water and waves that occasionally splash over the edges, it would seem close to impossible to get anything other than fish blood or seagull crap.

"Do you guys usually use the FBI forensics lab?"

"We have some kind of cooperative agreement, I think. You could ask Detective Gora for more details on that."

I put on a respirator mask and pull out a sampling kit. "I'm just going to collect some samples."

"Have at it. Take the whole pier if you want."

I scrape some of the rotten timbers and look for mold under the railings. To be honest, I'm doubtful I'll find any trace of what I'm looking for here. This is not where Carl Dunhill got infected, if he got infected. But I'm here and I might as well give it a shot.

The similarities between this case and Marcus's are striking. The sudden change of behavior clearly stands out. Neither case involved a long-standing grudge or any other major trigger event. For Carl Dunhill, the file shows only a recent drunk brawl over a basketball score. In Marcus's case, it was a bad performance review. These aren't big triggers that push a normal person over the edge. They would only activate the hair trigger of a psychopath.

"Anything else I can do for you?" asks Newell.

"No. Thank you. I'll probably be calling Gora with a hundred questions. But first I've got to drive to Pennsylvania to see another crime scene."

"Is it connected to this?" he asks.

"I hope not."

CHAPTER SIXTEEN

RUMPUS

The houses on Worth Avenue are all run-down in different ways. Some of them are missing entire panels, exposing insulation. Others have overgrown yards or broken windows patched up with cardboard and duct tape. It's like each home expresses its own kind of failure: economic, health, old age.

It's dark out, and the one working streetlight is flickering on and off. I'd be more concerned for my safety if it didn't look so abandoned.

Raskin, Pennsylvania, police detective Duffy is waiting inside her car when I pull up to 4428 Worth Avenue. She glances up at me from her window. "Cray?"

"Yep."

She gets out of her car, and I see she's wearing black slacks and a jacket. Her auburn hair is cut close and she isn't afraid to let some of her gray show. Although she's short, her green eyes look straight through me, unafraid.

Duffy seems immune to the cold, while I've got my hands in my pockets to keep them from turning white.

Her words are punctuated by vapor clouds as she speaks. "I spoke to Benjamin Pale's mother at the hospital. She gave us permission to look around the home. His brother, Robert, will probably be there."

Benjamin Pale, a thirty-eight-year-old factory worker, was convicted of trying to murder a supervisor at his workplace. One day he went ballistic, grabbed a box knife, and started to slash at his boss, almost killing him on the spot before someone intervened, slamming a chair into his head, knocking him out cold.

When police conducted a search warrant on his home, they found the bodies of two prostitutes under a pile of boxes in the basement. They'd been killed only days before the incident at the factory.

Pale's mother, an invalid who requires oxygen—living at home then, now a hospital inpatient indefinitely—had no idea what the noises were coming from downstairs. His brother is a truck driver who had been away when the murders happened.

"Just so you know, both the brothers are kind of odd," says Duffy as we walk toward the one house on the street with a light on.

"Odd? How do you mean?"

"When we searched the home and found the two victims, we'd originally pegged Robert for the murders. He seemed more the type. Benjamin wasn't really the angry sort."

"Tell that to his foreman," I reply.

"Well, yeah. Both of them are a bit on the spectrum. They've never left home, never been married, and I don't think either has a friend to speak of. Anyway, we thought Robert killed the girls in the basement, but he'd been out of town, and we got a sample from Benjamin that matched."

"Does either one of them have a history of violent behavior?"

"No. Kinda surprising. Nothing. Not even a domestic disturbance. Although I'm not sure they have any neighbors. Most of the houses here have been foreclosed on for years."

We reach the front steps of the two-story house. One yellow light illuminates a dull-gray porch with two sad-looking wooden chairs supporting plastic crates of car parts and empty bottles.

Duffy knocks on the door and gives me a grimace as we wait for someone to answer. She pounds louder, rattling the light fixture next to the door.

"Mr. Pale! It's the police. We need to finish up a few things about the case."

The neighborhood is quiet. The only noise is a dog barking in the distance and the low hum of cars on the distant freeway. Duffy bangs her fist against the door again.

From somewhere inside the house, we hear a squeak and a door shutting. Footsteps can be heard coming toward the door.

The dead bolt unfastens and a man half a head taller than I stands there in a dirty white tank top. He's got black hair with gray streaks and an unshaven face.

"Yup?" he says.

"I'm Detective Duffy. Remember me? We're here to clear up a couple things about your brother's case," she explains.

"What kind of things?"

"Procedural."

He shakes his head. "I'm kinda busy right now."

I watch Duffy and can tell that she's a little suspicious of his behavior. "It's okay. We won't be long. Your mother told us we could have a look. And she still owns the house."

"Yeah. Fine." He pushes open the door and waves us into the living room.

The inside of the house reminds me of a Sears catalog from 1982—with the expected wear and tear of the intervening decades.

Time seems to have stopped while everything fell apart. I suspect that the time-capsule effect was created when the brothers' father died.

Mrs. Pale never bothered to change anything, and the sons were in no hurry to move on.

I can relate. I lost my own father when I was young, and all my interests were sort of frozen at that point. I tried to be a doctor like him, and it didn't work out, but I still feel his shadow to this day.

Duffy makes her way to the kitchen. The sink is full of dishes, and garbage is piled up in the corner. Dirty footprints are all over the floor. I hear the jingle of a dog collar, and a shaggy, gray-black, medium-size mutt comes running up to us.

Duffy kneels down and scratches the dog behind the ears. "Hey, Thomas! How have you been?"

The dog soaks up the attention and does an excited spin. Robert seems indifferent to the animal. "Who are you?" he asks.

"I'm a researcher helping the police department build some statistical software."

Duffy glances at me out of the corner of her eye. She doesn't say anything about my lie but understands my hesitancy to tell him the same story I gave her—which involved using my government project as an excuse.

"We're going to have a look in the basement," Duffy informs him—not asking.

"Whatever." Robert gestures at a door in the kitchen, then walks down the hall to the living room and picks up a newspaper.

Duffy leads me down the stairs into the basement and flips on a light. I'd been expecting some dank, dungeon-like space.

Instead it's what I guess they used to call a rumpus room. There's a pool table at one end, couches at the other, and an old television. It's actually the cleanest part of the house—then it dawns on me.

"What was it like when you found it?" I ask.

She shakes her head. "A nightmare. Wall-to-wall boxes, newspapers, everything. The place was practically a garbage pit. We had to haul it all out in case there were more victims." She makes a face. "And the rats.

Good lord. We had to put barriers in the kitchen to keep them from infesting the rest of the house."

She aims her flashlight at a far corner. "That's where we found the first body. Nora Morrant. She was a heroin addict that had been working around a liquor store ten blocks from here."

"She was killed in Benjamin's car?"

"Yes. Before the act or in the middle, they started to fight. We still don't know over what. He beat her, then choked her to death. That's when he panicked and drove the body here, throwing her in the basement.

"The second woman, Shiri Lanham, was almost the same exact thing. Then he flipped out and tried to kill his boss the next day. Funny thing how a guy can just snap like that."

Creaking sounds come from the floorboards above us. Duffy's eyes go upward, then land on me. In a hushed tone, she whispers, "Is it me or was Robert acting kinda weird?"

"I don't know his baseline, but yeah. He seemed very interested in that newspaper."

"Who reads newspapers anymore?"

"Who reads newspapers from July 2004?" I reply.

Her eyes narrow at my observation. "I'm going to have a look upstairs."

CHAPTER SEVENTEEN

Vapor

Robert Pale is back in his chair in the living room when we return upstairs. This time he's reading an old Clive Cussler novel while Thomas sits at his feet, ignored. He looks up from the book he's pretending to read. "You done?"

"Almost," replies Duffy. "We're going to have a look upstairs." She watches for his reaction.

"What for?" he asks.

"We want to take a look at Benjamin's room."

"I got rid of most of his stuff. Whatever."

As we go up the steps, I can feel Robert's eyes boring into our backs. I can't tell if it's suspicion, fear, or something else.

There's a jangle of dog tags as Thomas decides to follow after us, dashing between our legs and then waiting for us at the top of the landing with a "What took you so long?" expression on his face.

Duffy reaches down and pets the animal again. "Poor little guy." She casts a glance back at the living room, maybe thinking about saying something, but decides otherwise.

The first room we encounter is Mrs. Pale's. The lamp on the nightstand is on, revealing pink wallpaper and overstuffed cabinets holding dolls and crystal figurines. Oxygen tanks and medical equipment surround the bed. Pill bottles cover most of the available horizontal surfaces.

She was clearly not a well woman before this happened. I can only imagine the toll it has taken on her health.

A small air purifier is whirring away on a chair by her bed, still blowing a breeze over the spot where she normally lies. A stack of paperbacks stands at her bedside, most of the books bearing stickers from library sales.

We go down the hall toward a closed door. I can't help noticing the faded pictures along the walls. They show family photos from the 1980s. Two boys, I assume Robert and Benjamin, are in the images. They look relatively normal, if not a little subdued in their expressions. I don't notice anything weird.

They just seem like a quiet family—the kind you see at a Shoney's wordlessly eating a meal together, their internal lives far more interesting than the ones they share with each other.

The threat of an airborne pathogen is weighing at the back of my mind, but I don't think a brief exposure would be enough. All the same, I avoid touching my face and decide to use a Vaseline nasal rub in the future to keep my nostrils from drying out and making me vulnerable. Wearing a mask or a hazmat suit might alarm people too much.

"This is Benjamin's room," says Duffy as she pushes open a door. It's a teenager's room straight out of the late 1980s. Posters of muscle cars and bikini-clad women fill the walls. The floors and closet are bare. I assume his clothing was taken as evidence. Like the basement, it has a picked-over appearance.

There's a shelf of books, mostly fantasy novels and a few role-playing games. I point them out to Duffy. "Did he have any friends?"

"Not that I'm aware of."

I walk over and take a look at the games. Some of them are new. I hold up the latest edition of *Advanced Dungeons and Dragons*. With it are several filled-out character sheets. "You check the local comics shop or game store?"

She shakes her head. "Nope."

"They might know him. Not that it makes a difference now. But he might have had a few friends there."

I get the impression that Benjamin wasn't antisocial—well, except for the whole murdering hookers thing—he was simply an introvert. You don't role-play if you hate people. You play these games if you don't know how to interact with others and are looking for a way to connect. The rules and routines of RPGs make it easy for even the most socially awkward person to spend a few hours in the company of other people without worrying about what to say.

When I was dealing with the loss of my father, I'd go play D&D over at an older kid's house. There was a small group of us that would game on Sunday afternoons. I never spent much time with them socially because of the age gap, but when we gamed, I could lose myself in an adventure and not stress out about how I was going to make it through life without Dad there to help me out.

Without those gaming sessions, I probably would have stayed in my room all the time. I never told my mother or the psychologist she had me see about my D&D habit. I'm sure they would have thought it was deviant behavior, tantamount to Satan worship.

I actually think schools should encourage role-playing games. It helps kids with limited social groups find something in common with others and learn how to interact. I don't have the data to back that up, but that's what it did for me. And maybe it did the same for Benjamin. For a time, anyway . . .

I put the games back and follow Duffy to the bathroom. This also looks cleaner than it should. The forensics department probably searched the drains for evidence.

There are dirty shoe prints on the tile, and the hamper is overflowing with sweat-stained clothes. Thomas pokes his nose into the room and stares at us for a moment before going on about urgent dog responsibilities.

Bam! Duffy and I both flinch at a loud sound coming from downstairs. We rush to the stairs, where the dog is standing at the top step.

"Fucking thing!" yells Robert.

We hurry down the steps to see Robert banging a wrench against a heating unit on the wall.

"Goddamn thing doesn't do shit," he growls.

He sees us watching, and his hand tightens around the wrench, his fingers going pale. After a tense moment, he relaxes, letting the wrench clatter to the ground near a toolbox, and sits back down in a recliner.

"I can take a look," I offer.

"Don't bother." He starts to rub his forehead.

"Migraines?" I ask, fishing through his toolbox.

He stares at me with a look that could kill. "You a doctor? I said, don't bother."

Technically . . .

"Sorry. Sometimes headaches can be caused by dehydration." I stand, leaving the toolbox alone.

"Thanks for the tip," he replies insincerely. "You done here?"

"You been to visit your mother?" asks Duffy.

"I've been busy," he replies.

"Clearly."

Robert tenses up. "Those cunt nurses said I had to come during visiting hours. Fucking bitches." He says the words as he stares right at Duffy.

She doesn't let it faze her. "Well, she'd love to see you. Maybe you can find a way for Thomas to visit her, too."

"Yeah, whatever." He starts to sort through a stack of books, feigning interest in them.

Thomas is watching us from the top of the stairs. I think Duffy's contemplating taking the poor dog with us. I'm not sure Robert would care.

"You good?" Duffy asks me.

"Thank you, Mr. Pale," I say to Robert.

"Mmm. Okay."

We let ourselves out and walk until we're beneath the one functioning streetlight and out of earshot of the house.

"He's nice," I say sarcastically.

"Actually, he wasn't that much of an asshole when we first talked to him. He was the calmer, more mature one. Of course, that was before his brother was charged with murder and his mom ended up in the hospital."

"And no forensics tied him to the victims?"

Duffy gives me a look. "No. And, like I said, we have hard evidence he was out of town when it happened."

I nod, thinking. "I guess he's just stressed." Actually, I'm even more suspicious. First his brother turns serial killer and now Robert is acting like . . . a psychopath.

"Well, let me know if you need anything else. I have my own troubled kids to go home to."

"Thank you," I reply as I shake her hand. "I appreciate your help."

"Good luck with your project." She gets in her car and leaves me on the empty street.

I get into my rental and start it up. In the rearview mirror, I can see Robert watching me from the living room window.

I tell people it's not a gut instinct per se—it's a neurological response triggered by one or more stimuli that are either unconscious or barely at our sensory threshold. But, man, does my gut tell me something weird is going on.

Robert Pale makes me nervous.

I turn the corner and double back to the other side of the block.

I'm not done here.

CHAPTER EIGHTEEN

Rust

Robert Pale is an angry man. He hasn't been accused of anything, but neither was his brother until he decided to slash open his supervisor. Carl Dunhill wasn't known as an angry man, either, until his fishing buddies started to wash ashore. Daniel Marcus was a quiet, nonconfrontational forensic specialist until he murdered his coworkers.

Robert Pale's behavior felt like more than that of a man upset at being hassled by the police. If I had to put it into precise words, I would say he was acting like he had something to hide.

Still, Detective Duffy and I were able to peek into all the rooms. While a teenage runaway could be shoved into a closet that we didn't search, Pale didn't seem too concerned about where we looked.

Logically speaking, if he didn't have someone shoved into the couch under him, and he wasn't worried about us searching the house, then either he wasn't up to something or he wasn't particularly concerned that we'd discover what he was hiding.

A few things got me thinking. When he was at the door, he was wearing a tank top, yet he got upset at the heater for not being all that hot. Why didn't he have on a sweater?

There was also the dirt on the floor. The walkway from the street to the house was concrete. You wouldn't track in dirt unless you'd been walking somewhere else.

I get out of my car and walk up to the house that sits directly in back of the Pale home. It's a run-down structure with a foreclosure sign. A large sheet of plywood has been nailed to the front door.

I walk around the side of the house, stepping through a metal gate that comes to my waist. Sheets of plywood and garbage cans line the side of the house. The backyard is an overgrown jungle of weeds. A rusted swing set sits derelict in the corner, waiting for ghost children to come play.

Light is visible from the kitchen of the Pale house. A boulder is propping open the rear screen door. A small gate separates the two properties, maybe put there to allow neighbors to easily exchange lawn mowers and cups of sugar.

I think of poor Thomas trapped inside a home with an uncaring owner while his human mother is probably on her last legs in the hospital.

The dog seemed to keep his distance from his owner. He liked to follow us around, but when Robert was raging at the heater, Thomas stayed at the top of the stairs.

I retrace the sequence of events:

We showed up and Duffy pounded on the door. We waited a minute or more for Robert to answer. When he arrived, he seemed confused as to why we were there, even though Duffy told him through the door.

Why didn't he hear her?

Maybe because he was too far away?

The Pales' backyard is covered with overgrown weeds, but flagstones lead from the concrete deck to the fence where I'm lurking.

Just to the side of the kitchen door there's a garbage can.

It's an odd place for one if they're taking their trash to the street.

I reach down to unlatch the gate. Moving it only an inch makes a loud squeak. I stop, afraid Robert will burst through the back door.

Minutes go by and nothing happens. I move the gate more slowly this time and slide my body through.

I'm not sure if this is trespassing, because Mrs. Pale gave us permission to search the premises. Either way, my curiosity and concern are too strong to stop.

I creep over to the trash can and carefully lift the lid, afraid that I'm about to come nose first with Thomas's yard droppings. Instead, the can is empty—or mostly empty.

There's a rag at the bottom. I peer closer, but it's too dark to see what it is. I decide to use just my thumb and forefinger to raise it out of the can and into the light of the porch.

I hold up a dark flannel shirt for inspection.

The pattern is hard to make out, but something glistens in the light. At first, I think it's water from the bottom of the can; then I notice a dark drop fall from the frayed edges at the bottom.

Blood.

Robert answered the door in a tank top . . . He was wearing this right before and threw it into the trash. That's why he was cold. And why it took so long for him to let us in.

I lower the shirt back inside and return the lid to the top of the can as quietly as I can. Still, the metal-scraping-metal screech sounds loud to my ears. I wince when I hear the sound of Thomas's dog collar as he comes running to the back of the house to inspect the source of the noise.

Damn it.

You're a good dog, Thomas. Too good.

I wait for him to start barking and call attention to my presence, but he doesn't. I can hear him sniffing at the door, but he just puts his nose there and waits, I assume.

Good boy.

I turn to the postage-stamp backyard. I didn't notice any dead hookers as I walked across the flagstones.

Dead hookers . . .

Damn it, Theo. You just used a dehumanizing punch line in your own train of thought. Were any of the young women I dug up in Montana punch lines? When I see their faces in the middle of the night, do I want to laugh? Do I belittle them for the horrible things that happened to them before I found them?

Words have meaning. While I'll argue until I'm blue for my right to use whatever words I want to, that doesn't mean I have to desensitize myself.

I sigh and scan the grass again. I still don't see any bodies. A body is a neutral concept. Impersonal, but not judgmental.

I'm a scientist—neutral is good. Neutral is where I want to be.

So, it doesn't look like Robert picked up his brother's hobby.

Or did he?

What assumptions am I making? What am I forgetting? When we knocked on the door, we heard a metal squeak—like a gate closing. Like the gate I just slipped through. The gate leading to the abandoned house behind the Pale home.

I look to the abandoned house's dark rear porch. A sheet of plywood is next to the back door, not over it. Someone removed the barrier.

Damn.

What have you been up to, Robert?

CHAPTER NINETEEN
DUSK

There was a haunted house in my hometown outside Austin. Or at least the other kids in the neighborhood tried to convince me the house was haunted. The middle-school playground buzzed with stories about the Ox House or the Barrow Place. The specifics were fuzzy.

The broad strokes were that the large, single-story ranch home with the half-acre lot used to belong to a group of Satan worshippers who murdered children and fed them to their ox god—when they weren't in the middle of a Dungeons and Dragons campaign.

Kids talked about investigating the place all the time. Well, Rodney Chuff, Frank Donovan, Emilio Paz, and I finally agreed to inspect the house, which had had a **FOR SALE** sign on it for as long as anyone could remember.

The night we were going to do the deed, I remember pedaling my Mongoose BMX bike to the house in the fading light of dusk, speculating on all sorts of horrific sights we'd see—but knowing deep down that ghosts weren't real.

That was my first personal paradox: I knew ghosts weren't real, but I was scared.

What am I scared of? I asked myself as I came to a stop on my bike and saw the creepy house—a rock-and-cedar fortress that looked like a southwestern tomb. The sun had almost set, and I remember thinking, *If Dracula lived in Texas, this is where he'd be.*

I put my bike in a stand of trees and walked around the house. The sole member of my group to arrive, I figured the others had chickened out. All the schoolyard talk was only that. To heck with them. I was going to see some ghosts, or not.

The back porch had been collecting tumbleweeds, but the yard had been cut, probably because of some management deal with whoever controlled the property.

I found a dog door on a side entrance and was able to push the inside cover upward. It might have kept raccoons out, but it wasn't eleven-year-old–proof.

I slid through the hole and onto the linoleum floor. Orange light from the fading sun cast an otherworldly glow around the house. I was as nervous as I'd ever been and decided this was what a house on the edge of hell must look like. Then a different part of my brain took over and I imagined that this was what it would look like on Mars or a planet that orbited a red sun.

What if ghosts were alien visitors?

I took out my blue plastic flashlight with its weak beam and probed the nooks and crannies of the empty house. There were no ghosts. No aliens. Just an empty house.

I spent an hour roaming the barren rooms, imagining Martian hieroglyphs and strange sarcophagi containing extraterrestrial mummies.

When I climbed back through the dog door, night had fallen. I knew something about myself as I dusted off my pants on the back patio. My curiosity was more powerful than my fear.

The next day at school, I didn't even bother telling the others I'd been inside the house. Wandering the rooms with my light, exploring that alien tomb, had been my special moment. If I told them, it wouldn't be the same. They'd have destroyed the sanctity of it with laughter or literally tried to destroy it with vandalism.

Standing behind the Pale house, I know I should call Duffy and tell her we need to look at the derelict home behind the Pales', but I don't. I'm afraid of what I'm about to find but, perversely, I'm excited about finding it on my own.

This is dangerous.

I take a glance back at the Pale home, then climb up the steps to the wooden porch of the other house. The wood around the lock has been scraped away with a crowbar or some other tool. When I push the door, it slides open into a dark interior.

I leave my penlight off until I'm inside the home. I'm afraid that Robert might see the glow and become suspicious. After I step past the threshold, I close the door and find myself in complete darkness.

I don't turn on the light just yet. I focus on my senses.

The wind is blowing around the house, and the wood is making creaking noises. Somewhere water drips and animals scurry through crawl spaces.

As my eyes adjust, I can make out the faint light coming from the edges of the boards blocking the windows. Most of the house is dark pools of nothing, but I have a sense of the boundaries of the space.

I step farther into the kitchen and spot the outline of a door, just like the one that led to the Pales' basement.

I turn the knob and pull the door open. A musty scent greets my nostrils. For some reason, I still don't turn on my light.

I walk down the basement steps, taking each slowly, afraid that I'll land on emptiness and fall into a bottomless void or trip and break my neck.

As I make my way to the bottom of the steps, the hair on the back of my neck begins to rise. This is that nongut instinct telling me something.

I'm not alone.

My skin flushes as my fear response goes into full effect. I flip on the light and pan it across the basement.

Boxes obstruct my view, but I see something move out of the corner of my eye.

"Hello?" I call out, suddenly realizing that I can't be sure Robert's still back in his house. He could be down here.

I move toward a wall to put my back against it and sweep the light around, trying to get a better glimpse of what I saw.

I remind myself that the advantage of a flashlight is that whatever I'm aiming it at is blinded.

"Hello?"

I spot a leg behind a stack of boxes. A black shoe and blue trousers.

I move closer, and the rest of the body becomes visible. It's a man leaning against the wall. He's an older black man in a United States Post Office uniform. His hands are bound, and his letter bag is a few feet away, its contents spread across the floor.

He's moaning.

I step to the man and kneel at his side. "Can you hear me?"

Groan.

I use my light to check his pupils. They dilate. Good. But the bruises on his head don't look so good. Blood is trickling out from his shirt under his jacket.

My first take is that he was beaten with something blunt and then stabbed with something sharp. Maybe a wrench? Like the one Robert was assaulting his heater with?

I glance around and spot a screwdriver sitting in a small pool of blood.

That would explain why he didn't want me attempting to fix the heater. Asking for a screwdriver could have led to an awkward silence.

I check the name on the uniform. Clay.

"Mr. Clay, my name is Theo. I'm going to open your shirt and have a look. Okay?"

Groan.

I rip open the shirt. His white undershirt is mottled with blood-stains. I don't like the one by his liver. It's wetter than the rest. I raise the shirt and see a trickle of blood pouring out.

"Mr. Clay? I need you to hold this." I slide his wrists free, then place his hand over the wound and press. "Hold it tight. I'm going to call for help."

I set the light down and reach for my phone. The hair rises on the back of my neck again as a familiar sound rings through the air—Thomas's dog collar.

I can hear him run down the steps behind me, and then a cold nose touches my hand.

"Looks like my helper is here, Mr. Clay."

Thomas walks over and sniffs the man. Clay makes an effort with his other hand to pat the dog but is too weak to complete the motion.

Thomas doesn't seem bothered. He sits and watches.

My phone lights up, and I dial 911.

"Nine-one-one Emergency Services. What area are you calling from?"

"The house directly behind 4428 Worth Avenue. I have a man here who I believe has been stabbed. I need a paramedic at this location and a police unit to respond to 4428 Worth and apprehend Robert Pale."

"Hold on one moment . . . May I have your name, please?"

"My name is . . ."

I freeze.

"I'm sorry, what was that again?"

Someone's walking down the basement stairs. Thomas didn't get here by himself.

I've been in too many scrapes at this point to make the same mistakes. The first time I had my ass kicked outside a diner in Montana, I realized that I was wholly unprepared for that kind of thing.

I'll never forget the pathetic face Jillian made at me when I stumbled into her restaurant, looking to her like some john who got rolled by a hooker and her pimp.

That was a long time ago.

Time to move.

I roll away from Mr. Clay and shine my flashlight directly at the sound on the stairs.

"Fucker!" screams Robert.

No sight of the man, but I hear a hollow metal clang. He's got a pipe or a metal bat.

It doesn't matter.

I am already on my feet and closing the distance between us as quickly as possible, flashlight off. At the last moment, I put my arms in front of my face and launch myself at where I think his body should be.

I make contact, and the two of us fall onto the basement stairs. A hand reaches up and grabs at my face, trying to claw at my skin.

I unleash a barrage of punches at his head. Some of them hit the steps; some of them land. I clutch his hair in my left hand and start pounding my right fist into his left temple.

The hand trying to claw me goes limp. I let up for a moment and check his pulse on his neck.

He's still alive.

Now I'm faced with a dilemma. I don't have any handcuffs.

I need to check on Mr. Clay but can't risk Robert attacking me.

I grab him by his wrists and drag him off the stairs and drop him next to where the flashlight landed. Thomas comes over and inspects him but seems indifferent to what's happened.

I search Robert for a belt and come up short. I take mine off and cinch it around his wrists then hog-tie it around his ankles.

It's not the best binding, but if I keep my eye on him, it should be enough.

I return to Mr. Clay. "You hanging in there?" Groan.

His hand has fallen from his side. I put mine there and press hard. My other hand searches for my phone.

"Hello?" I call into the phone.

"Are you okay?" asks the dispatcher.

I hide my sore knuckles in my armpit. "Yes. But we're going to need two ambulances."

CHAPTER TWENTY
ECHO CHAMBER

I'm sitting on the curb, rubbing my knuckles, as paramedics load Mr. Clay into one ambulance and Robert Pale into another.

There are seven police cruisers in the street, and what few people who live in this neighborhood have gathered just outside the imaginary boundary to watch.

Thomas is sitting on the curb next to me, watching Detective Duffy as she has an animated discussion with her superiors. Occasionally a finger is pointed in my direction. I simply stay seated and pet Thomas.

Duffy breaks away and walks toward me. I can't read her expression, but I don't think she's bringing me good news.

She stands over me like a giant. "Holy crap, Dr. Cray. How hard would it have been to call me up and say, 'Hey, I think there's something weird going on—you should check it out'?"

"You knew there was something going on," I reply.

"Yes . . . but . . . who gave you the authority to go into the other house?"

"Authority." I say the word as if it's a foreign expression I've heard for the very first time. "What about me makes you think that's a word I care for or yield to?"

"We don't get to write our own rules."

"Of course we do. We do it all the time. I could lead you down the sequence of events that led me to decide that someone was either dead or dying in that house, but there's really no point. How is Mr. Clay?"

"The paramedics say he's going to make it. Robert Pale, too, if you care."

"I do," I reply, massaging my swelling right hand.

"From the look of his face, I'd say otherwise."

"I had a gun on me. I could have shot him."

"What? You didn't tell me you were armed."

"I have DoD authorization. My point is I could have shot Pale as he walked down the steps."

"Instead you fractured his jaw and gave him a concussion."

"I'd put it another way: I risked bodily harm to myself to avoid killing him."

She shakes her head. "This is why I'm talking to you instead of Captain Schmidt interrogating you right now. When he comes over, you need to tell him that Robert Pale swung at you with the bat while you were helping Mr. Clay."

"I can say something to that effect."

"Something to that effect? Whatever." She pats her leg. "Guess who's coming home with me?"

"That's very kind of you," I reply.

She flips me off as Thomas comes running up to her. She pats the dog and leads him down the street to her car.

I stand up and cross my arms, thinking things over. When Duffy's captain approaches me, I'm still lost in thought, trying to put the details in order.

"Dr. Cray? I hope I'm not disturbing you," he says sarcastically.

I resist the urge to say that he is. "Sorry. Crazy night."

"So, you heard moaning coming from the house?"

This is new. I glance over at Detective Duffy as she puts Thomas into the back seat. She's watching me.

"There was moaning coming from inside the house." This is true. Maybe not audible to a human, but true.

"And that led you to go inside, where you found Mr. Clay?"

"I was suspicious and went inside."

"And that's when Robert Pale returned, probably to finish Mr. Clay off?"

"Possibly."

"And you tried to pass him on the stairs?"

"We collided. He seemed very agitated."

Schmidt nods. "Okay. Good enough for me." He reaches out his hand. "I'd like to thank you for your help. I'm sorry your research took a dramatic turn, but I'm sure Mr. Clay's family is grateful."

"What about Robert Pale?" I ask.

Duffy returns without Thomas and listens to the conversation.

"We'll have Pale checked out and then take him to lockup. With any luck he'll be in a cell next to his brother," says the captain.

"You need to have Robert get a full MRI. I'll give you the name of a doctor in Atlanta. Send her the scans. She needs to have a look at them."

"For what?" asks Duffy.

"I didn't kill Robert because I think he may be just as much of a victim as Mr. Clay. The same as his brother."

"What kind of bullshit is that?" asks the captain.

"The brothers may have been infected with a pathogen that makes them prone to violence." I think this over. "First Benjamin, then his brother. But why the delay?" I ask rhetorically.

"Hold up, there," says Duffy. "Are you saying they got infected with something that made them violent?"

"It's a theory."

"A bullshit theory," says Schmidt.

"Any theory without sufficient evidence is bullshit. True. That's what I'm trying to find out. The curious thing is that neither Dunhill's nor the Pale brothers' environments were remotely like the one where Marcus may have been infected."

"What is he talking about?" Schmidt asks Duffy.

"Hell if I know."

"Sorry," I reply. "Just sorting things out aloud. I was expecting some kind of dank murder-dungeon hangout. In both cases I found neither."

"I'll leave you two alone," says Schmidt, walking away.

"Do I need a paramedic for you?" asks Duffy.

"No. I'm fine. This is me being very confused. I've been operating under some assumptions. They've turned out to be false, yet the signal is much stronger than I . . ."

She cocks her head, waiting for me to finish. But the world is falling out from under me as the realization hits.

"Holy shit," I mutter.

"Dr. Cray?"

"Theo. Call me Theo. Excuse me. Holy crap," I say. *No.*

Damn it, no.

I'm feeling cold, exhilarated, dizzy, focused. I'm high on endorphins as something clicks together and terrifies me.

"No!"

"Theo?"

I take off running through the yard and vault the back fence. A group of uniformed cops stares at me in confusion as I bound up the stairs and into the Pale home. Far back in the distance, Detective Duffy is yelling at me.

I race into the living room and dump the toolbox over at the base of the wall heating unit. I sort through the tools, searching for a Phillips head, and find one. As I start on the corner of the heating unit, I stop.

Duffy comes running in. "What the hell?"

I pull a bag of paper air masks from my pocket and hand one to her. "Wear this," I command as I slide one over my head. "Don't let anyone else come into the house."

"What's going on?"

"Just do it!"

"Do we need the bomb squad?"

I stare at her. "No. Make sure nobody comes inside."

She rushes to the back to yell at the other cops, then returns to the living room as I'm unfastening the screws on the plate over the heater. I set them aside then pull the vent off the wall.

There's a spongelike material covering the heating coils.

It's dark black and has a porous texture.

"Don't touch anything!" I yell at Duffy as I run to the kitchen.

I yank open drawers and search the cabinets until I find what I'm looking for, a large roll of plastic wrap. I race back to the living room and unroll a long sheet and wind it over and around the material and the entire wall unit.

"Go to the fuse box and pull out the one that says central heating or something like that."

Duffy obliges while I add another layer of wrap to the unit, taking extra care to go around the edges. When I'm satisfied that I've contained the unit, I sit on the floor and stare up at it—amazed and terrified.

"What's going on?" asks Duffy.

"Ask your captain to call whoever handles bioterrorism threats—whoever you'd call if you had anthrax or something like that—and have them send a containment crew."

"Oh shit," she breathes, peering at the foam under the plastic wrap. "Is that the pathogen?"

I nod, trying to figure out the implications of all this.

"Are we safe?" she asks.

"Probably. I think. Unless he decides to go after either of us."

"Who? Robert Pale?"

I slowly shake my head. "No. The man who put this here. The Pale brothers, Dunhill, Marcus, the others in my files. They weren't accidentally infected." I measure my words, because I don't like what I'm about to say. "They were targeted. Someone deliberately turned them into killers."

CHAPTER TWENTY-ONE
MICROGRAPHIA

The monitor in front of me displays a grayscale universe alien to my own experience. Fibers crisscross a plain so boundless that if I were to climb onto one of them and walk to the edge of the plain, it would be like trying to cross a continent.

Veronica Woodley, the Penn State professor operating the electron microscope, is watching my expression. We're literally on a fishing expedition and our search area is the size of an ocean.

I talked the Raskin police into letting me take a few samples of the air filter in the wall heater from the Pale residence. I sent one to the FBI, another to my lab back in Austin, and brought the third to Veronica. Our paths have crossed at conferences, and we seem to share a maverick attitude when it comes to science.

Trying to spot the pathogen with the electron microscope, not knowing anything about its kingdom, size, or appearance, is a foolhardy endeavor. But I had to see the real scene of the crime with my own eyes—albeit enhanced by an electron microscope.

When you start to see the world through magnification, the deeper you go with more powerful tools, you begin to realize that the world we're familiar with is just the thin skin on the outer surface of a metaphorical apple.

Glass balls filled with water and other simple instruments were used to observe objects on a micro level, hundreds and even thousands of years ago, but it wasn't until a few hundred years ago that we started making the great leaps forward as glass-making technology improved dramatically.

Robert Hooke's 1665 book *Micrographia* revolutionized the way we looked at common objects and life-forms. He made detailed anatomical illustrations of fleas, showed us what a fly's eye looked like up close, and coined one of the most important terms in all of biology when he noticed the particular structure of plants and called the base unit a cell.

Just a few years later, his secretive contemporary, Antonie van Leeuwenhoek, shattered what we understood about the world around us when he looked through his specially designed microscope and discovered that there were entire kingdoms of organisms that couldn't be seen with the naked eye.

He was the first person ever to see an individual bacterium and prove once and for all that there were worlds beyond the one we knew. Belief in "humors," spirits, and other supernatural components of our world faded quickly away as we realized that illness and life itself could be better explained on a microscopic scale.

Veronica centers on a group of sharp-edged boulders. "That would be old-fashioned house dust." She spins a dial, and the image flashes over to a different location. "Let's zoom in to a fiber. You said this air filter was on a heater?"

"Yeah. A gas heater. There was a small blower at the back. This was just stuck over it," I explain.

"Interesting. A heater would kill most things over time, or at least dry them out. I don't see any dust mites."

A fiber grows larger until the surface fills the screen. "We can see some common fungi at this level." She points to a fibrous mat at the edge of the image. "They can look like that. Of course, they can look like anything. What magnification do you want me to use?"

"Good question. Try anything."

While we're visually inspecting the material, my lab is running two other tests. One is a simple filtration assay. They soak the sample in purified water and then let it drip through a series of filters with increasingly smaller diameters.

Big things like dust mites, which are large enough to be a house cat in Abraham Lincoln's lap on the back side of a penny, get caught at the top layer.

Heftier bacteria tend to get snared a few layers below, and so on, until the smallest layer, where we can collect viruses that aren't too small.

This process can be helpful when spotting known organisms and families, but nature plays by its own rules, and recently we've discovered bacteria as small as viruses and viruses as big as bacteria. And there are proteins like prions that behave a lot like viruses in some respects but are technically not life, because they don't have DNA or RNA.

While I have my suspicions about the pathogen, they're only that. This could be a devious protein or some kind of brain amoeba with a complex genetic structure.

The third process, and the most hopeful, is the genetic assay my lab is conducting. We've taken a sample of the foam and washed all of the beasties living and dead into a chemical bath, in which we'll extract their DNA en masse, then feed it all into a sequencer.

This is the equivalent of taking all the animals in a zoo, putting them into a blender, and then looking at the genes in the resulting soup.

In theory, unless you were looking for a specific gene, you wouldn't know if a particular sequence came from a parrot, a rhinoceros, or bacteria in the monkeys' stomachs. In theory . . .

I have an updated approach to whole-genome sequencing that uses some algorithms to speed up the computational requirements of sorting all the genes in the soup into different organisms by looking for certain markers that indicate genome length and frequency and making first-pass guesses based on a machine-learning model. It's how I spend my Friday nights.

The short of it is that I think we can get a good inventory of what the hell is in the filter—as long as it's not something that doesn't use DNA or RNA. Then I'm fucked.

Stanley Prusiner spent years trying to convince people that prions were a real thing and the likely cause of mad cow disease. Although he won a Nobel Prize for his research, some people are still skeptical. This doesn't give me much help if I can't find a pathogen similar to one we understand.

All of this has me anxious. I take out my phone and call Sheila.

"Hey, boss man, what's up?"

"I wanted to check on the lab tests and see how they're coming."

"Oh, one sec." She puts me on hold for a moment. "Todd Pogue put those on hold. He told the lab to get back to whatever they were doing before."

"What the fuck?" I yell into the phone. Veronica flinches at my explosive reaction. "Put Todd on the phone."

"Hold on . . ."

The long pause only makes me seethe more. Pogue is drastically overstepping his boundaries here. Not to mention derailing my case.

"He says he can't come to the phone right now, he's in the middle of some lab work."

I take a deep breath to avoid yelling at Sheila again. "Did it look like he was doing important lab work?"

"I'm not a scientist, but, um, no. It's Todd being Todd."

I mull firing him over the phone but decide I need to go back there in person and handle the situation. "All right, Sheila. I need you to go over to the main lab and announce that they're back on this project; then ask Todd to call me. If he objects, call me right back and I'll fire him on the spot."

"Can I listen in?" she whispers.

"Sure," I reply, then hang up.

"Tough day at the office?" asks Veronica.

"I'm growing to hate humanity."

"Took you long enough." She points to the screen. "I may have found something. See these smooth bubbles here? I remember something from some tests I was hired to do for a pharmaceutical company. They look a lot like a time-released polymer used to administer drugs. The one I tested worked off body heat. They could adjust the chemical to respond to a fever, coma, whatever."

"Using a heater, they could be timed to release over a steady period of time?"

"Exactly. Every time it's turned on you'd get a wave of infectious particles. The problem is, they could be anything. The size really didn't matter. I hope that's helpful."

Damn.

"It is. I have to make some urgent calls before I get back to Austin and kill my lab manager."

CHAPTER TWENTY-TWO
CONTROLS

Todd Pogue eyes me with indifference from across the conference room table. He's got an "I don't have time for this" look on his face. He clearly doesn't understand the boss-employee dynamic.

Granted, I'm a horrible boss, but not in the aggressive, yell-at-you or sexually-harass-you kind of way. I'm an absentee boss. Even when I'm here. I boss the way I want to be led—which is to say not at all.

My interactions with the eight lab technicians tend to be through email and randomly popping in to see how they're doing things. I don't do meetings. I don't do pep talks.

If you have a question, ask me. If I have a problem with your work, I'll tell you. Other than that, I leave everything to Todd in the lab and Sheila in the overall operation of the business. Although calling it a business feels silly. We get checks from the Department of Defense, and a handsomely paid grant writer handles all of the paperwork.

My eyes are on the door, waiting for Darnell, a UT Austin biology graduate student I put in charge of doing the testing.

I don't even know where to begin with Todd. I start with the obvious. "Why did you tell the lab to stop working on the field project?"

"We're already running behind on the DoD work," he replies.

"Sheila said we were on track."

Todd rolls his eyes like a tool. "Did she?" He hesitates for a moment, then replies, "I spoke to General Figueroa on the phone. He wanted to know the status of the T-gene project."

"What?" I almost spit my coffee. The last thing I want in the world is Todd talking to *him*—especially about that bullshit project.

Todd gives a slight shrug. "He called. You weren't here. I took the call."

This is beyond insubordination. I have to fire him, but I can't do it right now. "What did you tell him?"

"The truth, that it wasn't high priority." *Son of a bitch.*

Todd continues. "He ordered me to make it our priority. I did. He is our employer, after all."

Calm, Theo. Stay calm. "No, Todd. He is not your employer. I am. The man may be a general, but there are no stripes on your sleeve. He's a client."

"He seemed to feel differently."

Todd is faking this obsequiousness. I know what he's trying to do. The slimy bastard is trying to set up his own relationship to get his own lab like mine. I should have seen it from the start.

He's also baiting me, trying to get a reaction. Todd probably knows the story about how I got my own lab, making an end run around the guy I was working for. Maybe that's how he thinks it works.

Maybe it is.

I have to separate my emotional reaction from my logical one. What do I want? I want to know what's in that sample. Okay, long-term, what do I want? I want to be left in peace.

Todd is disrupting that peace. I can't have someone ready to stab me in the back walking an inch behind me. So, the answer is confirmed: Todd's gone, but not right now.

I need to handle this like someone smarter than me. What would Jillian do if she had a bad baker but needed them to finish out the shift?

She'd probably tell them to take a hike and run the shop herself.

She's capable of doing that. I'm not. How would she really handle it?

"I understand your perspective, Todd. From now on, let me handle all contact with General Figueroa and let the lab pursue projects as I deem necessary."

He's waiting for the other shoe to drop. I say nothing. "Okay?"

Todd blinks, confused. It's almost like he *wanted* me to yell at him. "And the T-gene project? We're no longer pursuing that?"

I'm about to say it's nonsense and we're not going to proceed. But I notice something odd about Todd. He's wearing a jacket. Normally he's in shirtsleeves or a lab coat.

If I were a suspicious man, I'd think he was trying to get me to say something out loud so he can get it on tape. Is he recording this conversation?

That's beyond illegal and unethical—unless his goal was to take it straight to Figueroa.

Damn, Todd. You're beyond scum.

I could order him to turn out his pockets. But then what?

What if he does have a recorder? It'd be a felony to illegally record a conversation like this. We're an ITAR-regulated facility. However, that would leave me short a lab manager and a long bureaucratic nightmare, plus whatever lawsuit he decided to file.

I call his bluff. "T-gene *is* a priority. I think General Figueroa's instincts are right on this. I just need to do some more research. The optics on this, particularly for him, could be bad if we don't proceed cautiously."

Todd's reaction tells me this takes him by surprise. His eyes dart to his left chest pocket, as if he's subconsciously afraid that the general's somehow listening right now.

"So . . . is it okay if I do some preliminary work on the project?" he asks, hesitantly.

"No. You have a full workload. This isn't for you." I let the last sentence hang there: *If not for him, then whom?*

I have no idea. While there's a stack of potential hires collecting dust on my desk, I want him to at least think that I'm considering bringing someone else in—potentially to replace him.

There's a knock on the door. "Come in."

Darnell pokes his head inside. "Okay to come in?"

"Have a seat. Todd was just leaving." *My life, hopefully.*

Todd gives Darnell a suspicious glance as the younger man takes his seat. I don't need Todd trying to undermine him, too.

"What do you have?" I ask Darnell after Todd leaves.

"I did the genome assay as you requested." He spreads some printouts filled with ATGC in various arrangements across the table.

Darnell is good. Quiet, not very creative, but very, very thorough. If I can just get him to start asking bigger questions, we might have a great scientist on our hands.

"I did a fungus comparison like you asked for. Even looking for entomopathogens like *Ophiocordyceps unilateralis*."

My zombie-ant fungus. Entomopathogens by definition affect insects, but that doesn't mean there couldn't be a human analogue.

"And?"

"Nothing came up on that."

Damn. I mean that's good, I guess. I'd hate to see a human version of *Ophiocordyceps unilateralis* that causes a stalk to grow out of the brain of a human as they're frozen in rigor mortis in some location where they're likely to spread the fungus's spores over other people . . . like an attic.

I have to make a note of that. I wonder how many bodies are found in attics or water supplies with unknown pathogens leaking out?

I realize Darnell is staring at me. "Sorry. Just had a train of thought. Go on."

"No worries. We call it the 'Theo seizure.'" He smiles, then catches himself. "Um, sorry, no disrespect, Dr. Cray."

"None taken. What did you find?"

"I decided to take a scraping of the material itself."

"You were careful, right?"

He gives me a look like I asked if he washed his hands after using the bathroom. "I used the containment hood. You said to treat this like it was virulent."

"Okay, good." Heaven help me if I got my own lab infected with this pathogen.

"I found some sequences. There was no way to tell if they were DNA or RNA, of course. But I found several interesting genes. Some unknown, but a few that came up with a proximal match to a variant of a *Lyssavirus*."

Damn again. "And the genes in common were?"

"The ones we usually only find in neurotropic viruses."

His voice is grave. Although Darnell has no idea what I'm looking for, he knows what he found. A neurotropic virus affects the nervous system—including the brain. And *Lyssavirus*? That's the genus that rabies belongs to.

"And there's another thing," adds Darnell. "I did a protein analysis and found something odd."

"Go on?"

Darnell shakes his head. "This will sound crazy. I was looking for signs of a viral envelope, the outer protective layer, but I found something unusual. It's almost like a polymer. A kind of coating. Nothing the virus would produce, I don't think. But like it was encapsulated in something to make sure it could survive open air, common sterilization, maybe even UV, but break down in the bloodstream. Apparently, there's something like that used in viral therapy. It's a way to take a weakened virus and protect it so it can deliver its payload to a subject."

It's also the perfect way to take a virus that wouldn't survive outside a host and preserve it long enough to infect someone. Mother of god. It's like a time bomb.

"Crazy? I know," says Darnell. "Who would make something like that?"

"Thank you, Darnell. Make sure everyone stays clear of the sample area. Can you make me a detection chip?"

"Already on it."

I call Agent Nicolson and deliver the bad news: we have confirmation that we're dealing with not only a virus but also a mad genius who's intentionally infecting people with it.

CHAPTER TWENTY-THREE
HYDE

Lev Vanstone is precariously balanced on an exercise ball as his arms wave in excitement while discussing over Skype the virus file I sent him. He's twenty-three, so slender that his *Rick & Morty* T-shirt fits him like a tent, and has a mop of black hair that makes him look like a Muppet. A mad-genius Muppet.

I had him as an undergrad at fifteen. He was able to overcome whatever educational damage I did to him and go on to become one of most brilliant virologists I've met. Currently he works at the Glassman Research Lab at MIT, using computer modeling and artificial intelligence to study viral behavior.

"This is insane, Dr. Ted," says Lev. "Is this something you cooked up in your secret government lab?"

"God no," I blurt out. "And for the last time, it's Theo. Also, it's not a secret government laboratory." I can only imagine what people think I'm up to. They'd probably be disappointed to find out the truth.

Lev taps away on a keyboard and stares at another monitor as he bounces up and down. I'm reminded of how he'd start asking a question in class and *then* raise his hand. I loved his questions and enjoyed his enthusiasm. The other students, not so much. I found the happy medium was to let Lev sit with me at lunch and barrage me with his inquiries and ideas. Now I'm seeking his advice.

While I'm pretty sure of what my lab has found out, I need an expert outside opinion. This is because my lab—being my lab—will likely reinforce whatever conclusion I've arrived at. Good science requires having your ideas challenged, and that's often difficult for the people whose paychecks you sign.

"What's your assessment of it?" I ask. I told Lev next to nothing about the virus other than it was extremely dangerous.

"It's a Frankenstein," he replies. "I thought maybe you made it. The thing has all sorts of genes stuck on to it. Although not in the elegant way I'd expect from you. Still, it looks functional."

"Okay . . . but what can you tell me?"

"Is this a test, Dr. Ted?"

I give up on correcting him. "Let's say it is. How would you identify this?"

"Classifying it is tricky, because like I said, clearly it's man-made . . . I think."

"You think? That's odd, hearing you second-guess yourself."

"All right. Here's what I know. Part of the genome says *Lyssavirus*—but not quite. And there're at least two other parts clearly pasted on."

"Pasted on?"

"Yeah. There's coding for the viral envelope twice. Once where you'd expect and then again at the end of the sequence. That's two separate locations—which can happen. But the placement of the last one and the alterations are like a software patch added after the fact. It looks like something a person inserted."

Lev is dead-on with this part of his assessment. "Okay, so we have the envelope coding. What's the second sequence?" I hadn't noticed another one.

"Well . . . I'm not sure what it does."

"Then how do you know it's patched in?"

"The head and tail of it basically have nonfunctioning headers used as gene markers. It's a sequence I've seen before. Kind of like software-patch coding that says, 'This is a patch.'"

"What does the rest of it do?" I ask.

Lev shrugs. "I don't know. I'm not even sure if it's functional. The entire sequence is about four hundred pairs. Who knows? I could make a functional copy and try to boot it up . . ." His eyes widen with mischief.

"Don't even try it. This thing is evil."

"How evil?"

"Zombie plague–level evil."

"Oh. Got it. So, the other part that has me confused is the *Lyssavirus* part. While part of me wants to put it in that genus, or at least *Rhabdoviridae*, there are some other sequences from different families entirely."

"Engineered?"

"It's kinda sloppy. Conventional wisdom says that viruses can't exchange genes across families . . ."

"But conventional wisdom is wrong." The mitochondria in our cells are living proof that wildly different species can exchange genetic material. We even have DNA in us that was left by viruses.

"Correct. I've been reading some interesting papers about all the weird ways viruses can trade genes. There's evidence that some viruses use tricks to interrupt the replication process of other viruses and start producing ligase protein to glue their own genes inside. It's speculative. Anyway, like I said, this is a Franken-virus."

"So is it man-made or not?" I ask, still processing the implication.

"Some of it. But I think the weirdness I was talking about is natural. Or at least the product of a seminatural process. Like someone found a freak and then made it even freakier."

Damn.

"What *is* this thing?" asks Lev, as if I know.

"I'm not sure, but I think it turns people into murderers. The virus somehow attacks part of the frontal lobe and makes it hard for people to control their impulses to violence."

"Wow. Kinda like Dr. Jekyll and Mr. Hyde."

I nod. "Except we have a lone-wolf Dr. Jekyll using it to turn unsuspecting citizens into Mr. Hyde."

"Where did you find it?"

"In the home of two men who have either committed or attempted murder."

Lev stares at the screen, unblinking, considering the implications.

"So," I say, "my question for you is where the other part came from."

"Which part?"

"The not-quite-*Lyssavirus* part. I can't find anything in the database that's a match for that. Do you think that part of the sequence could have been engineered?"

"I guess it could have," he says. "Maybe it had to be." He shakes his head. "It's weird, though. It has the mutation frequency you'd expect from something that occurs naturally. And the brain-eating part was around before. But nobody's recorded seeing this version before. Why is that?"

"I don't think we've been looking in the right places. Maybe it's been there all along."

"Causing people to kill each other?" asks Lev.

"No . . . not quite. Maybe some percentage. But we're not getting off that easy. But let's say for a moment that people infected with this are more prone to kill. Then what's in it for the virus?"

"I guess that depends on how it's spread. That's the goal—go forth and procreate through infection. How does this thing spread?"

"Well, in the cases I'm looking at, it took a little human intervention to get it to spread. What's the natural life cycle of a murder virus? How does it go from one person to another? Why?"

"Maybe you should ask Dr. Jekyll," says Lev.

"I need to find him first."

Lev nods slowly, his mind attacking the problem as he looks into the webcam. "Dr. Ted?" he says after a moment.

"Mm-hmm?"

"Say this virus existed in a similar form for a long time. Then it's discovered. If your bad guy who's using it also found it . . . well, that's really unlikely. What are the odds someone that evil would be the first one to find a virus like this?"

"Pretty astronomical. Unless he went looking for it."

There's a morbid thought. Our Dr. Jekyll isn't just some sociopath who knows how to use CRISPR to cut and paste genes—he's someone who knows more about virology than Lev or me.

"Lev, I need a big favor. Start asking around discreetly for names of anyone who might be capable of making this. Or anyone doing research into this sort of thing. I'm not sure if they'd pop up in a database, but they could be a person who shows up at conferences and asks odd questions."

It's a long shot, but at this point I'll take any shots I can get.

CHAPTER TWENTY-FOUR
INFERENCE

My flight was an hour late into Atlanta, and I almost take the wheel from my Uber driver out of frustration. As soon as I landed and texted Agent Nicolson to say I'd be late to the conference, he replied, **Don't worry.** This for some reason has me worried. As the receptionist guides me to yet another conference room, I resist the urge to ask if her heels are the most practical shoes for getting around the building quickly.

Take a deep breath, Theo. You can't barge in there like a raving madman again. You've done that too many times already. Just make your case. Break it down and offer your solutions.

Solutions?

I stare at the ceiling as the world's slowest elevator crawls upward. What *are* my solutions?

We have an insane genius infecting people with some designer virus that turns them into homicidal maniacs. What's the solution for that?

Step one is finding the asshole. Step two is figuring out all the people he infected . . . Oh man, I hadn't even thought about that.

I've only been thinking about the outlier cases Gallard showed me. How many other murderers has Dr. Jekyll created? The elevator comes to a stop, but my stomach feels like it's sinking.

"Dr. Cray?" asks the receptionist. "Are you okay?"

I'd been worried about the biology of the virus, trying to figure out how we can create a vaccination for it and maybe a way to reverse the damage. I haven't even considered how many cases of infection we don't know about might already be out there.

I glance up at the air vent in the elevator suspiciously.

In how many places has Jekyll placed his little air filters of death? Dozens? Hundreds? Thousands?

Even if contracting the virus requires long-term exposure, that could be achieved in an office or school.

A school.

The image of a bunch of berserk high-school children chills me.

I realize the elevator doors are open and the receptionist is holding them for me.

I follow her down the hall to a different room than I've been in before. When she opens the door, I'm ready to offer my apologies to everyone waiting, but there's nobody there.

"Just have a seat. Agent Nicolson will be right with you," she says.

"Nicolson? What about Gallard? Is anyone else joining us?"

She shrugs. "Oh, here he comes."

Nicolson steps into the room. "Thanks, Nikita."

After she leaves us, Nicolson takes the seat across from me. "Thanks for flying in. You didn't have to do that."

I stare at the empty chairs, dumbfounded. "Is this it?"

"Dr. Warner will be stopping by. I told him you're here."

"Warner?"

"He's on loan from the CDC. I was able to get him to help us out."

I guess that's something. "What about my report on the virus?"

"I read it. Most of it is over my head. When Warner gets here, you two can discuss that. The good news, or at least sort of good news, is that we think we've narrowed down the cause of Marcus's freak-out."

"The virus," I reply.

Nicolson is silent for a moment. "You can talk to Warner about that. Actually, we found out that Marcus had an accident in the gym a day prior to the murder, which may have caused more damage than we realized. It's possible that it was enough trauma to push the previous injury over the edge. Kind of like football players building up brain damage."

The door opens, and a short, bald man with a thick black mustache enters the room. "Dr. Cray! So good to meet you."

"Dr. Warner," says Nicolson.

Warner shakes my hand, then drops down next to Nicolson, spreading over the table like a gargoyle looming over a church square. "This is very exciting. Very exciting. And we owe a big thanks to you."

"The virus?" I reply. "What about the virus?"

"Uh, yes. I had a look at your report. Interesting. Very interesting."

"And?" I say impatiently.

"Your background is computational biology, correct?"

"It was my primary area of research."

"Yes, yes. It's a wide-ranging field. Very exciting. But virology isn't your specialty? Is it?"

I see where this is going. He's trying to undermine my expertise. "Is it yours?"

"My research is primarily in vectors for the spread of disease, but I work very closely with the virologists at the CDC."

"But you're not a virologist?"

All cheerfulness fades from his face. "No. And neither are you."

"Correct. But Lev Vanstone is. And he confirmed my findings."

"Vanstone? Isn't he the kid that published the paper suggesting we look in the structure of RNA for messages from extraterrestrials?"

I hate this guy. "Yes. And he also just released a new field-test kit for Lassa and Ebola that gives a faster and more precise estimate of antibodies and treatment protocol. He's up for a World Health Organization award for that."

This blunts Warner's attack for a moment, but he quickly recovers. "That's wonderful. I'm glad he's been able to grow up and focus some. That said, I did run this by Dr. Ling, and he echoed my observations. While you may have found something new, it's not entirely surprising. There are untold numbers of viruses out there we haven't encountered, and new ones are being created by nature all the time. That doesn't mean they pose a threat."

I start to respond, but Warner pushes ahead.

"As you pointed out, this virus, your 'Hyde' virus, doesn't possess the tools to spread from person to person on its own. It doesn't sound like a particularly lethal virus."

"Tell that to Marcus's coworkers. Or Mr. Clay."

"Clay? Who's that?" asks Warner.

"The postal worker I found half-beaten to death by someone infected with Hyde." I turn to Nicolson. "Seriously. Who is this guy?"

"Dr. Warner is a friend of the associate deputy director, and he's worked with us in the past. We brought him in after you suggested there might have been some kind of contamination at the Oyo residence."

"I looked over their procedures extensively," replies Warner. "The micron filters on their masks were more than adequate for blocking the virus you forwarded to us."

"Assuming they followed all protocols," I reply.

"Which we believe they did."

"*And* that the Hyde virus wasn't sprayed *inside* their masks."

Warner blinks. "I think that's a highly unlikely scenario."

He clearly hasn't thought about it. "Unlikely? Like an FBI employee going berserk and killing two coworkers?"

He waves his hand in the air. "You're jumping to conclusions here. I expected better of you."

I'm about to jump across the table and strangle him. "Are you saying that it's impossible for that to have happened?"

"No. Just unlikely. Let's apply Occam's razor. Which is more likely? That Marcus was undergoing severe stress and a non-work-related injury exacerbated a preexisting brain trauma, resulting in violent behavior? Or that an evil scientist who is both a brilliant virologist and geneticist we've never heard of before created some kind of rage virus and decided to sneak into a well-protected FBI crime scene and infect our employees in the middle of dozens of armed men?"

There are so many things to take apart in that response. I focus on the most important one. "And yet we have the virus."

"No, Dr. Cray. *You* have the virus. I didn't want to go down this path, but have you entertained the possibility that maybe this is an example of contamination? Perhaps from something you made in that little secret lab of yours? I've spoken to some of my Russian colleagues. They know an awful lot about you over there. Which is kind of curious, don't you think? Unless you'd been working on some kind of designer kill virus or something like it."

He raises a hand to stop me from responding.

"Now, I'm not saying this was deliberate on your part, but when I look at the facts of the matter, the one consistent piece of data across everything is you. You, Dr. Cray. My theory is that what you sent us is something you had loose in your own lab at worst. At best, and this is me being charitable, possibly you found something that nobody has seen before—but more than likely you have tools and resources we in the civilian world don't have access to. Not even at the CDC.

"Thankfully this thing isn't very contagious. Otherwise I'd be pushing forcefully for you to be shut down and investigated. Instead, it looks like a failed experiment. Perhaps something made to get attention and perhaps gain funding so you could be the one to stop it. Yet again, Dr. Cray intervening to help out the bumbling government bureaucrats."

I sigh and turn to Nicolson. "Is this the FBI's official position?"

"We don't have one. The accusations against you aside, Dr. Warner has made a very compelling case to us."

"Did the part where he emphasized 'non-work-related injury' fail to tip you off? They brought him in because he's able to exonerate the FBI—which they don't need, in my opinion, because nobody could have foreseen this."

"I understand your point—"

"I'm not sure you do," I snap. "And to be honest, you're trying to make a decision about science you haven't studied. Your bosses have given you an expert that says my expertise doesn't count. So now you've been given permission to ignore me—even though you don't understand what's going on."

Dr. Warner interrupts. "Isn't that the point of expertise? To tell those less informed who to believe? In my case, I'm the government-appointed authority. Shouldn't my expertise carry a little more weight?"

"Maybe if your opinion made sense. Are you listening to yourself? *Expertise* simply means experience. And we don't *tell*, we inform. And as scientists, we certainly don't preach what anyone should *believe*. We talk about things that are scientifically likely to be true."

"Thank you for the lecture. Why don't you take your own advice to heart?"

"I have. We retested this in our lab. I then got Lev to weigh in. Now I'm begging the CDC to search for the virus in other locations and look for symptoms in the suspects."

"I wish we had the resources to chase down every little theory someone suggests. But sadly, we don't. Thank you for coming in. And as a bit of personal advice, you really should double-check your laboratory procedures for the possibility of cross-contamination."

My fist wants to contaminate his face. "What about Gallard?" I ask Nicolson.

"He's no longer helping us on this one. He went back to DC." Nicolson's voice is subdued.

"I see."

This is very, very bad.

CHAPTER TWENTY-FIVE
DATA POINT

"You're kind of an asshole," Gallard tells me over the phone.

I'm sitting on a bus bench, watching Atlanta traffic drive by as the sun sets in the west. Long shadows creep toward me, reflecting my mood.

I called Gallard because I didn't know whom else to talk to about this. His first words to me weren't meant to be unkind, just to set the facts straight.

"I've been told that before," I reply.

"Yes. And once a person gets to know you, that doesn't change, but you become one of those tolerable a-holes, like a great film director. When I first heard about you, I loathed you. Here was another dilettante telling us what to do. Then I realized that you were actually brilliant and had a different way of doing things that we can't do in the justice system."

"I'm not a vigilante," I reply.

"Let's agree to disagree on that part. What I mean is that I have to answer to people. Most of us do. Nicolson, Weltz . . . they're not the disease. They're the symptoms of the disease. They can only stick their necks out so far before they're cut off. You don't have that problem."

"I can't teach because I stuck my neck out," I reply.

"You seemed to land all right. For us it's different."

"Why did they send you back to DC?" I ask.

"Because I stuck my neck out. When Dr. Warner was brought in and started telling them exactly what they wanted to hear, I was told that my time was better spent back in Quantico teaching. Maybe I could have put up a bigger fight, but to be honest, I don't really know how anymore. Maybe I don't fully understand what's at stake."

"More death. Not counting the ones we don't know about. If this guy's still out there, who knows what he's doing with the Hyde virus? And there's the possibility that he's not done tinkering with it. Dr. Warner's satisfied that Hyde can't transmit from person to person. But he doesn't get it."

"I gather that. When I was there, he was talking about how easy it was to make a virus that looked scary. But he said to actually get it to boot up and replicate in a cell was a different matter entirely. He didn't seem to think much of Hyde."

"He thinks I made it," I say.

"He did imply that."

"Which is insane. Because if he thinks that I actually made some kind of rage virus, then he isn't acting terribly concerned about it."

"I think he's afraid of you," says Gallard. "Or is afraid to take you seriously, because that means he has to stick his neck out to implicate you."

"What a douche," I say. "You know I had other people check my work. Smart people. People smarter than me."

"I believe you. But that's like telling me that the Ministry of Magic approved your spells. It's all magic to me."

"Thanks for that, I guess. So, you're sidelined. Now what?"

"I'm officially sidelined," says Gallard. "But unofficially I'll do whatever I can to assist you."

"Assist me? With what?"

"What do you mean, with what? Aren't you going to go after this guy? Isn't that what you do?"

"No. I stare at lines of code and fill out forms all day. This is a thing I just sort of get pulled into."

"And now you're pulled into this. I know enough about what's going on inside your head to tell you that you're not walking away from this. Sure, I've seen the petulant side of you storm out of the room when everyone wasn't complimenting you on how brilliant you were, but I also know that you can't walk away from a puzzle."

This guy cuts close to the bone. "Man, you're kind of harsh."

"Then let's just jump past the part where you debate with yourself whether or not you should pursue this and I tell you to let the FBI handle it. We both know what we are and what we want to do."

"Yeah," I reply. "We need to find this guy. Any idea as to how?"

"I was hoping you'd have a suggestion."

"I caught two guys that nobody was looking for but who left clues when you knew where to look. This guy . . . he's bold enough to walk onto a crime scene and infect FBI employees. I don't think he's going to make the same mistakes as Oyo or Vik."

"Unless he wants to be caught," says Gallard.

"Are you serious?"

"It's a theory. Maybe this is part of some bigger strategy. He's done a very clever thing. Maybe he wants to be known for this? Really brilliant killers sometimes want recognition as much as they want anything. Kaczynski, for example. Even smart spree killers often try to justify their actions after the fact with letters to the newspapers. They're trying to reconcile their madness with their intellect. If this man . . . or woman, or group, is really intelligent, then they're going to want to be seen as such."

"And has the FBI received any letters from someone like this?"

"None that's come to my attention. But let me ask you this: If *you* did this, how would you tell people?"

"Why do I feel like this is some form of entrapment?"

"We didn't start off on the best footing," Gallard admits. "But you are a suspicious person."

"True. How would a homicidal version of me tell the world how smart I was? I don't know."

"What about putting coded messages in research papers?" asks Gallard.

"Too much chance they'd be changed or take forever to get published. No offense, but that's pretty amateurish."

"Okay. Then what's the cleverest way you can think of to hide a message?"

The word *message* sets off something in the back of my head. For a biologist, words often have different meanings.

Message is one of those words.

Messenger RNA is the little bits of code that DNA sends to the ribosome telling it what to build. DNA is the blueprint; mRNA is the work order going to the factory to tell it what to do next.

But the message I'm looking for could be more literal.

Researchers have encoded text and image data into bacteria. They've even developed ways to encrypt data and prevent mutations from corrupting it. That's how I'd hide a message. I'd do it right in the virus itself.

"Theo, you still there?" asks Gallard.

"Yeah, Lev Vanstone said there were some extra genes in the virus. That could be our message . . ." I start to send Lev a text message.

"Seriously? Like in the virus itself? You can do that?"

"The entire book of life is encoded in DNA, from amoebae to zebras. Why not a message from a maniac? It would be trivial to insert it."

Lev texts me back: On it.

"Who knows?" I tell Gallard. "We might know who this is real soon."

"Your guy can 'read' the DNA? Just like that?"

"Yup. But that doesn't mean it'll contain anything worth reading. Our Jekyll may want to send a message, but that doesn't mean he's going to give up that easily."

Lev texts me back: Took the sequences and converted it to binary. Ran a search . . .

I reply: And?

Lev: I hate this fucker.

Me: What???

Lev: It's Unicode. For an emoji . . .

Me: Which one?

Lev: You're not going to like it . . .

I hate Dr. Jekyll. I hate him with the white-hot fury of a thousand suns. The lives he's ruined, the people who have died—he doesn't care. It's all a game to him.

Fine, asshole. Play your game. Then ask yourself how the game ended for Oyo and Vik.

"Now what?" asks Gallard.

"We're going to find him. But it's not going to be pretty."

CHAPTER TWENTY-SIX
FURY

Half a century ago, a collection of bones was unearthed in Yorkshire, England, launching a debate that has yet to be settled. The bones, dating back to medieval times, had been chopped into fragments and resembled something out of a massacre.

Some speculated it was cannibalism. Others weren't convinced. As scientists found other unusual burial sites across Europe, a theory began to emerge.

These adults and children may have been mutilated posthumously. The reason for doing so was to keep them from coming back from the dead.

In Bulgaria, several skeletons have been found with stakes through their chest cavities—precisely how ancient lore says you kill a vampire.

While I don't think these people were actually besieged by the undead, I'm actually sympathetic to their conclusions. In the absence of modern science, a supernatural explanation is at least an explanation.

As I sit in my hotel room looking at the video projection on the wall, trying to make sense of the red dots associated with Dr. Jekyll, I'm at a loss for a rational explanation.

How did he choose his victims?

Right now, all I have for certain is the virus itself and the cases involving people infected by it. I've made a number of unproven assumptions but have little else to go on.

Jekyll could be a man or a woman. He could even be a group of people. For his part, Gallard tells me that his nascent profile suggests that Jekyll is a single person. Possibly with a high degree of academic experience but teaching at a small college or a place with less prestige. He could also be a lab technician with experience in virology who never went on to pursue a formal degree.

Gallard also believes that there's a nonzero chance this man (most likely a man) may have come from another country, with Russia and Ukraine leading candidates.

That narrows it down to several hundred thousand possibilities.

That's why I'm staring at a map thinking about vampires. All of the crimes we've connected have been on the East Coast, but that may have more to do with the way the crime lab was collecting data. I see no reason why Dr. Jekyll couldn't hop on a plane to Tempe, Arizona, and wreak a little havoc.

Gallard speculated that Jekyll might be limited by where he could drive, as he might not want to leave a record with the TSA of where he's been.

For the sake of making my life easier, I've decided to put the cases into two categories. One category is Dunhill and the Pale brothers. These are people I believe may have been test subjects for Jekyll.

In the other category I have Marcus.

Although I can't prove that the Oyo residence contained the disease vector, I strongly believe that Jekyll was at that crime scene. I think that's where he infected Marcus and the other techs by spraying their masks with his virus.

When I ask myself why, I don't have any good answers. Did Marcus piss him off? Was Jekyll getting bolder, trying to taunt the FBI directly? Maybe.

There's also the question of why he chose that site.

Gallard suggests that Jekyll may be a lurker, someone who gets a thrill out of visiting crime scenes.

While I don't dispute that, I think there's something more to it. I keep going back to my earlier hypothesis that perhaps Jekyll was there to gather research material.

Could he have been looking for killer viruses?

A viral component to violent behavior might be too convenient a scapegoat for our murderous past, but it's not impossible. Stranger things have happened.

While struggling to figure out what the life cycle is for Hyde, or how it could emerge, I've come up with another hypothesis for an imaginary pathogen that follows along the same logic as *Ophiocordyceps unilateralis*—the zombie-ant fungus.

I had been thinking about a pathogen that affected humans in literally the same way, but what if I took a higher-level approach and looked at the pathogen from that perspective?

Ophiocordyceps unilateralis makes ants climb until they're in a strategic position to distribute the fungus: in this case, by killing the host, bursting out of its brain, and dropping spores all over the unsuspecting ants that wander by.

A virus wants to spread. That is, viruses that have the genetic tools for spreading are more likely to survive and propagate.

I keep thinking about Hyde in a modern context. But what about Hyde in the context of the majority of human history, when we lived primarily in small tribes of a few hundred people?

It was much harder for a virus to spread back then. Our immune systems were vulnerable, maybe more so than today, to viruses (and maybe less so to bacteria); rare interactions with outside pathogens could easily be fatal.

European diseases wiped out millions of Native Americans. The ancient Greeks may have been pushed to near collapse from early forms of Ebola that made it all the way up to Athens from Africa.

So, in an age when viruses didn't have airplanes or even established trading routes, how did they spread? Or did they?

Plagues may have been an extreme rarity in Neolithic times, unlike their regular frequency from the Bronze Age forward.

There are other vectors for spreading pathogens—including atmospheric air currents that can send them around the world, which would only work for the heartier kind of bugs that can handle the UV exposure.

But for a virus like Hyde, which may not survive long in the open air, how could it get from place to place?

My scary theory is that a virus like Hyde may have been more common in hunter-gatherer populations. When it was time to spread, Hyde would cause an increased amount of aggression, which would lead to intertribal conflict, possibly victimizing women and children first, and ultimately causing the tribe to venture away from their locale to attack another tribe and deliver Hyde to that population.

It's a harebrained theory for which I have no supporting proof, but it's a starting point. I now have one idea on how Hyde could find it advantageous to turn the hosts homicidal.

The weak evidence I have to support this is the extremely high homicide rate of hunter-gatherer societies, even to this day.

There's even the notion that weak infection with Hyde could make you slightly more aggressive, and if enough of your population acts slightly aggressively, it would still result in higher rates of homicide and a greater chance of belligerence.

I can see how Hyde's becoming a dangerous catchall theory. I can also think of a million different ways I'd try to test for it. I'm sure Dr. Jekyll has, too . . .

Do you even know what you've found, Jekyll? Why have you done this with it instead of telling the world?

In case he did try, I've looked for research papers in hopes of finding Dr. Jekyll but have come up blank. Nothing I've found describes Hyde. But that doesn't mean he didn't try to publish.

It's a morbid thought to think that he caused all this mayhem because some research journal rejected him.

Find him and you can ask him all the questions you want . . .

But how to find this man?

I'm at a dead end. I need to step outside and get a breath of fresh air . . .

Vectors. Vectors. What are his vectors? Try to connect the dots of Dunhill, Pale, and Oyo . . . What do they all have in common?

What is the persistent thought at the back of my mind? Yes, I'd like to talk to him. He's a student of death, just like me. What else do he and I have in common?

We've both been in the same places. Three at least. While I visited the Pale house and Dunhill's beach because of what Jekyll did, I found Oyo because of what Oyo did. Or rather, what I did to uncover him . . .

Am *I* a vector?

I check my watch. It's still early in Montana. I call Bill McDougall, the attorney who is handling Joe Vik's estate.

Currently the families of Vik's victims are suing the estate for damages. Vik left behind a large amount of money and no heirs because he murdered them all.

"Hello?" says McDougall.

"Hello, I was wondering, was there a posthumous MRI done of Joe Vik?"

"You again? How come I never heard back? I could have used that in the pretrial hearing."

Oops. I was afraid of this, as I'm not exactly McDougall's favorite person.

"I'm sorry . . . I've been swamped."

"You can't even pick up the phone? Yeah, I had the MRI done and sent the files and blood samples like you asked. But you never responded. Oh, and another thing? Nobody even heard of you. What are you, some kind of quack trying to write a book? I'll sue your ass if you use those scans."

Oh my. McDougall thinks I'm someone else—someone who asked for MRI scans and blood samples from Joe Vik's corpse.

I have to tread carefully.

"I'm terribly sorry. Can you tell me what address you sent them to?"

"Ugh. Hold on. Let me have you talk to my assistant." I'm embarrassed by my own excitement.

CHAPTER TWENTY-SEVEN

Vector

The Beaman Pack & Ship hasn't had a visitor since it closed at 6:00 p.m. I've been waiting for three days outside this small North Carolina shipping store in the hopes that Dr. Jekyll will come pay a visit to his post office box. So far he hasn't reared his head, as far as I can tell.

PO Box 44 is the address he gave McDougall. The name he gave was Watson Franklin Crick—the three last names of the codiscoverers of DNA. *Ha ha.*

I placed a small camera above the door, disguised as an old alarm unit. The owners, an elderly couple, haven't noticed it yet. It helped me find Oyo—it'd be stupid not to try it again.

The camera transmits a signal that I can pick up on my computer, showing every face that walks inside the shop. I can then compare each person to a database of faces pulled from social media and DMV records. It's fairly comprehensive.

The owners of the store drew a complete blank regarding who rented the post office box. They had a hazy recollection of a young black teenager bringing in a certified check and prefilled paperwork.

No doubt an intermediary for Jekyll, someone hired from TaskRabbit or a service like that.

That said, I've been keeping an eye out for the kid as well. Who knows? He could be some angry young genius.

If Jekyll's smart—and not just about biology—he has probably decided only to use this mailbox sparingly. He asked for Vik's records months ago, so it might've been a onetime-use situation.

Back in DC, Gallard's trying to find out if a similar ruse was used for the other murders.

My phone vibrates. It's Jillian. I was supposed to call her an hour ago.

"Hey, babe," I answer into my Bluetooth.

"When you're dating a mad genius, at what point do you decide he's more mad than genius? Asking for a friend."

I sigh. "I wish I knew."

Jillian knows the broad strokes of what I'm up to. I'm not sure if she's truly distressed or has simply resigned herself to the fact I'm going to vanish on a whim.

"I guess you wouldn't. You'd be the last to know, right?"

"Probably. My internal compass is no guide to what's normal."

She laughs. "We went hunting for corpses on our first date."

I watch a homeless man in camo pants and a thick black peacoat shamble down the street. He's got a leathery face and sun-bleached hair. I'd guess his age as midfifties.

He stops at a trash can in front of an old movie theater and reaches inside. His hand comes up empty, and he curses aloud.

"You there?"

"Yeah. Sorry. I'm just watching someone suspicious."

"You looked in a mirror lately?"

"Har, har. How's the bakery?"

"Fine. How's the serial-killer hunt?"

"Uneventful."

I crouch down in my seat as the homeless man gets closer to the shipping store. Although I'm parked in an alley down and out of direct view, I'm the only one here right now and must look a little suspicious.

"That doesn't sound very inspiring."

"It's not," I whisper.

The homeless man checks the door of the store, looks over his shoulder, then enters.

"Theo?"

"Gotta go."

I climb out of my car, carefully closing the door without slamming it. When I'm sure the homeless guy can't see me, I cross the street and hide behind the small brick divider between the shipping store and the real-estate office next to it.

I peer around the corner but can't see what the man is up to because of some stupid signs placed on the windows. And my video feed is only visible on my laptop.

I could get a closer look, but if I spook him, that would be game over.

Instead I have to wait.

I spend an eternity waiting for the sound of the door to open again. Too afraid to check my phone, I can only listen and count my breaths.

Finally, the door opens again.

I push myself flat in case he walks this way. The steps go back the way he came.

I peer around the corner and spot the man halfway down the strip mall. I start following, keeping enough of a distance that my footsteps don't alarm him.

He reaches the corner of the structure and walks around it. *Damn. Did he see me?*

I pick up my pace and race to the corner. When I reach the end of the walkway and turn toward the parking lot, the man is getting ready to climb a chain-link fence.

Now what?

"Wait!" I yell to him.

The man sees me and then starts to pull himself up faster.

I reach him right as he's about to throw a leg over the top. "Stop!" I grab at his ankle.

He kicks at me, hitting me in the nose. I stumble backward but catch myself before he climbs over.

With my right hand, I grab the fabric of his pants. With my left hand, I pull the stun gun from my pocket and send a crippling charge into his leg.

"Fuck!" he screams.

I yank him down. He crashes into me, and I shove him to the ground.

Terrified eyes look up at me. "I just . . . I just wanted something to wipe my ass with!" He pulls the corner of a FedEx envelope out of his pocket.

"Who are you?" I demand.

"D-D . . . Don Spilling," he stutters.

"Prove it."

He fumbles in his pocket and pulls out a leather wallet attached to a chain. "H-h-here."

I glance down at a driver's license. It could be real, but that doesn't prove anything. For all I know, he could have checked the mailbox, then grabbed the envelope as a ruse.

"Get up," I order him.

"Who—who are you?"

I activate the stun gun, triggering hissing blue sparks. "Follow me."

I lead him over to my rented SUV and make him sit on the curb while I watch the video replay of my camera aimed inside the store.

True to his word, Don walked inside the store and started riffling through the mailing displays, looking for something to do his business with. He never even glanced at the boxes.

"You a cop?" asks Don.

"No." I pull my wallet from my pocket and take out all the bills. About two hundred dollars. I hand them all to Don.

"What's this?"

"My penalty for being an asshole. I'm sorry. I'm real sorry."

Don counts the bills. "I've had worse happen."

"You live around here?" I ask.

"No. Just making my way through to Tampa."

"You need anything? Like a phone or something?"

Don pulls out an older Android phone. "My sister got this for me."

"I'm sorry again. How long you been in Beaman?"

"About a week."

I look across the street at the shipping store. "Want to stick around a little longer and make a thousand bucks?"

CHAPTER TWENTY-EIGHT
RUSH

"Halsey, Virginia," says Gallard over the phone. "A week ago. A guy flipped out and killed the parking-patrol officer who was writing a ticket."

"What makes you think this is related?" I ask.

"They found his wife and kids dead at the house. I know someone in the police department there. I'll see if we can get a blood sample, but it sounds a lot like your Hyde virus."

"Maybe," I reply. "But people have been freaking out long before this. When did it happen?"

"Five days ago."

I feel gut punched. I was hunting Jekyll by then. If it was him, then these deaths happened on my watch. "Damn it! We can't watch 'em stack up like this."

"I know, kid. But what can we do? You spent how many days watching that mailbox? I'm working my end. I even have some guys doing some after-hours digging. I owe some big favors."

"We need to do more."

"Like what?"

"I don't know," I say. "I sometimes imagine what I'd do if I had every resource in the world. Even that doesn't help. I don't know what this guy looks like. I don't know anything about him other than he has a science background. You know more than I do."

"All I have is a flimsy profile. How'd you find Vik and Oyo?"

"They had hot spots. Areas that they frequented. Habits I could detect. Whatever connects these victims is beyond me, and if I had to guess, most are chosen at random. That would be the scientific way to do it. And I mean random. Like have a random-number generator help choose your targets."

"So, no connection?"

"Almost none. They fit a broad profile. Each one lived in an environment where Jekyll could expose them to the virus. But the Pale brothers have no idea who put that there. I suspect Jekyll broke in when nobody was looking."

"And Atlanta?" asks Gallard.

"Well, there's that. A high-profile murder scene like that, I don't think he could resist. He had to go there."

"Along with the other cases. That's his tell. He likes to visit murder scenes. Want to bet he's been to all the big ones? Like the Manson murders? Dahmer's apartment?"

"I wouldn't put it past him." I think this over for a moment. "He's a souvenir hunter."

"Looking for the virus? Right?"

"Yes . . . but maybe not just that. Hold on. What if he's been at this for a long time? Looking for something like Hyde?"

"Okay," says Gallard. "But what does that get us?"

"Well, he may have thought there was a pathogen—which could mean anything from a fungus to a prion. He didn't know what he was looking for. So that would mean he'd be collecting anything he could find in these locations. Soil, mold, bacteria. Anything."

"And then he found a virus," says Gallard.

"Right. So, he had to have the knowledge to know what it was. He may have found it in a couple murder scenes. Maybe in the suspect's blood . . ."

"What's that tell you?"

"I don't know. But on another tangent, that tells me that he's got a field kit for collecting multiple samples. He probably still collects everything."

"From crime scenes?"

"Yes. Fresh ones. He's able to travel at a moment's notice and get behind police barriers."

"Okay. This helps my profile. He might disguise himself as something. Not a cop, because he'd be recognized as a fake. And we don't let reporters in that close."

"Maybe he changes it up. Maybe he pretends he's from some other agency. I don't know. But the critical part is that we know he went to at least one crime scene after the fact, and likely others."

But how does that help us?

"We could just wait for the next high-profile serial killer to get caught and see if Jekyll shows up."

"I can't wait that long. But there's something to that idea."

"I kind of meant it as a joke," says Gallard.

"Yeah, but it's not a bad idea. If it were really horrific, our guy couldn't resist."

"Do you think he'd show his head now, given that we're after him?"

"Why not? He doesn't necessarily know we're after him. Maybe the FBI's institutional inertia is working for us."

"That's a first," says Gallard.

"We need a honeypot . . . something to attract him."

"What about a revelation about an old case?"

"I don't know if that'll do it. Jekyll's still looking for something. Maybe he thinks there's a more virulent version of Hyde to be found? I don't know. Oyo clearly excited him."

Gallard doesn't respond, thinking it through.

A thought occurs. "He may have gone to Joe Vik's house. I could ask around and see if there were any weirdos that were seen in the area. Of course, after the massacre every news agency in the world was there."

"Okay. Suppose you had a flamboyant, new murder scene. Then what? This guy has slipped in and out before. What would you do to catch him?"

"Surveillance. I'd hide cameras everywhere. We'd monitor every face and cross-reference them—but secretly."

Gallard breathes into the phone as he considers it. "Yeah. I don't think the surveillance part is that hard. Although getting the FBI to go along with it could be tricky."

"We might have to arrange for our own secret surveillance. I could probably drop a few drone cameras around a scene, leave them on rooftops, and set up our own perimeter surveillance. I even have some contractors I could hire."

"Are they good enough to spy on the FBI?" asks Gallard.

"Half these guys are former CIA and DIA. Yeah, they're good enough. They have toys the FBI doesn't have. That's if I even need them."

"Too bad they can't provide a murder scene," says Gallard. "I wouldn't put it past them. But some things you don't ask for . . ."

"Although . . ."

"Theo?"

"Hold up. I'm thinking something over." *It's insane . . . but it might work.* "Ethical question: How far would you go to stop the next family from getting murdered?"

"Pretty far," Gallard replies without hesitation.

"Okay, so we're in agreement. We can do this."

"You do realize, though, that without bodies you'll have about two minutes before the jig is up."

"Who said we won't have bodies?"

CHAPTER TWENTY-NINE
BASEMENT

Ned Rayner is waiting at the front gate of his compound when I pull up. A large fence on rollers stands between us as he appears to be deciding whether or not to unlock it and let me drive my rented cargo van inside.

Set back in the woods just outside Raleigh, North Carolina, the house is a large one-story structure that resembles a pillbox more than a family home. A driveway off to the side leads to a basement garage. Two industrial air conditioners sit on cement pads next to the house. A white van with rusted paint is parked next to a brand-new Toyota Tacoma and a sporty BMW.

Business is good for Rayner, whose business falls into a gray area of legality. Given the suspicious glances he's giving me, even after I gave him a plausible alibi, I'm certain that some of what he does is decidedly not legal.

Ned Rayner sells human body parts. Or to put it in precise legal terms, he provides services to entities looking to obtain human tissue. Selling human body parts is illegal, but it's perfectly fine to charge for preparation, transportation, or any other fee you can come up with that basically amounts to charging for the donated tissue.

The problem arises when body parts are collected from funeral homes and hospitals without the donor's or family's permission. This happens more frequently than people realize. Femurs and other bones are removed from the deceased and replaced with plastic pipe so the body doesn't bend like Gumby when there's a viewing. Other tissue, like ligaments and veins, can be taken without anyone being the wiser.

Rayner, a tall, bald, imposing man in his late forties, looks me over, unlocks the gate, then tells me to park next to his truck.

"Tendons? Right?" he asks.

"Yep."

He presses a button on his key chain, and the garage door rolls up, revealing a Dodge Hellcat and a large workshop. A large refrigerator stands at the far end next to a sink.

Rayner opens the refrigerator, revealing an almost empty interior. A foam cooler sits on the middle shelf.

"This is less than two days old. I've got calf and thigh from three cadavers. How many do you want?"

"All of it," I reply.

Over the phone, I told Rayner I was a broker working for a biotech start-up doing research on skeletal muscles.

"All of it?" He thinks for a moment. "That will be four thousand dollars."

I pull out my phone. "Venmo? PayPal? Bitcoin?"

"Venmo to BDT Pharma Services."

I send the money to him, and his phone buzzes.

He checks the screen and nods. "That was easy."

"My clients are desperate," I say. "They're trying to beat a competitor to some patent I don't understand."

I watch Rayner's face as he thinks this over. He realizes that I must have just made a much larger profit than he did. Good. I want the greedy part of his brain to overwhelm reason.

I check my phone as it buzzes from a timed call. "I gotta run. Gotta fly to Arizona to get some brain tissue."

Rayner's eyes drift toward a door off to the side of the garage, directly underneath the large air handlers. "Brain tissue? How much?"

I shake my head. "It's kind of weird. I had to source someone across the country."

"Weird, how?" he asks.

"I mean their request's a little unusual. They're not just after brain tissue. They need an intact optic nerve system and inner ear. They told me to get whole heads if possible."

Rayner lets out a laugh. "A whole head?"

"Heads," I reply, putting the emphasis on the *S*. "I think they may be working on some kind of trauma drug."

"Whole heads?"

A human head contains several different tissues that have a ready spare-parts market. Corneas, teeth, gums, and parts of the brain can be used either in transplants or the preparation of medical treatments. While there are legitimate ways to purchase these parts, waiting lists can be long and supply can be limited.

While it's one thing to swipe a few tendons or veins from the body of a person who never volunteered to donate, taking the head would cause some alarm at the funeral.

Which makes finding heads difficult—at least in the United States. In China it's a different matter entirely. The state government is the largest supplier of human body parts, many of them harvested from political prisoners and religious dissidents. Some speculate that thousands of practitioners of the Falun Gong religion may have been disposed of this way.

"Whole heads," I reply. "I think my source has a line into some Chinese ones. Ideally we'd like to get some Caucasians, too."

"How much?" asks Rayner.

"Per head? I'm paying five thousand for each one in Arizona."

Rayner strokes his chin, then takes out his key chain. "Follow me." He walks to a side door and unlocks the massive lock above the door handle.

"I have a source in Ukraine," he tells me. "They have a problem with families not paying medical bills for the deceased. So I run a charity that provides assistance."

"To the hospital?"

"Basically. They provide me with research materials." He opens the door to reveal a brightly lit refrigerated room lined with large shelves. Entire bodies wrapped in plastic lie there like shiny mummies.

"Holy shit," I murmur. There have to be at least eighteen bodies here, including several small ones that make me cringe.

"Yeah. What do you need?" he asks.

I count up how much money I have in my bank account and what I can borrow. "How much for the whole lot?"

CHAPTER THIRTY
SERIAL

Thirty years ago, Butcher Creek Boy Scout camp was filled with tents, cabins, and wooden buildings in good condition. Now it's a rotting ghost town overtaken by the surrounding Kentucky forest. It was also the site of not only several Bigfoot sightings, but at least one UFO, dutifully reported by the scouts inhabiting the camp at the time.

When I'm done with it, Butcher Creek is going to reemerge into the shadow world of conspiracy theories and folklore. I plan to do something truly horrible to it—turn it into the scene of the Butcher Creek Massacre.

The setting sun even has me spooked as the trees go darker and the sky starts to fade away. Evil-sounding frogs croak while owls make threatening calls to their evening prey.

I chose this location from Google Maps. It sits on federal land, guaranteeing FBI involvement. All the roads into it can easily be surveilled, and I found ample locations to hide cameras disguised as US Forest Service monitors.

I created a Wi-Fi network that transmits to a satellite dish I hid farther in the woods. Should an investigator look for a hot spot, they'll see a bland-looking USFS router that can't be traced back to me.

It's a perfectly creepy spot. An interstate highway passes by a half mile away up a ridge, which offers a good vantage point from which to watch the part of the camp where I assume the police and federal vehicles will park. That'll make this roadside perch perfect for television news trucks.

I've got the location, the filming equipment, and even some ready-made press releases to send anonymously to both investigators and news agencies. All I have to do now is put my actors in place . . .

Yeah. Easier said than done. Rayner sold me the bodies with the promise I would never mention his name. No problem.

He assured me that they were all Ukrainians who died of natural causes. He claims they were flown into the United States aboard a cargo plane carrying medical equipment only two days prior.

I'm not sure if I believe him, but it's not important. The more pressing matter was trying to figure out a way to explain the presence of preserving fluids to the first investigator who takes a whiff of the bodies.

My solution was to make that a feature, not a bug. I can't just throw a bunch of bodies around and have people jump to the conclusion a serial killer is at work. The more likely assumption would be that a funeral home dumped off a bunch of bodies that were supposed to be cremated. That's hardly the catalyst for headlines.

No, unfortunately, I can't simply bury the bodies. I have to hack them apart and then bury them in plastic bags with formaldehyde and leave creepy little notes.

I already wrote the notes using a typewriter I bought at an out-of-state flea market in Raleigh. For the text, I bought a few copies of old science-fiction novels and plagiarized them.

Words can't describe how horrible I feel about this.

Creating a horrific hoax like I'm about to do is going to cause a strain on local law enforcement, make people panic, and do who knows what to the families of my victims when word reaches them in Ukraine about the impossible fate of their loved ones.

It's for a good cause, I've convinced myself. If Jekyll shows up here, then we have a chance to catch him before he kills again. And to make sure he's going to show up, I'm making sure what he really wants is here as well.

I purchased a sleeping bag and some camping equipment, which I now set up inside one of the cabins. For cinematic effect, I nail photos and maps of constellations and planets I pulled from old magazines. The centerpiece is a telescope with a cracked lens that I etched with Egyptian symbols.

A skilled investigator like Gallard might think the thing looks a little too staged. That's fine. I don't want the FBI to take too long to figure out what really went on here—except for who did it. I just want it to make the news and for Jekyll to drop by.

I sit on a log that forms part of a ring around a campfire and stare at the naked corpse lying on the tarp before me and then at the hacksaw in my hand.

"What the hell are you doing, Theo?" I ask myself.

I used to wonder at what point the serial killers I pursued realized they were messed-up human beings. Was it a moment like this?

I didn't kill the young man staring at the sky, or the young girl lying next to him, or the dozen more still in my truck. Arguably, I'm giving them a better purpose than the one fate had chosen. They're going to save lives.

That is, the mutilation of their bodies is going to save lives. The horrible, sacrilegious desecration of their bodies, by me, is going save lives. Hopefully.

As I stare at the fading orange reflection of the sun on the stainless-steel saw blade, I ask myself another profound question—why the hell didn't I bring a power tool?

The time for introspection is over. I'm sweating my balls off in my protective suit, and I don't want to linger too long out here and get shot by some vigilante hunter—who, by rights, wouldn't be judged too harshly for killing me in cold blood.

Even I'm appalled by what I'm going to do.

"Okay, Steve, time to save some lives," I tell the nearest naked body. I have no idea what his name is. But I'm going to call them all Steve.

I place his arm over a cinder block and get a good grip . . .

Come on, Theo. You've seen death a hundred times. You've dissected corpses and even mutilated one to save your ass from Joe Vik. How hard can this be?

Part of me is worried that all the Steves and Stephanies may not have died of natural causes. While Rayner's claim to the bodies made sense, part of me wonders if this wasn't a convenient way to get rid of some political enemies in Ukraine.

A number of the bodies clearly show signs of blunt trauma.

At least two have bullet wounds. Only half have autopsy incisions . . .

Let's put a pin in that for now. I can make Rayner tell me where he got them later on. If I find out there's some kind of homicidal European strongman up the supply chain, I'll pay him a visit.

Okay?

I find myself looking into Steve's glassy eyes. "I promise you. Deal? Okay, then."

I'd say a prayer if I were religious, but I'm not. But I'll bet Steve and his friends are.

Okay.

"Um, God, uh, forgive me for not believing. And forgive me for what I'm about to do. Uh, may they all rest in peace."

I look up to the sky as if I'm expecting Morgan Freeman to look down at me and wink, giving me his approval.

I'm seriously losing it.

I put the blade to Steve's pale skin. Something touches my leg.

"Ack!" I yell.

It's my phone buzzing. I tap the Bluetooth in my ear. "Yes?"

"Hey," says Jillian.

I forgot I was supposed to check in with her. "Uh, hi."

"What are you up to?"

"You don't want to know," I reply. I make a quick goodbye and go back to work.

By the fifth Steve, it has stopped feeling weird.

That's what scares me the most.

CHAPTER THIRTY-ONE
VIRAL

I haven't been on Facebook since I left to go study ponds in Montana and ended up being accused of murder. My Twitter account has one post made at the behest of a teaching assistant. I couldn't put a name to a face of any current television celebrity. In many respects, I'm about as pop culture ignorant as possible. That said, after watching the media explosion over the Joe Vik murders and then the Oyo case, I've had firsthand experience in how something sensational blows up. I went from one lone voice trying to call attention to the freakish number of missing persons in Montana and Wyoming to having cable-news crews knocking on my door at four in the morning to get a statement about the latest development.

What I learned with Joe Vik was that it wasn't always easy to call attention to something that seemed plainly obvious. I literally had to drive the bodies I was finding to police stations. Even then, I witnessed a strange kind of mental blindness as they tried to not see what lay before them.

There's an apocryphal story, probably completely false and maybe a bit racist, that the Indians of the New World couldn't see the arriving Spanish ships anchored off their coast because they were so alien to them. We'll ignore for the moment the hundreds of other first encounters indigenous peoples had with large sailing vessels in which they saw the ships perfectly fine, even swimming out to them—and instead accept that in some cases we don't want to see the truth before us.

I have to make very sure that my manufactured massacre gets the attention it deserves, even if it means prompting the authorities and media rather overtly.

After I cleaned up whatever traces of Theo Cray I may have left at the scene of the crime, I packed everything into my rental truck and drove it two hundred miles back to North Carolina, where I returned it to the agency I borrowed it from.

My alibi, if I'm ever asked, is that I purchased lab equipment, moved it with the truck, and then had it shipped. I have receipts from a liquidator because I've learned that those tiny details are important to keep a story from falling apart. Should this ever come back to me, I don't want to sit there with a dumb expression if I'm asked why I rented a cargo truck in North Carolina.

Safe inside my motel room, with my massacre clothes stuffed into a garbage bag inside a dumpster a hundred miles back, it's time to try to make this blow up.

Step one: Call the cops.

I use a virtual private network and launch a calling app on my computer that routes through Europe. To dial Reed County emergency services, I have to use their direct number and not 911.

"Nine-one-one Emergency Services. What's the nature of your call?" asks a woman with a mild Kentucky accent.

"My son and I were just hiking in the woods near the old scout camp near Butcher Creek, and we saw part of a human body sticking out of the ground."

"Can you give—"

I hang up. Now at this point, the operator is trying to decide if this is a prank call or not. Either way, she has to report it to the sheriff's office. Depending on how seriously they take it, someone could arrive in a half hour or a day. I don't have that kind of time. So I escalate things.

I dial the direct line to the sheriff's office.

"Reed County Sheriff's Office. How may I help you?" says a polite man.

"I saw a body over at Butcher Creek, by the scout camp. I wanted to check, but I heard a gunshot. I'm sorry. That's all I want to say. Please send someone by there."

I make two more similar calls. One to the US Forest Service and another to the neighboring sheriff's department so they'll call Reed County and make them aware of it.

I begin to time the response . . .

Seventeen minutes later, a Reed County SUV flies past my first camera on Route 22—followed by three police cruisers. Four minutes later, a Colton County SUV screams down the road after them.

Huh. My hat's off to them.

The lead SUV drives up the gravel path to the camp, going past camera number two. I can clearly see the faces of the occupants. A younger deputy is driving and an older man, maybe the sheriff, is sitting in the passenger seat.

They fly off camera and show up a minute later coming to a screeching halt at the upper left frame of my wide-angle camera disguised as a rain gauge.

The two men get out of the truck and, despite the urgency with which they arrived at the scene, walk into the camp at a casual pace. I'm relieved they didn't tumble out with guns blazing. They're actually handing this quite professionally.

Let's see how they handle the scene I left for them.

While I buried most of the body parts in leaking bags and used a propane tank to saturate the soil so methane probes would go berserk,

I still needed to make sure the first responders took this very, very seriously.

Once more, I'm horrified by what I did. If this doesn't lead to the capture of Jekyll, I'm going to be haunted by the image of what these two men are going to see for the rest of *my* life.

It's not enough to randomly place some hacked-up body parts around an old camp. If investigators get suspicious about the large amounts of embalming fluid and broken jars and suspect that this may not be a murder but instead some weird hoax, then Jekyll will never show.

I can't have all this go to waste. I can't have Steve's and all his friends' deaths end in a poorly planned ruse.

I need the first people on the scene to have a visceral reaction. Even if they don't think it's a serial killer at work, I need them to think something evil happened there.

That's why I did what I did.

Steve forgive me, but when I saw the camp's firepit and started thinking back about the chopped-up bodies found in Yorkshire, England, I got a terrible idea.

There's one term even more sensational and headline grabbing than *serial killer*.

As the sheriff and his deputy approach the still-smoldering firepit and see the arm sticking out of the embers with its flesh partially eaten away, I can almost read their minds:

Cannibal.

CHAPTER THIRTY-TWO
FRENZY

After the first police officer makes a phone call, I wait twenty minutes, then call the tip lines for the two local television news stations. I get an answering machine on one and a bored producer on the other. My message is the same each time: "How come you aren't reporting on the body found at Butcher Creek?"

While that alone isn't enough to cause a news truck to be sent to the remote location, the ensuing phone call to the sheriff's office from the producers is likely to arouse interest. A "No comment" response will make it sound newsworthy.

In the event that neither television station feels inclined to look into this, I also send an email to five online reporters I found by Googling local newspapers.

I then sit back, watch the responding police on my surveillance cameras, and click refresh on my laptop until one of the local news outlets picks up the story.

It takes two hours. The *Blue Mountain Packet* is the first to run an item from their crime-beat reporter. The headline is fairly nonsensational:

Police Investigating Body Found at Butcher Creek Scout Camp

That's a start, but I need to goose this a little if I want it to catch fire before the hoax is revealed. I forward the link with an anonymous account to twelve different blogs and Facebook sites that cover serial killers, with an added note:

> My brother was one of the first on the scene. He says they found a half-eaten woman and multiple body parts including babies. FBI being called in. They think it's a serial killer.

I added the incorrect embellishments to avoid being too spot-on. If the authorities decide to track down the early leaks, I don't want to call attention to myself by knowing things nobody should know yet.

Even though I'm using anonymous email accounts, a browser in incognito mode, and a VPN, there's a chance I slipped up somewhere. While I doubt investigators would bring the full force of the NSA to track the rumor leaker down, I can't be too sure.

In case things don't go viral, my next step, and a slightly risky one at that, is to create my own ghoulish serial-killer Facebook page and spend several thousands of dollars to promote stories about the Butcher Creek Massacre. By targeting Facebook users with what I assume are Jekyll's interests—genetics, crime, virology—I can probably get it in front of him, if he even bothers with Facebook.

My bet is that he gets his news about serial killers through Google News Alerts. This service constantly searches the headlines and sends you updates when ones matching your criteria are published.

By 11:00 a.m., the police have roped off the scene, covered the body in the firepit, and started using dogs to search the area. After doing an initial sweep, the sheriff did a good job of clearing the camp so his people wouldn't trample on evidence.

Investigators from the Kentucky State Police start to arrive at 1:00 p.m., along with a forensics van. Three men and a woman in uniforms take photographs. Supervisors wearing ties and windbreakers show up as well and confer with the sheriff and his deputies. Uniformed forest service personnel also arrive, and I watch three of them fan out from the camp, combing the grounds.

I count at least twenty people on my cameras. Everyone seems to recognize one another, but I'm still grabbing close-up shots and adding license plates to my database.

I'd be shocked if Jekyll showed up this early in the game, let alone even knows about this yet. None of the major news sites is saying "serial killer" or "cannibal" yet. On the news stations' websites, they're still reporting that a body may have been found. There's nothing sensational in the articles. The crime blogs are a little more hyperbolic, using "serial killer" in their headlines, but they don't carry the same kind of weight as traditional news sources.

I blame the lack of hysteria on Sheriff Ward. He's too damned professional. Ward has the scene locked down and has managed to placate the local news. I'd been hoping for more leaks, but so far, I appear to be the only person breathlessly saying there's a serial killer.

Damn law enforcement and their professionalism.

I need to get a little more drastic. It's risky, but I can't chance having the jig be exposed before Jekyll shows up. Then the horrible, horrible things I did will be only that.

After the Joe Vik killings, I was hounded by the press. I got asked to go on every news show, requests for interviews from the *New York Times*, you name it.

I ignored all of them. The fact that I didn't want to talk to them about it only made me even more newsworthy. When I caught Oyo

Diallo, the media went insane. Jillian and I had to buy our house using a front company and go to extreme efforts to maintain our privacy.

The last thing I wanted was to be a talking head on television news, offering my uninformed opinion about whatever was the scandal of the day. Fox offered me six figures to be exclusive to them. I declined. I declined them all.

While I'm not ready to trade my privacy for a brief amount of attention, I can use the hundreds of email addresses and phone numbers from the media in my Gmail account for my benefit.

I start with a producer from CNN, one Sandy Garrett. I dial her number and get her voice mail.

"Hey, this is Dr. Theo Cray returning your call about the Butcher Creek serial killer."

Sandy, being a good producer, will probably check her messages in the next hour or so, or at the very least scan the transcriptions and spot my name. Clearly, she knows I didn't call her before, but she'll assume I made a mistake, thinking I was calling another producer at a different news organization.

If all works right, I'll have attracted attention, created desire, and implied scarcity.

She calls back two minutes later.

CHAPTER THIRTY-THREE
Hook

I ignore the CNN producer's call. And her second. And her third. I wait an hour before calling her back. During this time, she's more than likely done a Google search for "Butcher Creek serial killer" and ended up finding the local news items about the body being found, but no mention of a serial killer.

However, the fact that I left a message about a serial killer has her attention. I keep checking the CNN website to see if they're running anything yet, but they aren't. No worries. I can fix that.

I call her back. She picks up within a second. "Cray?"

"Yes. Theo Cray. Sorry I missed your calls. I called you by accident," I say hurriedly.

"Wait! What's this I hear about a serial killer in Kentucky? Are you investigating it?"

"I'm sorry, um, Sandy? I pulled your number from my email when I got a garbled voice mail and accidentally got the wrong producer. My apologies."

"Which producer are you trying to reach?"

"I already spoke to them." Let her think I'm talking to Fox or MSNBC. I add, "Off the record."

"Wait . . . what can you tell me, off the record?"

"I really don't think I should. The other producer promised me it would be confidential."

"I can guarantee that!" she blurts out.

"Um, let me think about it." I need to make her feel the pressure.

"When can you call me back?"

"Uh, I don't know. I'm going to be pretty busy. I have to catch a flight."

"To Kentucky?"

"Er, I can't say."

"Come on, Dr. Cray, give me something."

"Ah, I don't know. But I guess I can, off the record, confirm the rumor."

She plays coy. "Which rumor?"

Two hours ago, a sheriff's deputy found the plastic bag containing a human head sticking partially out of the ground. I'm sure that's known locally.

"About the first victim being found in a firepit and appearing partially eaten. I don't know about the condition of the other body parts elsewhere."

"Other parts," she repeats as she writes this down.

"This is off the record? Right? I get asked to help out, but I try to keep it confidential."

"Of course. Of course," she insists. "But could I get a statement from you *on* the record?"

I mull this over. The pro is that it will make the story go further, faster. The con is that it will put my name right in the story, which is risky.

"I can't have it look like I'm your off-the-record source," I reply.

"I have other sources. Don't worry," she lies.

"Okay. Then can it just be a statement?"

"Sure. Go ahead."

I give it a moment's thought. "This is unlike anything I've ever heard about before. Is that okay?"

"Uh, okay. Can you tell us on the record if you'll be going to Kentucky or that you're working with the FBI?"

"Sorry," I reply, confirming it but keeping her from saying so. "I have to go."

The first headline shows up thirty minutes later next to a map showing Butcher Creek: "Serial Killer at Work in Kentucky, Sources Say."

The news copy makes a slight mention of unconfirmed reports of cannibalism and then says, when reached for comment, "Dr. Theodore Cray, investigator behind the Grizzly Killer and Toy Man murders, says this is unlike anything he's ever heard of before."

Fair enough.

An hour later, CNN has a reporter on the ridge along with a KRTN news truck. A written statement from the sheriff's department says flatly that this is an ongoing investigation and they have nothing to report.

Just after 5:00 p.m., the first FBI agents arrive on the scene. By now, Sheriff Ward's deputies have found a third body part. A foot.

Ugh, I remember sawing that foot off. I almost cut off my own thumb. Leaving my blood in that scene would be very, very bad.

Just in case I did somehow contaminate the crime scene, my thin, very thin, excuse was that I was following up an anonymous report a day prior but didn't see anything. I don't know how convincing that would be, but given my reputation for bumbling into crime scenes, it might buy me enough time to get a really good lawyer.

God knows how I'm going to pay for that. I can't even figure out how I'm going to tell Jillian I spent the money for the extension on our deck to buy a bunch of corpses.

Um, maybe I don't tell her that part. The better option would be for me to try to convince her I've been keeping a ten-thousand-dollar-a-day cocaine habit a secret.

By the time of the East Coast evening news, the Butcher Creek Massacre has made headlines. The watershed moment I'd been hoping for happened when someone leaked cell-phone photos of the crime scene to a local news reporter. The shots then went worldwide.

I'm sure Sheriff Ward would love to wring the neck of whoever did this. Presently, only the reporter who got the photos and I know the identity of who released them.

It was Payne Heskins, a Kentucky State Police uniformed officer, who took the photos when nobody was looking. Except for me on my hidden cameras.

Thank you, Payne, for your lack of professionalism.

While most media outlets have pixelated the photo of the arm, the creepy image of our Butcher Creek Butcher—that's the name that stuck—has already made the rounds. The Reddit thread is already more than three thousand posts long.

If Jekyll doesn't know about this now, he's either dead or has given up his serial-killer fixation.

The next step is to watch my screen and wait for someone to show up who doesn't belong there.

Sheila has tried calling me several times, but I don't want to get into office politics right now. I need to catch a killer. Ideally while he's still there.

As night falls and more people show up on the scene, I keep scanning the shadows, hoping to see Jekyll lurking somewhere in the background like a ghoulish Bigfoot.

CHAPTER THIRTY-FOUR
Extras

Two days later and all I have to show for it is a growing midsection from all the crap food I've been eating in my motel room, a stressed-out girlfriend who's totally fine but not fine with it, an increasingly frantic office manager I've been avoiding, and hours and hours of footage of a diligently managed crime scene.

Sheriff Ward has kept tight control of the location by establishing several perimeters. He's blocked off the surrounding forest a half mile out in either direction and has deputies patrolling the outer edges on a regular basis.

My roadside camera caught a sheepish photographer being escorted out of the woods while a deputy held on to his camera.

While some news trucks have gathered by the overlook where I guessed they'd want to do stand-ups, Ward has established a media base camp two miles away at a ranger station. His deputies routinely chase off anyone on the ridge trying to take photos.

Ward himself has made regular appearances and said precisely nothing to the frustrated media. All he says is that it's an ongoing investigation and they're working with other law-enforcement agencies.

While he clamped down on his own deputies after the leak of the photos, other people have been talking. It's hard to keep a secret like this from your friends and family.

All the large details I planted have made it into the news, including several that I didn't. Oddly, Ward has started circulating a sketch of a person of interest.

I panicked when I first heard about this. Did someone get a glimpse of me? Was I going to get arrested in my motel at any moment—a strange replay of what happened back in Montana?

Thankfully the sketch looks nothing like me. In fact, it bears a strong resemblance to the actor Lance Henriksen—which makes me suspect that someone decided to put himself at the center of attention by claiming to have seen something.

I get up from my computer and decide to take a walk around the motel. While leaving the screen takes a certain amount of willpower, thanks to the wonderful world of open-source software and GitHub, I was able to cobble together a Python script that grabs frames as they come in, finds faces, and categorizes them.

I've counted 314 unique faces in the media area. One hundred and two inside the outer perimeter. And twenty-seven at the crime scene itself.

I've been able to attach names to less than half of them through public records and social media. The others I've given titles like Kentucky State Police Sergeant 3 or County Official 8.

What I've been paying the most attention to is anyone who doesn't look like they belong. However, so far everyone seems to know everyone else and I'm able to identify which agency they work for.

There's no way that Jekyll is local to here. The only outsiders that I've seen on the crime scene are FBI agents, and they seem to know each other. None of them is connected to the other crime scenes from Gallard's files, as far as I can tell.

That said, I haven't been watching twenty-four hours a day. It's possible I've missed someone. I'll have to go back and identify all the faces later on to be sure. My biggest area of focus, other than watching for some random interloper on the crime scene, has been studying the faces of the people in the media area. As I watch them watching the crime scene, I've wondered whether Jekyll could be posing as a freelancer. Heck, he may actually *be* a freelance photographer who works these scenes under different names. That would give him a reason to go there and help him slip under the radar.

I'd bet anything I've already seen his face—he could have been holding a camera or doing something innocuous while he surveyed the area.

When the deputy caught the photographer in the woods, I got excited until I was able to look him up and rule him out. No surprise. Jekyll is cleverer than that.

I step outside into a cold breeze and stretch, letting the bracing wind wake me up. The glowing signs of a Waffle House and a Taco Bell beckon to me in the night. I've already had my fill of Cracker Barrel takeout.

I walk down the narrow strip between the parking lot and the rooms, catching a glimpse of the few inhabitants of the motel. In the five rooms with their lights on, four of them have their televisions playing. I can never stand to have one on in the background, but I guess that's one of the ways that I'm wired differently.

The newspaper dispenser by the office has a copy of the *Lexington Herald-Leader* with the headline "Police Silent about Butcher Creek Butcher."

I have to say that I'm disappointed that the media ran with "Butcher Creek Butcher," because it's so redundant. Oh well.

The newspaper also has front-page stories about previous crime sprees in the area that I had no idea about, going all the way back to the time of Daniel Boone.

My phone buzzes, and I realize it's Jillian calling me.

She's already sent five unanswered text messages.

"Hey, what's up?" I ask.

"I know you're real busy, but Sheila has been calling me, trying to get hold of you."

Damn. I've been putting off my office manager for too long. In fact, I haven't spoken to her in three days. "Did she say what about?"

"Other than the fact that you've been MIA? No. I just assumed that you're working on the Butcher Creek thing. Are you trying to track him down?"

"Uh, in a roundabout way." I check the time. "Let me call Sheila. Bye, love you." I hang up in a hurry and probably increase the odds that my clothes will end up on the front lawn.

"Cray, where the hell are you?" Sheila demands the moment she answers.

"Deep-cover thingy. What's going on?"

"What's going on? You're about to lose the lab and everything else if you don't get your ass back here ASAP."

"Hold on. What's the deal?"

"General Figueroa. He's been trying to reach you. Apparently, he's pissed and coming here."

"When?"

"Tomorrow."

Damn it. Jekyll could show his head at any moment. While my cameras can still capture him on video, physically capturing him could prove impossible if I'm a thousand miles away.

I want to call Figueroa myself, but I know trying to placate him over the phone at this point won't work. Clearly Todd the Rat has been getting into his ear. I can only imagine what he's been telling him. Time to go back to Texas and solve yet another crisis.

CHAPTER THIRTY-FIVE
BLACK OPS

Todd Pogue drops into a chair across from me in the conference room with a stack of folders, waiting for me to ask why he's here. I just look up from my laptop and nod, then return to work. General Figueroa is due to arrive any moment, and I don't want Todd to know to what degree I've been aware of his machinations.

On the flight back to Austin, I tried to figure out what Todd's angle was. Why did he seem so sure he could go around me and win over the general? Somewhere over Arkansas it hit me: the general's aide, Lieutenant Osman.

Osman has visited the lab a few times but always acted unimpressed. For some reason, he hasn't taken to my sparkling personality or my government research. I'm certain that Todd made contact with Osman behind my back and bent his ear, probably telling the lieutenant that everything he suspected about me was true.

While it would look bad if Todd went directly to Figueroa after I talked to him, undermining me to Osman would be equally effective. Osman could tell the general that his "insiders" had been informing him that Dr. Theo was incompetent and not following directives—technically true. This would then set Todd up in the perfect position, not to get his own lab, but to take over mine.

If the DoD decided to investigate me, I'd be given a few options. The least painful one would be to let the lab continue under the supervision of someone else—likely Todd.

Diverting my attention from Jekyll at this point is killing me. It's only the fear of losing the lab that got me onto the plane. And while the lab feels increasingly like a noose around my neck, I'm not sure what I'd do without it.

One thing is sure: I'm not going to let Todd take it away from me. I'll burn it to the ground before I let that prick have it.

I finally acknowledge Todd's presence. "I'm glad you're here. We have some things to go over with the general."

"That we do," Todd replies.

He either suspects I have no idea he's the reason behind the visit, or that I'm going to try to defend myself in front of Figueroa when the general broadsides me with Osman's inside report.

I think what Todd wants more than anything is for me to accuse him of going behind my back in front of the general, making me look like I don't have control of my office.

What I plan to do is to sidestep that entirely. Hopefully I can bluff my way through the terrorist-gene-project checkup. Thankfully I did a little more planning than Todd knows. It might be enough if my other plan doesn't nuke him from orbit at the beginning. The trick is to control the general's attention. If I can't do that, I could be out of the lab in an hour. If the general is feeling particularly aggressive, he could have me audited and even put under investigation for misappropriation of funds.

While I have clean books, as far as I know, if Todd really is the son of a bitch I suspect, he could have put some booby trap in there I don't know about, like ordering ten MacBooks sent to my house, billed to a DoD project.

Sheila opens the door, gives me a smile and Todd a cold nod. "The general's here."

Todd starts to stand up, then realizes I'm still sitting and falls back into his seat. The moment his butt hits the chair, I get up and walk around the table and greet Figueroa as he walks in.

"Cray," he says with no warmth. Osman is behind him.

"General. Lieutenant."

All right, let's see if my gambit works . . . I call to Sheila in the hall, "Could you make a copy of the T-gene report for Lieutenant Osman?" T-gene sounds so much better than *terrorist gene*.

I notice Figueroa take a sideways glance at Osman right after I say this. Todd is behind me, so I can't see his face; I doubt it's happy.

I take my seat across from Figueroa and close the lid of my laptop.

"You have a T-gene report?" asks Figueroa.

I wait a moment, pretending to be surprised by the question. "Of course. You asked for that, right? I hope it was okay that I went ahead and did an expenditure from the general account on feasibility."

Next step, pretend to be afraid that you were too proactive.

In about two seconds, I'll know if I was right about Todd's plot . . .

Osman speaks. "You've moved forward on the T-gene project?"

I hold up my hands. "Wait? Was I not supposed to do that?"

Osman flashes a glance over at Todd, then returns his attention to me. He wants to speak but doesn't want to look too obvious. He turns to Figueroa.

"I would like to see that report," says Figueroa.

"Yes, of course." I slide a folder out from under my laptop. It's not too thick, and little more believable than the bullshit file the FBI gave me back in Atlanta. "It's probably better if we discuss this after we go over some security issues at the lab. If that's okay."

"Security issues?" asks Todd.

I ignore him and speak directly to Figueroa. "I need to disclose certain things to you as our compliance officer. It's really embarrassing and could be a serious issue." I slide another folder out from under my laptop. "We may have a breach in our network."

"A breach?" The general's face turns grave. "How serious?"

I pull a printout from the folder. "I don't know. I've just contracted a security specialist to take a look. I was going over our server logs and noticed a large amount of traffic going out over our network to a VPN."

As a government-backed lab, we have an extremely well-protected network, and we have to follow an exhaustive list of rules about what we can and cannot connect to the network, the apps we use, and what data we bring out of the lab.

While reluctantly flying back to Texas, I started to think about the last time I spoke to Todd. What was going through his head? What did he think I was going to do?

I realized that Todd might have assumed that I would have been impulsive enough to fire him right after the meeting. Todd being Todd, he would have done whatever he could to protect himself—first and foremost, making copies of all the emails and files he could, not to mention whatever research he had access to. Or in case this little plan of his to oust me worked and he was afraid I was going to be spiteful, he wanted to make sure he had backup copies of our data.

I tried to think like Todd and foresee what Todd would do. I was disappointed at how predictable Todd was.

Two hours after my last in-person meeting with Todd, he started copying files from the lab and sending them to a server that had a very similar name to the one we use for backing up our data.

Our backup is with a service that uses a URL named MonolithArchive. That night, data started uploading to Mono1ithArchive—in which the lowercase *l* is transposed with the number *1*.

It was a very sneaky maneuver and only possible because Todd has administrative controls over the lab network. He was hoping that, on the off chance I decided to inspect our server logs, I'd read right past the typo.

I almost did. But when I refused to believe that Todd didn't do something dirty, I checked the IP addresses and realized that he'd added new permissions.

Figueroa takes a look at the list of addresses on the printout. "What is this?"

"Not all those are our servers."

"I'm not sure I follow."

"Simply put, someone uploaded a hell of a lot of data from our computers to a foreign computer."

"Foreign?" blurts Todd. His face has lost its color, but he's clinging to this word, hoping I think it's the Chinese or the Russians.

"I mean *foreign* as in not ours," I reply.

Todd glances over at the printout. "It looks like Monolith to me."

"That's what I thought. But someone used a server spelled with the number *1* instead of the lowercase letter *l*. It's very deceptive."

"So, you were hacked?" asks Figueroa.

"That's what I thought at first, but then I started looking at the rest of the server logs and checking for evidence of a worm. I can't speak definitively, but I think this may have happened inside the lab."

"Are you telling me that one of your employees did this?" asks Figueroa.

I look down at my hands. "I'm embarrassed to say that it looks that way. Only a few have network access. Todd and I are the only ones with full admin privileges, but it's possible someone observed our passwords."

I watch Todd out of the corner of my eye. He's sweating.

This whole experience is worth it to see what he's going to do next.

"Any idea who?" asks Figueroa.

I shake my head. "I trust everyone. I guess that's the problem. If someone has been leaking information behind my back, then I guess I'm guilty for not paying attention."

Figueroa glances over at Osman, who now looks uncomfortable himself. I've turned his back-channel communication and uploading into a possible security breach. While Osman didn't do anything wrong that I know of, he's now thinking Todd is damaged goods.

"We have some new people," says Todd, finding the strength to speak and probably fearing that his silence is suspicious.

"Like who?" I ask, baiting him.

"Darnell is a good guy, for example, but he may not understand the protocols."

Wow. He just threw the kid under the bus.

"I don't know, Todd. I'm not ready to point a finger at anyone right now. Our best bet is to change our passwords and let the forensic investigator go over our logs as well as our computers at home."

"Our personal computers?" Todd says with alarm.

"Well, yes. We'll need to give him full access, passwords and everything, in order for you and me to be ruled out. After all, someone used one of our passwords."

"You don't know," Todd shoots back.

I wasn't expecting that visceral of a reaction. What else does Todd have on his computers that he's afraid of exposing?

He probably uses incredibly tight security on his home computers. When he concocted his plan to upload lab data, he was thinking in the worst-case scenario the FBI might seize his hard drives and try to access the data, but they'd fail because of encryption.

What he never conceived of was that I would corner him in a way that *not* giving the government access to his computer would make him guilty in the eyes of Figueroa and Osman.

"Do we need to shut down the lab?" asks Figueroa.

"I don't think so. At least, not if we can trace the leak."

"Are you sure it was someone who works for you?"

"I don't know, General. But we should start by investigating me first, then move on down."

I don't know in a scientific way, but I *know*.

Todd looks visibly ill. His little scheme has now put him in the crosshairs. He could be going to jail for a long time.

The smartest thing he can do is go home, wipe his computer, and refuse to participate with the probe. I think that's what's going through his head right now.

"We'll do everything we can," I tell Figueroa.

He nods. "Can the rest of you clear the room?"

As Osman and Todd leave, Todd glances back at me with hatred in his eyes.

After they're gone, Figueroa looks right at me. "What's really going on, Cray?"

CHAPTER THIRTY-SIX
INTENT

Do I lie to General Figueroa? Telling the full truth about my recent side project and my avoidance of the T-gene research could be enough to make him pull my funding on the spot and have me investigated . . . if he so chooses. Yet lying to him will only exacerbate the issue. I'm stuck between a rock and a weird moral area—says the guy who just three days ago was sawing corpses up in the middle of a Boy Scout camp.

I decide to stick to small truths. "Running a lab is hard."

Figueroa stares at me for a long moment, possibly inviting me to elaborate. I leave my statement as is.

"T-gene?" He taps the folder. "What am I going to find?"

"Everything so far. I did a meta-analysis of the genomes we have of known, captured, or killed terrorists. I then cross-referenced them with the locations of certain genes associated with the behavioral inclinations we're looking for—sociability, oxytocin response, adrenaline response. Plus, some other possible correlations based on the different kinds of profiles we have of terrorists. Some of them travel to other countries to fight. Others build bombs," I explain without explaining anything.

"And?" asks Figueroa.

"There are problems. First of all, our definition of a terrorist. While you and I may define that specifically as nonstate actors who primarily use violence against civilians, that's still too broad. The temperament of a mastermind who funnels money and weapons around the world is very different than a manic-depressed suicide bomber who got talked into blowing up a shopping mall. A lone white supremacist who builds pipe bombs is different from a community activist who decides to plan a riot and smash the nearest Starbucks."

"What are you saying?" asks Figueroa.

"We can't even decide what a terrorist is, much less determine whether certain genes incline one toward the activity."

"Then we focus."

"Okay. Do I look for the charisma genes that Osama bin Laden had? What if George Washington had them too?"

Figueroa's nostrils flare. "Are you comparing Washington to bin Laden?"

"What? No! Washington fought on the front lines and put himself in harm's way. Bin Laden was a coward who hid behind his women and human shields. I should have been more specific. What may stand out about both men might be simple things, like both were tall. Height may be an advantage when it comes to persuading people to a cause. I can't be too indiscriminate. Genes often work with other genes, and many of them may not be active."

I think about Figueroa's visceral reaction to my clumsy Washington comparison and come up with a strategy. "Let's say we find that suicide bombers have certain genes? Maybe it's some kind of extreme emotional swings, plus an adrenaline addiction? What if we find that some of our best special-forces troops have the same genes? How would that look to someone on the outside evaluating our research? Are we making our guys equivalent to the bad guys?"

Figueroa leans back and thinks this over. I've given him enough of an idea of the complexity of the issue to realize that this could backfire on him if not done properly.

When I first raised the idea of the terrorist gene, I was casually thinking about a highly specific behavior and wondering why some personality types might be more inclined to partake in it. Everyone else heard me say that there might be one gene that makes a terrorist—which is an astronomically stupid notion if you have a basic grasp of genetics and behavior. The problem was that I was talking to a roomful of people that didn't understand the basics beyond the misleading headlines they see online about genes that allegedly explain away entire conditions or behaviors.

The gay gene is one example. While science can eerily tell who is likely to be gay and who is not through certain genetic markers and environmental factors, it's not like there's one gene that makes you straight or gay.

Figueroa shakes his head. "This isn't very satisfactory. We promised people something more specific."

He doesn't seem angry at me as much as disappointed about the overall prospects of the project. It's easy to forget that he has bosses to answer to as well. If I can't make them happy, I might be in jeopardy, which means closer attention paid to aspects of my life that I'd rather not have exposed right now.

I think of telling him about the Hyde virus. The prospect of a virus that influences homicidal behavior may be extremely interesting to the military—but that's also the problem. While I trust that Figueroa isn't the kind of man to unleash something like that over North Korea, that doesn't mean that someone else wouldn't—or worse, that research could fall into the hands of someone less morally sympathetic to civilians.

"What I'm trying to do right now is focus specifically on suicide bombers," I decide on the spot. "While ten percent of the population could be radicalized into doing something like that, if we had a good genetic profile and behavioral background, we might be able to figure out who to focus on when choosing surveillance targets."

This is so Orwellian I want to throw up. Am I playing the game or making it worse?

"A behavioral profile for genetics?" Figueroa asks.

"Yes. It could tell you who is more likely to commit a violent act. It's not a tool for implicating guilt, but how to efficiently use resources in an investigation."

This still makes me uncomfortable, but if used as a forensic tool, it might do the least damage. And if it's a bad tool, it'll more than likely be abandoned.

I hope.

"We can work with that," says Figueroa. "How far are you?"

I think of the stack of research I threw together in the folder and suddenly realize that I'd asked for permission several months ago to work with an Israeli lab on a different project, but whose research could apply to this.

"Right now I'm being held up by red tape," I reply.

"What red tape?" he asks.

"I want to confer with some researchers at Sandstone Labs in Tel Aviv but need clearance first. I asked about it shortly after we talked about the T-gene." I'll let Figueroa fill in the blanks.

"The Israelis? I bet they'd love this, assuming they haven't already done their own research. That could be good. Real good. He'll love hearing that we're working with them on this."

I don't ask who *he* is. It hits me that Figueroa's superior may be much, much higher up than I realized.

"If you can facilitate that moving through, that would be a big help," I tell him.

But not too quickly.

"Yes. I'll get on that right away. I can probably have the clearances in a day or so."

"That would be wonderful," I lie. "And once we have our security check completed, I'll feel comfortable moving ahead on that."

"Right, right," says Figueroa. "We need to get on that." He looks toward the door. "It's that Pogue guy? Isn't it?"

"I don't really know," I answer cautiously.

Figueroa chuckles. "Cray, I've seen enough turkey shoots to know one when I see it. You set that little fucker up to dangle in the wind like a pro."

I shrug. Todd is minor league compared to the other sociopaths in my life. "I have concerns."

"Right. Now, do we think he's talking to foreign intelligence?"

I shake my head. "No. I think he just wanted to get rid of me. He backed up the data in case I cut him off or wiped everything in the event of my dismissal. He wants to work for you."

"He wants to be you," Figueroa replies. "I think he's been plotting with Osman."

I shrug. "I wouldn't know."

"I'll handle this. We'll put tabs on him," says Figueroa. "Just keep doing what you're doing."

"I appreciate the help, General."

This is turning out better than I expected.

"It's why I'm here. Just one more thing."

I begin to stand up. "What's that?"

"What were you doing in Kentucky?" I sit back down as my legs go numb.

CHAPTER THIRTY-SEVEN
CYA

I feel like Todd must have felt when I brought up the network intrusion. His perfect little plan was only perfect as long as it played out the way he thought it would. In his mind he was safe because his files were heavily encrypted, and not even a court order could decrypt them if he didn't want them decrypted. What he hadn't thought about was that I would preemptively use his unwillingness to cooperate as a way to imply his guilt.

Now it's my turn.

Figueroa is no dummy. When Osman went to him with Todd's talk of my erratic behavior, Figueroa clearly decided to check up on the eccentric Theo Cray. I can only imagine what resources he has at his fingertips. Whatever they are, they told him I was in Kentucky. Anything else Figueroa knows, he's keeping close to the vest.

I have to play another game of little truths. Telling him the whole scheme might get me off easily, but it also runs the risk of creating another T-gene problem.

"I'm hunting another serial killer," I reply.

"This Butcher Creek Butcher?" asks Figueroa.

"It's related," I say vaguely.

"Related? Like he's working with someone else?"

I think over the word *he* and the reality hits me: *I'm* the Butcher Creek Butcher. While I didn't kill anyone, I did butcher people . . . corpses, but still bodies of people.

"I don't know that," I reply. "I've been tracking down some other seemingly unrelated murders that I think may have a . . . an unexpected component."

"Could you elaborate?" asks Figueroa.

"It's too early to say." That's a horrible answer.

"Well, let me put it to you this way: Could you elaborate in a way that would help justify why you're using laboratory resources on this investigation?"

Damn. Figueroa knows way more than I suspected. What if Todd isn't his only source on what goes on here? I start to think about Sheila, Darnell, and the others . . .

Focus, Theo. There's a chance he already knows about the Hyde virus. Hell, I told the FBI all about it.

Okay. Assume he knows everything. Respond, but spin it. "It's a very radical idea. I spoke to the FBI, and they dismissed it outright. But I decided to persist."

"I've noticed that your far-fetched hunches have a habit of turning out to be correct," Figueroa replies.

Yeah, except the time I was seven and tried to dig a hole in the backyard to what I suspected would be an entrance to Middle Earth.

"It's actually tangentially related to T-gene," I explain. "We know that some genes aren't activated unless there are certain environmental factors . . ." My voice trails off as I think about an aspect of the Hyde virus I've never considered—even though it's right in front of my face.

"Cray?" says Figueroa, interrupting my minifugue.

"Right. I had a thought. Anyway, some genes are turned on by starvation, the presence of bacteria, deficiencies, abundances, et cetera. What if there are genes that control behavior that can be switched on and off? What if there was a gene that regulated psychopathic behavior? Or a group of genes that could be triggered by a pathogen?"

"Something that makes you a killer?" he asks.

That's what I'd originally been thinking; now I don't know. "Maybe something that flips some genes and changes the way your brain works. A virus that exploits an on/off switch. One controlling violence." Let's steer him away from Hyde. "I'm looking for genetic profiles of killers that may suggest a vulnerability to an infection."

Figueroa considers this. "Interesting. Very interesting. This sounds a lot like the T-gene project."

"Well, yes, but it's very speculative. I didn't want to encumber that project any more than it already is."

"How many of your lab employees know about this?"

I think this might be a test to see if either this is a real explanation or there's a reason that Todd didn't tell Osman the whole picture. I take a gamble on the latter.

"I've compartmentalized this information. It's not even on the network. Todd Pogue knows some. Darnell, one of our lab techs, has been running tests. But other than that, I've kept the full scope of it secret."

"And funding for this?" asks Figueroa.

"Other than lab time, which has only been a few days, it's been self-funded."

"Self-funded?"

"I was asked by the FBI to give some advice. It didn't seem appropriate to use our funding for something that's their problem."

"Right. Right. If they want any more, they should fund you themselves."

That'll happen right after the first snow-cone machine in hell opens for business.

"Agreed."

"Okay. I think I understand now. We can fold this into the T-gene project."

"We can?"

"Yes. Doesn't it seem obvious that this is related?"

I guess it does, but I don't want the two connected, even if it means that I'll have a little more freedom. After it's all done, I'll have to package this and present it to the DoD. God knows what will happen next.

"There's been some research into this before," Figueroa continues. "It showed promise but then didn't really go anywhere."

"It could be another blind alley," I reply.

"Okay. Is your fieldwork in Kentucky done?"

I guess it is. I already have my cameras in place. I'm twitching to check the latest feed. "Yes. Until they catch the bastard. I'd love to get a look at his genome."

"I bet you would. Anyway, get your lab back in order. Figure out staffing. And get that pissant out of here as soon as you can."

I'm on sketchy legal grounds if I fire Todd. I need to walk lightly and let Figueroa be the one who sends him packing. In the short term, that still means having Todd around the lab.

"Will do," I reply.

Figueroa thinks something over. "Excellent. I'll need you in Washington in four days to do a formal presentation before the committee. They've been hounding me for a progress report. It's probably better if I let you do the talking. To be honest, I can't tell which is bullshit and which isn't, but as long as you show results, I guess it doesn't matter."

"Ha," I reply. *Washington? Fuck my life. This is the last thing I need.*

"And Theo," he says, using my first name, "as a personal favor, don't go hunting any more serial killers without telling me. You're a valuable government asset at this point. I need you out of harm's way and under the radar."

That's a difficult ask, considering that my handiwork is now being shown on the news around the world.

CHAPTER THIRTY-EIGHT
FLOUR

I'm sitting on a stool at the back of Jillian's small bakery after hours, watching her knead dough. There's something attractive about the determined look on her face as she works her fingers through the thick paste while flour splashes liberally all around.

My computer back home is processing the images from Butcher Creek, so I decided for the sake of domestic tranquility to drop in on Jillian.

"Want to try?" she asks.

I think it over for a moment. The chemistry of cooking fascinates me. I love watching how Jillian can combine unrelated flavors or ingredients and come up with something that tastes spectacular. Her salted crusts and chocolate crème pie can leave me awake at night. The way she uses just a hint of lemon with her vanilla frosting is a trade secret she's threatened to kill me over if I ever divulge it.

As much as I want to step over to the counter and push my fingers through the dough, sliding through the spaces between her fingers as I smell the light lavender bath oil scent on her neck, I decline.

It wasn't that long ago that these hands were used to do unspeakable things to dead bodies. The thought of the gore somehow lodged underneath my fingernails, or the fatty oils absorbed into my own pores mixing with Jillian's pure white dough, is too unsettling.

The rational part of my mind thinks about all the bacteria and other organic matter that drifts into the things we eat in even the most sterile kitchens, but it's not the physical aspect that bothers me the most; it's the *acts* these hands have taken part in.

"I'm good. It's more fun to watch," I explain.

"It's more fun to eat," she replies, giving me a smile over her shoulder.

I love the way her ponytail bounces around her neck as she gives me the grin. There's something so girl-like about her that's never going to go away.

Strangely, I can see that smiling face under a Kevlar helmet in the middle of Iraq, still keeping her spirits up even as her friends are dying all around her.

And when things were at the worst, when she had to bury her husband, I can still see that face carrying a kind of inexhaustible resolve that helped her through the darkest of times.

Our relationship started as a heat-of-the-moment fling that kept going. My occasional emotional inaccessibility somehow completes that part of her that will never be able to love another man like her husband. My absences and aloofness aren't so hard on a widow who's already gone through the most extreme absence a lover can offer.

Still, I'm afraid of drifting apart from her without realizing it. Like a boat stretching its anchor line to the point that one day it snaps without warning.

"You know I love you more than anything," I tell Jillian.

"I know," she replies.

But is that love good enough for her? I've made her life as easy as possible. The house is everything she's wanted. The bakery started as an act of charity on my behalf but turned out to be the opposite.

She grabs a cherry from a bowl, holding it by the stem, and dips it into some molten chocolate, then lets it cool in the air.

"I know you have your little projects and plans, Theo." Jillian walks over to me, dangling the cherry at eye level. "And I know you're dealing with some dark things." She raises the cherry to my lips. "Just promise me you'll let me know before it swallows you whole." At the last moment, she devours the chocolate-covered cherry.

"Cruel," I reply.

"I don't know how long this phase is going to last. I'm prepared for it to be forever. I hope not, but I'm prepared for it. I've also resigned myself to the idea that one day you'll stop calling or texting," she says seriously.

"I'd never forget about you," I reply. "I sometimes get lost in my work."

"It's not your work I worry about. It's that someday you'll get too close to one of these killers or maybe cross some line you're not supposed to cross, and then it's no more Theo."

"That sounds pessimistic."

"Or realistic? That thing in Kentucky. The Butcher, is that you?"

For a fleeting moment, I'm afraid she's literally asking me if I'm the Butcher Creek Butcher, the answer to which is technically yes. But what she means is this part of the case she saw me leave the airport to go pursue.

"Yes. It's something I'm working on."

"I thought so. Did the FBI ask you?"

"No," I reply. "They stopped listening to me. I had to go out on my own."

"Hmm."

"What's that mean?"

"I told you I was okay with you helping them out, but this has already turned into a one-man Theo crusade. I hoped you were over that."

"Over it? How can I be over helping people? If I don't do something, people will die."

"And if I don't send all the things I bake to feed people in starving countries, they're going to die. And you know what? I don't send them there. Why? Because there's only so much I can do. You, you at least have a choice between the right things you can do."

"What's that supposed to mean?"

"Carol has gotten more ill. The treatments aren't working. When I sat on the couch, holding her hand, I couldn't stop thinking, *What would Theo do?*"

Carol is her mother-in-law. I never even asked Jillian how the trip went. I am a horrible person.

"I'm sorry to hear that, but I don't follow."

"Theo, you're the most un-self-aware self-aware person I've ever met. It's like you're constantly standing two feet in front of yourself, watching yourself go through the world without ever seeing your place in it all. You're brilliant, not in the smartest-guy-in-the-room kind of way, but a one-in-a-million kind. I run into people in the shop from the university who know you. They tell me how they all thought you were going to win a Nobel Prize or do some kind of groundbreaking research. Instead, in their eyes, you became some kind of glory-seeking monster hunter."

"That's insane. I'm trying to help people."

"How many people would you help if you tried to cure Carol's condition?"

I shake my head. "It doesn't work like that. It takes years."

"And you can do that kind of thing faster. I don't know what you should be doing. But I do know that if you were doing what you originally set out to do—cure diseases—more people would be alive today than the number of potential victims if you'd just let Joe Vik do his thing."

"That's . . . that's absurd."

"Maybe. But another part of me wonders if you do know how smart you are, but you've never tried to tackle a bigger problem because you're afraid you'll fail and then . . . well, and then in your eyes, you'll be a failure to your father."

I can't respond, because I still haven't even processed it all. My face feels like it's been slapped. Where did all this come from?

What if she's right? What if monster hunting is some kind of easy kill for me that makes me feel better while avoiding the larger issues? Hiding away in my lab doing bullshit work for the government was my way to find time to pursue my hobby. What if my hobby is just a way of avoiding the harder problems?

I'd be out of my league trying to cure Carol, but there are plenty of diseases in the third world I might be able to tackle with my methods. There are even treatable ones I could help with if I were willing to follow the same kind of outrageous impulses that led me to Butcher Creek and apply them to a big problem.

Damn it. What am I doing?

"I can tell by watching you that's food for thought," says Jillian.

"I don't know where to begin," I reply.

She grabs my hands and places them on her hips. "Think later. Do me in my kitchen now."

CHAPTER THIRTY-NINE
Pattern Recognition

"It's me," I say into the burner phone the moment Gallard answers.

"Theo? I didn't recognize the number. I'm glad to hear from you. This Butcher Creek thing, have you been following it?"

"It's not important. Did you get the email I sent you?"

"Email? What email?"

"It would be sent from a Eugene Chantrelle. I thought you might pick up on the clue."

"Uh, no. Let me check my inbox. Who's Chantrelle?"

"A French teacher who lived in Scotland and murdered his wife. Robert Louis Stevenson knew him."

"Stevenson?"

"The author of *Strange Case of Dr Jekyll and Mr Hyde*," I reply. "Chantrelle's a pseudonym."

"Oh brother. You do know I'm a *real* detective, right? Not the kind that sips tea on the leather couch of an English manor explaining why Lord What's His Face poisoned Colonel Whoever in the laundry room."

"Yes. Sorry. I just got carried away. Anyway, inside the email you'll find seven folders. Each one contains images of men I think could be our culprit. I was hoping this would help the case."

"The Butcher Creek case?" asks Gallard.

"No. Your Phantom case. The guy who cultivated the Hyde virus," I reply, frustrated.

"Who are these men?"

"Suspects."

"Theo. I get the concept of a suspect. Why are they suspicious to you? Why should I tell the FBI to find out who they are?"

"They're the seven people at the Butcher Creek crime scene that I can't find any information on. None of them came up in image searches. I suspect that at least six are county or state employees, but you have better resources to look into that. The images are too fuzzy to give me a solid match."

"Wait. These photos are *from* Butcher Creek? Inside the crime scene? How did you get them?"

"No comment."

"The angle is kind of high. What did you use, some kind of military drone?"

"Something like that. What's important is that one of these men is very possibly Jekyll. All you have to do is identify them. Ask around. See which person stands out as an outsider."

"So, he did show up at Butcher Creek, huh? I guess he couldn't avoid that. Great timing on your part in getting the photos. Was the Butcher Creek killer someone you'd been after, too?"

"Not quite. I wouldn't worry about the Butcher Creek thing." I try to decide how much to tell him. "Doesn't it feel a little staged to you?"

"Yeah, but with serial killers getting ideas from *CSI*, I don't know what's real or not."

"This one isn't real at all."

"What do you mean?"

I'm confident that if Jekyll showed up, he's one of the seven men I photographed. There's no point in letting this dumb charade continue any longer. I just have to avoid implicating myself.

"Can I tell you something confidentially?"

Aside from the fact I'm calling him from a phone that can't be traced back to me.

"Within reason."

"Your forensic people are going to find out that the victims all died of other trauma. They're not even Americans. They're cadavers from a hospital in Ukraine."

"That's one hell of an intuitive leap, Theo. Care to elaborate?"

"No. Focus on the images I sent you. Identify them and you have Jekyll."

"And ignore Butcher Creek? It's not that easy."

I simply can't tell him that I set it all up. I broke a lot of laws—even if the intent was noble.

"Call hospitals in Ukraine. Send them photos of the victims. You'll get a match."

Unless Rayner lied to me about the source of the bodies.

"Yeah, well, it's more complicated than that, Theo."

"How so?"

"I can't get into that right now. But I'll take a look at the photos you sent me. How exactly did you take these?"

"I can't tell you," I reply, then add ominously, "I may have used assets meant for other purposes."

It's a lie meant to reinforce Gallard's earlier assumption that I used some secret military tech to get the images. Let him believe what he wants.

"Okay. I'll ask around."

"Gallard, Jekyll is very likely one of the men I sent you. We don't have time to sit on it."

"I get it, Theo. But understand that right now the FBI is more concerned with catching the Butcher Creek killer. I'll follow up your Ukrainian-hospital tip, but the authorities already have suspects."

Suspects for an imaginary crime? *Oh man. What have I done?*

They probably rounded up a number of local men with rap sheets. Hell, I'll bet some crazies called and claimed they were the Butcher Creek Butcher.

I kept fearing that the hoax would get exposed too quickly—I never stopped to consider the implications if the authorities never caught on. Real lives could be at stake.

I toyed with the idea of planting some kind of clue or evidence that it was fake but dismissed it because I didn't have the time and couldn't think of something that didn't run the risk of being found too soon.

"Besides call Ukrainian hospitals, can you give me any other insight?" asks Gallard.

I could tell him how the science-fiction books were selected and how their excerpts were spread around with the victims or how to find the autopsy marks I concealed, but all of that would point the finger right back at me. And despite the friendly relationship Gallard and I have, there's nothing stopping him from telling his colleagues at the FBI that they should be paying a lot more attention to Dr. Theodore Cray.

"Tell them to look at the embalming fluid inside the veins. Being soaked in the liquid won't get it that deep into the tissue."

"Okay. I'll do that, but . . . you're kind of scaring me. You know a lot more about this Butcher Creek . . ." There's a long, awkward pause. "Damn it. You idiot. What did you do?"

"Remember our conversation about how far we'd go to catch Jekyll?" I reply. "I took it seriously."

CHAPTER FORTY
Breathe

Jillian is asleep in the bedroom while I sit in front of my monitors, reflecting on my life. On one screen are the seven male faces, one of which could belong to Jekyll. On another is a map of the world. The third monitor contains a list of all the things I could be doing with my skills besides faking crime scenes.

Infectious-disease research stands out the most.

Increasingly we're finding that the cure to many pathogens can be found in the environment from which they emerge. Recently, a man with a life-threatening infection in his heart was cured by using a bacteriophage—a virus that infects bacteria—found within an hour's drive of where he contracted the infection.

As bacteria outpace the development of antibiotics, treatments like bacteriophages are looking increasingly like the solution. My interest in computational biology and fieldwork could be useful.

The fact that I've decided I'm okay with stepping outside legal frameworks could be an advantage as well. I'd have few qualms about setting up a lab in a less regulated country, provided I didn't put people at an unnecessary risk.

Scrolling through the list of the top infectious diseases in the world and places where treatments could be used the most, I realize what Jillian was saying is true. I could do a lot more good if I stepped back and paid attention to the world around me.

And yet . . . I still keep thinking of Jekyll. He's out there. He'll kill and kill again. Hyde isn't merely his murder weapon; it's also an experiment. I have a strong feeling that he's trying to turn it into something much more dangerous. But I still don't understand his endgame.

I pull up an image of Hyde's structure. I've been trying to think of a vaccination for it. A rabies vaccine may help prevent infection after the fact, but only right after infection. The disease works too quickly for the vaccine to be effective if you wait too long.

The only treatment I can imagine—and it's more science fiction than practical—is using stem cells to try to regrow the damaged part of the brain. Another possibility is boosting the brain's production of microglia to get it to repair itself.

There's been some promising research into this. But, as with everything else, time's the biggest factor.

It can take at least a decade from when you have an idea of how to treat something until you can actually try it on a human. If it doesn't work and you have to go back to the drawing board, it could add another five years.

I could probably make something that would stop Hyde in a few weeks. My approach would be to make a vaccine that had a dozen different vectors to attack the virus and then create a hundred random variations of it.

This method would let me test ten times as many vaccines at once. It's a beautifully simple approach that's perfectly fine to test on bacteria, but once you scale it up to humans, the paperwork alone could consume a researcher's lifetime.

There are dozens of little hacks I could do to increase the efficacy of laboratory research, but they'd all have to clear legal hurdles that would frustrate me to no end.

Granted, a number of these are important hurdles to keep mad scientists from killing people, but many delays kill more people than they'll ever save.

I've heard the argument made that simply doubling the budget of the FDA could save hundreds of thousands of lives by speeding up the approval process. The counterargument goes that, historically speaking, the increase in employees would lead to even more roadblocks and an increased misuse of the precautionary principle, killing even more people.

It's why I like my computer simulations. I can create entire universes where I don't have to ask permission to try something radical or genocidal.

I have an open offer from a philanthropist to fund any start-up I can think of. I'd avoided the offer because the thought of running a company didn't appeal to me. I took up Figueroa's offer because it sounded a lot like university research and he offered me certain protections.

I'm now wondering if I should have taken the philanthropist up on his offer. Maybe I still can.

If trying to cure disease directly is too frustrating because of the time involved and the regulatory problems, is there some other way I could speed up the development of drug discovery?

I'd been using my modeling program, MAAT, to make predictions about ecosystems before I used it to catch Joe Vik and Oyo. How hard would it be to apply MAAT to something like eradicating a disease?

If I were to describe to MAAT something like pneumonia and the different pathogens that can cause it, the system might be able to steer me into an interesting direction for research. My latest iteration of my modeling program has been using machine-learning models to understand relations between things at a much faster rate. I could give it a data set of the structures and genomes of bacteria and viruses that cause pneumonia and then a set of treatments that have some effect. MAAT might then be able to find a correlation or show where to look for possible treatments.

Doing this with the Hyde virus would be tricky because it's based on a strain that there's not a lot of treatments for. But when I have the time, I should try.

Most of the time, MAAT shows me approaches researchers have already thought about, but sometimes it's capable of surprising me. After I type in the structure of *Streptococcus pneumoniae* and ask MAAT to make a best guess for a bacteriophage to fight it, he tells me to check out the lungs of blue whales.

This doesn't mean that MAAT thinks that there's a cure to be found there, only that it's an environment worth looking into. If I had to guess why MAAT came up with that, it might be that since *Streptococcus pneumoniae* is a respiratory issue and blue whales have the largest lungs of any creature that ever lived, MAAT came to the conclusion that the whale's lung environment might contain a virus that preys upon *Streptococcus pneumoniae.*

Interesting . . . Even though marine animals can get pneumonia—especially in captivity—it might not be a bad idea to see if they don't have a slightly higher resistance to it.

I lose myself in thought and only notice my phone after the third time Gallard tries to call me.

"Hello?" I reply, vanquishing all thoughts of blue whale lungs.

"Bad news, Theo."

CHAPTER FORTY-ONE

INTENT

It's amazing how much thinking the human mind can do in the span of time between two words like *bad* and *news*. My mind races through a thousand different scenarios. Not so much complete thoughts as images. An image of another body.

An image of thousands of Hyde particles floating through the air in a kindergarten. An image of Joe Vik standing over Jillian's sleeping body. An image of myself covered in blood . . .

"What is it?" I ask.

"First things first. We didn't have this conversation. Understand?"

"Yeah. Got it. What's going on?"

"You have a good criminal attorney?" asks Gallard. That's never an encouraging question.

"Yeah . . . a couple. I had one help me out with the Oyo case. I also got a guy back in Montana who's been keeping them off my back. Why?"

"You're a clever guy, Theo. But not that clever. Those photos you gave me? I sent them around as you asked. You didn't tell me how you acquired them."

"I don't even know that I sent them to you . . ."

"Oh, let me back up. I didn't mention your name. But they couldn't help but notice the angle of the photos. It didn't take them too long to put things together. They found your little hidden cameras."

I don't know if the call is being monitored. I trust Gallard, I think, but I still don't know. "I'm not sure I know what you're talking about or how that affects me," I reply.

I was expecting them to find the cameras at some point. I sprayed them with a lab-grade degreaser to remove any fingerprints I may have left on them.

"Fine. Whatever you say. But here's the part you may not have anticipated. After they realized the corpses were . . . well, corpses, they started putting the squeeze on people involved in the tissue trade. They started asking questions and showing your photo. Someone pointed you out."

"Me? For what?"

"Illegal purchase of human tissue, or something to that effect. The point is that you're now the FBI's main suspect for the Butcher Creek whatever they're calling it."

Damn it. Rayner squealed. Why? Did he have some deal with them? Was he already under investigation?

It doesn't matter. The FBI has a suspect, and they're going to come knocking on my door any day now . . . literally.

I feel my lungs start to tighten. Everything is collapsing around me. Hubris. Pure hubris.

You thought you were smarter than them, Theo. But did you really think you were smarter than all *of them?*

To be sure, I thought I had the advantage of being a loner.

While they wasted cognitive overhead trying to decide among themselves what to do, I could act nimbly and outsmart them—until they turned their focus on me.

I should call Mary Karlin in Los Angeles. She's sharp.

I'm about to tell Gallard I need to go, then realize that I don't want to call Karlin just yet. If I'm already lawyered up by the time the FBI arrives, it'll only make them more suspicious. It's better if I let them take me in, then call her, then try to preempt any questioning.

I think.

Questions . . . that's how it will start. They'll have questions for me. They'll want to know why I was in North Carolina buying tissue from Rayner.

If I don't tell them anything, that will delay them. All they have, I think, is Rayner's word against mine.

Wait a second . . . what if he's their suspect? I'm sure Gallard's being straight with me, but what if he's jumping to conclusions? There's no doubt I'd be a person of interest if my name came up . . . especially if Rayner pointed my face out. But I am a semipublic person. Rayner's a more natural suspect.

There's also another angle I can exploit. Maybe.

I talk myself off the ledge a little, but only a fraction of an inch.

"What else have you got?" I ask.

"What else? I just told you that they're about to charge you with a felony!"

"I didn't do what they think I did. What about the photos? The seven men? What happened with that?"

"We identified six of them. The seventh, there wasn't a lot to go on. We don't have a name. Nobody remembered him being around for more than a few minutes."

The paramedic. He had on a hat and shaded glasses and kept to the outer edges of the crime scene. I remember he went over to assist one of the forensic people who'd accidentally cut himself.

"It was the paramedic? Right?"

"Yeah. We're trying to figure out which ambulance service he worked for."

"He doesn't," I reply. "That's Jekyll. That's the man we've been looking for."

Gallard takes his time to respond. "What makes you so sure?"

"What's the one person you'll let into any building without question? A paramedic. A fireman makes you wonder where's the fire. A cop arouses too much attention. Nobody wants to stop a man on the way to save a life." I should know. I was a paramedic for a short period of time. An uncomfortable new connection between Jekyll and me. "He probably calls in the incident himself sometimes. Plenty of ambulances show up, and he fits right in."

"He . . . uh, treated someone," says Gallard.

"I know. Have you talked to the tech and asked them what happened? Maybe the paramedic created an opportunity to talk to them. Maybe he spotted a preexisting injury and offered to change the bandage."

"Damn." Gallard is thinking this over.

"We need to check the 911 calls around the other crime scenes. Want to bet that they had someone calling an ambulance there, too?"

"I know it makes sense, Theo. But I don't know if we have anything else to go on . . . especially because of the chaos you created at Butcher Creek."

"Do I have to remind you that the only reason we know what he looks like is because of the chaos I may or may not have created?"

I take his silence as assent.

Finally, he speaks. "What are you going to do now?"

"Make sure my girlfriend knows how to reach my attorney."

I crawl into bed with Jillian and stare up at the ceiling.

My mind is pulled in a lot of different directions. At this point there's no point worrying about all the possibilities. They're endless.

I tell Alexa to play my audiobook for ten minutes until I fall asleep.

A moment later I'm wrapped in the comforting arms of John Lee's narration as he tells the story of the lives affected by the construction of a fictional medieval cathedral in Ken Follett's *Pillars of the Earth*.

My mind begins to forget my earthly troubles a few minutes before the audiobook fades out and I drift off to sleep.

I wake up as Jillian is getting back into bed and crawling underneath my arm. She places her head on my shoulder and holds me tightly. The sun is just starting to appear as a glow through the blinds.

"You okay?" I ask. I have a vague memory of a dream where there was someone knocking on the door.

"Yeah. I sent them away."

It wasn't a dream. "Who?"

"The FBI agents. They wanted to talk to you. I told them you were sleeping." She yawns.

"Oh," I reply. "You don't seem too surprised."

"I'm not anymore. Now shut up and sleep or play your audiobook. I have to bake sixty pies tomorrow." Then she adds, "And possibly a metal file inside a cake."

I hold her tightly, afraid to let go.

CHAPTER FORTY-TWO
Person of Interest

"Dr. Cray, can you tell us what you were doing in Kentucky last week?" asks the sandy-haired FBI agent who looks young enough to get stopped for truancy.

I glance at my attorney. Ron Holman nods to me. "I was there on business." I reply with the answer he gave me.

"And what exactly is the nature of your business?" asks Agent Lyford.

Lyford is sitting in the conference room next to Agent Llewellyn, who looks barely older than he does, although the wedding ring implies she's at least of the legal age to marry in Texas.

I look at my attorney again. He nods.

"I can't divulge the nature of my work," I reply.

"For god's sake, can you answer a question like an adult without having to turn to your attorney every time?" grumbles Agent Boyd Gordon, their immediate supervisor in the Austin field office.

"Sure," says Ron Holman. "If you want to turn off the recorders and grant my client complete immunity. No? Then as long as we're voluntarily cooperating, please allow my client to answer each question in his own time."

Holman warned me about Gordon's explosive temper—that he'd try to bully me into faster responses and get me to trip up.

I don't plan to let Gordon push me around. Underneath the table I am holding a pen. I won't let myself answer a question until I've uncapped it and recapped it. It's a silly little trick I'm using to avoid implicating myself—which I have a habit of doing.

"All right. Can you explain to me why you can't tell us the nature of your business?" asks Gordon.

Holman explains, "As we told you, Dr. Cray runs a top-secret research lab funded by the Department of Defense. I can't even ask him what he does, because attorney-client privilege doesn't cover state secrets of this level. You'll have to get a federal court order to allow him to explain—and even then, the DoD will want the right to clear any statements. And if you continue to badger him on that, I'll have to ask that they send an attorney here as well."

Gordon's face flickers with frustration. The last thing he wants is me sitting here with two attorneys—one of them a government lawyer.

"For crying out loud. Can you at least tell me *they* know what you were up to?"

"Yes," replies Holman. "I spoke to General Figueroa. He authorized me to say that he was fully aware of Dr. Cray's whereabouts."

"And he was sanctioned by the government?" asks Gordon.

"As it was explained to me," says Holman.

He's exaggerating considerably, but he made it a point to tell me not to give him anything other than the barest amount of information about what I did, so that he could spin it however he felt necessary.

"So . . . Dr. Cray was in North Carolina on government business that may or may not have involved buying human tissue from a body-part dealer?"

"I can't speak to any of that," says Holman. "But I can assure you that Dr. Cray fully understands the laws concerning human body parts, and if he were ever to acquire them for research, he'd only pay the legally allowed fees for preparation and transportation."

"And the cameras in the woods by the Butcher Creek crime scene? He had nothing to do with them?"

"We'll need to contact the Department of Defense if you have any more questions about Dr. Cray's purpose for his visit to North Carolina."

Gordon rolls his eyes in frustration. This isn't his office's case. He was asked by the Kentucky FBI field office to interview me here in Texas. He wasn't expecting I'd show up with a lawyer and start hinting that if I was involved in this, it might be some hush-hush, secret government research.

That, of course, could still lead to an FBI investigation, but if there's no murder, no stolen money, and no secrets going to the Russians, their degree of enthusiasm in pursuing this will drop dramatically.

Even the mention of a Defense Department lawyer defending me has Gordon deciding that he'd rather be doing something else instead of grilling me.

Gordon turns his wrath upon his own agents. "So, we got a witness in North Carolina who says Cray bought a bunch of dead bodies off him and then they show up in a national park all hacked to pieces like one of those awful movies my daughter watches? Is that it?"

"Yes," says Lyford. "There are a number of statutes involving human-tissue trafficking, disposal, and probably a dozen others."

"And how many of them happened in Austin?"

"Just his lab," says Llewellyn. "We don't know what goes on there."

"Nor should we," says Gordon. He turns to me. "Maybe you're a weirdo and in between interfering with investigations you like to play serial-killer pretend. Right now, I don't care. If I get asked to arrest you so the Kentucky office can pick you up, I will. Other than that"—he shrugs—"I find it hard to make myself give a damn. If those idiots out there couldn't tell an autopsied body from a murder victim, then that's their problem." Gordon nods to my lawyer. "Take your client and leave."

"We're letting him go?" asks Llewellyn.

"Kentucky wanted us to interview him. We did," says Gordon.

"We've still got more questions from them."

"They're not going to tell you anything."

"Thank you," says Holman as he takes my elbow and begins to usher me away.

"You're welcome," growls Gordon. "Llewellyn will see you out."

She stands up and gives me a scowl. "This way."

I keep my mouth shut until Holman and I are outside the building and sitting in a coffee shop five blocks away.

"You got lucky," says Holman as we sit down with our drinks.

"How do you figure?"

"Gordon sized you up on the spot. He thinks you're a weirdo, which I have to agree with, but he figures you're a government weirdo and more trouble than it's worth."

"Well, then, I guess it's good, then."

"I don't know. Here's the thing: it might have been better if we got your DoD lawyer in there and answered all their questions. If Kentucky sets its sights on you, they're not going to go easy. They'll dig up whatever evidence they can, get their witness to swear up and down that you're Jack the Ripper, and get a federal judge who won't be intimidated by the Department of Defense.

"As your attorney speaking, let's pretend you did the things they think you might have done. Your only way out of it will be to plea bargain, and that still means hard time.

"Otherwise, they'll have you tied up in federal court for years. If the DoD decides that it's easier to cut you loose than answer a bunch of questions, you'll be doubly, pardon the expression, fucked.

"This Butcher Creek incident is hugely embarrassing to them. They're going to want to blame somebody. If the body dealer says it's you, then the FBI's not going to let it go. They need a fall guy. Who better than Theo Cray?"

No good deed involving pseudo–mass murder and cannibalism goes unpunished.

CHAPTER FORTY-THREE
INTERFERENCE

I'm sitting across from Jillian at a bistro table next to the window inside her bakery. Cars drive past in the parking lot while the aroma of baked apple pie fills the air. She has her hands around a coffee cup.

"I've been thinking about getting a commercial-grade machine. Maybe a Keurig or something easy to maintain." She looks around the small dining area of three tables and a counter. "I don't want to turn this into a Starbucks, but it might be nice if people could get a cup of good coffee when they're here."

I nod and reply half-absentmindedly, "Coffee is so subjective."

"True. I've been paying attention to the different coffee shops around here." She opens her blue spiral notebook. "Petite Café is pretty decent in the early-morning rush, but then the quality goes down. I think they don't change the filters or clean out the grounds. The Velvet Donut is pretty mediocre all day long, but I estimate they make just as much from coffee as food. If I use a pod system, the cost per cup goes way up, but it's easier to maintain. I did the math, and one person could run the shop, serve five times the coffee, and still make it work."

I look at her handwritten tables. "Impressive. I didn't know baking was so math intensive."

"It is after living with you. I could do a special, like coffee and a muffin or something, and have a bunch of muffins ready-made. With three coffee machines, I think I'd be fine. It's real easy to increase. Why are you smiling?" she asks.

"I love this."

"The idea?" she asks.

"Well, yes. But sitting here and having a conversation about muffins and coffee instead . . . of, well, you know."

"I do, too. But . . ."

She knows me too well. "How much do you want to know?" I ask.

"Everything you need me to know. Do I have to worry about you going to jail?"

"Maybe. I don't know. That's not what has me worried," I reply.

"Uh, okay. So, what does have you worried?"

"He's out there. And, yes, I should move on from this *hobby* and do something more impactful."

"I didn't tell you to drop this. I said you need to think about why you keep getting pulled into this sort of thing," she explains.

"Right, right. Well, he's out there and probably killing right now. I gave the FBI my images."

"And then they came after you," she replies.

"I meant well . . ." Although it's a far cry to call what I did at Butcher Creek *well*. "They focused on me instead of Jekyll. They should be plastering his photo everywhere."

Jillian takes a sip of her coffee and looks out the window. "I'm not sure they've connected the dots as easily as you have."

"Gallard gets it." I've told Jillian about the FBI profiler.

"Yeah, but I think he's more enamored with you than the others," she replies.

"Enamored?"

"He studies behavior, right? Extreme personality types? Sound familiar? You're his favorite subject. Which makes him . . . less than subjective."

"Maybe so." I start to take a bite of my caramel crumb cake, then set it back down.

"You have to commit, Theo. Either you're all in or you're not."

"Yeah. It's the only way we're going to catch him," I reply.

"I was talking about my crumb cake. If you're going to eat it, eat it, damn it."

"Sorry." I start to take a wolfish bite, then remember how Jillian frowns on that. Her desserts are meant to be savored slowly, not used as meal substitutes—although there's about a week's worth of fruit in a slice of her pie.

"What's stopping you from catching this guy?" she asks.

"He knows he's being hunted, or at least planned for that. His victims are probably random . . . although some of them may not be. It's a possible area to explore, but without police and FBI assistance, it'll come down to more shoe leather on my part, and interviewing people."

"Which is not one of your strengths," she reminds me.

"Yeah. I could try a bunch of data analysis on the victims, but I'm afraid Jekyll will have expected that. He could have chosen some random factor, like they're all into model railroads, solely to get investigators chasing a false lead."

"You think he's that devious?"

I vigorously nod my head. "Oh, hell yeah. I'm also afraid that any forensic data could be another false lead."

"Sounds like this guy knows just as much about this kind of thing as you do."

"Jillian, he knows *more* than I do. He's also a skilled virologist and experimentalist. He's brilliant."

"An evil Theo," says Jillian with a smirk. "Maybe he's off in some evil government lab, just like you, but plotting death."

"Yeah, maybe." My mind follows that train of thought.

"Wait. Do you think he really could be?" asks Jillian.

"It's not as crazy as it sounds. You might be onto something."

"An evil lab?"

"No. Well, not exactly. I keep thinking about this guy operating out of some dark basement—and maybe that's what he's doing now, but the more I think about it, the more unlikely it is that it started there. This could have been legitimate research at one point that he took underground."

"Why?"

"He's a sociopath. The reasons could be anything from making money to his delight in watching people die. The point is that Hyde may have started as legit research. Maybe it wasn't even his idea. He could have been just one of the researchers . . ." I pause to think.

"What is it?"

"I keep thinking of Todd Pogue in my lab. He was trying to steal data right out from underneath me."

Jillian's jaw drops. "Wait . . ."

"No. No. Todd isn't Jekyll. I wish he was half as smart. I just mean that science has as many backstabbers as any other industry—maybe more."

"Okay. So, who is Jekyll?"

"He could be a scientist or a lab technician. I can't be arrogant enough to assume the smartest person in the lab is the one with the PhD. But a scientist with a PhD would have greater access to resources. He could even teach at a small college and have unsupervised lab access." I enjoy a bit of wistful nostalgia for a time when I had a little more freedom in my teaching lab.

"You said you searched for research papers on Hyde, right?"

"Yes." I shake my head in disbelief. "I'm an idiot. I'm such an idiot."

"I know this already. But tell me why you came to that conclusion," she says.

"I was searching *published* papers. Hyde would be the kind of thing studied in secret . . . like my lab. Most of what we do will never end up in a journal—that would be breaking the law. If Jekyll worked for a similar lab . . . or works for one now . . . then I won't find out about it in *PLOS Pathogens*. That kind of research would be shoved into a filing cabinet next to Indiana Jones's Ark of the Covenant."

"That's frustrating," says Jillian.

"Except . . ." I snap my fingers. "While the research results may be hard to find, there's probably one aspect that would be easy . . . if you had the right clearance. The funding proposal."

"Meaning?"

"If it was a government project, they had to ask someone for money at some point. Most likely the Department of Defense. Those records are electronic and go back decades."

"Can you access them?" asks Jillian.

"Oddly enough, I'm supposed to speak at the Pentagon tomorrow and explain my research. If I play nice, they might let me dig around."

"Right," she says. "Unless they decide to arrest you instead."

CHAPTER FORTY-FOUR
PROCESS

I'm sitting in a conference room in Virginia within walking distance of the Pentagon because in 1957 a backward, agrarian economy that had starved millions of its own population in a state-instigated famine had managed to be the first nation to send a satellite into orbit.

Until the moment the Soviets sent Sputnik around the world, the United States government paid more lip service than funding to science. While we'd leapfrogged into the twentieth century with the atomic bomb, other grand-scale projects didn't receive nearly as much attention.

After scientists and generals explained the military application of rockets and cutting-edge technology to Eisenhower, he decided we'd never be caught behind again. In less than a year, he established both NASA and DARPA, the Defense Advanced Research Projects Agency.

The problem wasn't really that we were technologically behind; we were simply unfocused. The Redstone booster NASA would use to launch its own satellite and ultimately Alan Shepard into space was originally the Jupiter-C ballistic missile designed under the supervision of Wernher von Braun, the former Nazi rocket scientist we brought to the United States to help develop our ballistic missiles.

Von Braun and his team could have beaten the Soviets to the punch, but interagency feuding prevented him from using the Jupiter to send an orbital payload in 1956.

It was because of Sputnik that von Braun finally got to build his dream rocket successor to the Jupiter—the Saturn V, which would ultimately take mankind to the moon and end the space race, for better or worse.

My place in all this is to explain to the DARPA overseers why my technology is both cutting-edge and, more importantly, worthy of continued funding in light of the gross mismanagement of my lab by yours truly.

I walked into this meeting expecting to encounter a bunch of General Figueroa clones; instead there are three scientists, an accountant, a colonel, and another general in addition to Figueroa.

I was relieved to learn that I was one of five meetings today and mine was scheduled immediately before lunch—suggesting that it would be very short or very long.

Dr. Geraldine Rosen, a DARPA scientist and administrator, starts the meeting. "Dr. Cray, thank you for meeting with us. We wanted to clear up a few questions about your research. We understand that starting a lab very quickly can lead to some problems further down the line, and we wanted to address those today."

This is a different turn than I was expecting. I've brought a stack of folders with updates on all the projects we'd been working on. I even put more substance into T-gene.

"Yes, I have to admit I'm a little out of my element."

"Our primary concern is the network intrusion you said you had. Can you tell us what may have been compromised? What should we be concerned about?"

"Lab data, primarily. Any paperwork related to DARPA was kept on a separate server, and I have no reason to believe it was stolen."

Rosen looks through a file in front of her. "Lab data? Anything about military operations or field locations where you obtained samples?"

"No. Definitely not," I reply.

"Why is that?"

"Because I keep all of that separate as well. Nobody in the lab has access to that."

"And you're sure you haven't been hacked?" she asks.

"I've had an independent audit done. The only incident we're aware of is the one I uncovered."

"And you're positive that was done internally?"

"Let's just say that I strongly suspect that's the case."

"And do you have any idea which employee that could be?"

"I have a suspicion. I've given that person nonessential duties while we investigate." Todd doesn't know that he's formally suspect number one, but I'm sure he's aware of the possibility.

"Have the FBI been notified of this?"

"Yes. They're waiting for the results of our internal security audit." I'd already spoken with the DC branch of the FBI that handles DARPA security issues. They're a million miles apart bureaucratically from the ones in Kentucky.

"But you're pretty sure who did this? Right?" asks Colonel Ashbrook, next to Figueroa.

"Very," I reply.

"Did you suspect them right away?" he asks.

"He was my first choice."

"Okay, then can you explain to me why you hired someone you didn't trust?"

I'm going to put it all out on the table, admit that I'm a horrible boss. "I had to staff up the lab as quickly as possible. I made some mistakes."

Figueroa shakes his head. "A big mistake. You know, you should have gone through my office. We can do talent searches and avoid these problems."

I wait to reply, letting the silence after his chastisement hang there for a moment. "With apologies, Colonel Ashbrook, *your* office did recommend the employee. As I said, I was trying to staff up quickly and just went with who you suggested. Todd Pogue was at the top of the list."

"Pogue?" he blurts out.

Uh-oh. There's a personal connection.

Figueroa turns to Ashbrook. "You know the man?"

Ashbrook hesitates, probably deciding it's not wise to jump on a grenade for his friend at this moment. "I've dealt with him in the past," he replies vaguely.

"Okay," says Dr. Rosen. "Please keep us updated on that. Meanwhile . . ." She flips through some notes. "General Figueroa did an on-site inspection and seems happy with progress. Unless anyone has anything else to ask, I believe we're done."

That's it?

Figueroa gives me a small nod from across the table when he sees my confused look.

I guess he told them it didn't need to be a long meeting.

Here's to friends in high places with missiles and guns.

I stand up and gather my folders while everyone else gets ready to leave as well.

"Dr. Cray?" asks Rosen.

"Yes?" I reply.

"Have time for lunch?"

I glance over at Figueroa, but he's in deep conversation with the other general. I'm one tiny cog in whatever machine he operates.

"Sure."

"Excellent. I have food waiting in my office."

CHAPTER FORTY-FIVE
Inner Circle

Rosen thanks her receptionist for the delivery box and starts opening containers of Indian food on the coffee table by her office couch, then turns her attention to me. "This is the real meeting," she explains.

I glance around the office with the glass windows and view of Arlington. It feels strangely exposed.

"Don't worry," she says. "The glass has vibration dampeners, and I won't ask you anything super secret." She hands me a plate of basmati rice and chicken vindaloo. "Here."

"Okay." I stick a fork into my food and sit back in my chair, not sure where this is going.

"T-gene? That's bullshit, isn't it?"

"Um . . ."

Well, this is odd.

"I mean, your research is fine, but it looks to me like you're dragging your feet. Wouldn't you say that's the case?"

Damn, she's sharp. I can't decide if I'm walking into a trap or not. Considering the fact that I'm sitting on a couch inside her office at DARPA, it's kind of moot. I'm already inside the trap—the question is whether I'm going to be skinned alive or kept as a pet.

"I'm not at a point where I think it will be as productive as my other projects," I reply.

"I can tell. You've only accepted the barest amount of funding for the project. You could probably get twice as much." She stares at something on her computer screen. "You're very cautious about everything and quite understaffed. You're taking on way more supervision than you need to. Don't you trust your employees?"

"Besides the one that's stealing secrets? I guess so . . . I just don't want to overwhelm them."

"Right . . . You know what your problem is, Theo? You've been working alone for too long. You don't know how to run a lab."

"Clearly."

She shakes her head. "I don't mean it that way. You don't see the potential here. I'll let you in on a poorly kept secret: Figueroa loves you. You're his warrior scientist. And while you think this is all about the projects, what he's trying to do is back people. Maybe none of this will pan out, but he's hoping that you'll come through with something eventually. Already you've impressed people with your biome-tracking project. That result could fund a lab ten times your size."

The biome-tracking system was a project to monitor where a person had been by analyzing the trace bacteria unique to every person on the planet. It didn't just tell you who someone was; it could help place where they'd been. While the results from the research didn't overwhelm me, it was enough for the DoD to have another lab pursue a field version of the procedure.

Other than answering some questions for them, I never followed up on what happened. I think Rosen is hinting that lab may have turned it into something even more lucrative than I realized.

"Do you get what I'm talking about?" she asks.

"Not a clue. Other than I'm an underachiever and a bad manager. I'll accept both of those."

She throws a paper napkin at me. "Wow, Veronica was right about you."

"Veronica?"

"Yeah, Veronica Woodley. She was one of my students. I asked her about you. I asked a lot of people about you. The consensus is either you're one of the most arrogant people they've ever met or the most brilliant. In my experience the combination of the former and the latter implies the latter is the likely case." She points to me. "I've read your stuff. All of it. I haven't encountered that many minds that can cross disciplines . . . or rather, that can and should."

"Thanks?" I reply.

"Which brings me to the purpose of this meeting and what I'm trying to spell out for you. There's a very big future for you. That small lab of yours could be a research park. We're looking to build an inter-disciplinary research group that could rapidly tackle problems as well as perform cutting-edge research."

"I'm not sure I follow." Or rather, I'm afraid I know exactly what she's saying.

"You could be a director of a much larger lab. You could do what-ever the hell you wanted and lend your considerable expertise to a lot of different projects." She hastily adds, "Management would be handled by people who *like* doing that. You wouldn't have the administrative over-head you have now. You'd just be Theo." She lowers her voice. "Some of the people who fund you know a lot more about what you do outside the lab than you may realize. There have been conversations about how someone like you could be used to speed up certain projects."

"Military projects?" I reply.

"Yes. Intelligence, too. The problem is that these people are a lit-tle worried about your extracurricular activities becoming a liability. Having the FBI show up at your doorstep to question you about a serial killer in Kentucky doesn't look good."

I get a knot in my stomach from the realization that she knows a lot more about me than I'm comfortable with. It would make sense, I guess. So far, the government has trusted me with millions of dollars. Apparently, that funding comes with methods of monitoring that I've not been aware of.

Suddenly I become a lot more paranoid. I've been careful enough to keep a step ahead of the police . . . well, mostly. But how do I hide from people who have spy satellites and surveillance equipment that I can't even imagine?

"Don't panic," she says. "You're interesting because you're a rogue. We just need to make sure you're not too rogue. Think about what you could do with your own research institution. We could steer a few low-hanging contracts your way, staff you up, and then throw more interesting problems at you, like Moscow."

I think this is what are called golden handcuffs. Big, huge, diamond-studded, golden handcuffs. But not everything adds up. Is the only catch that they want me to stop hunting serial killers? *Done.* That was never my choice.

Rosen has an agenda here, but I'm not smart enough to see it.

"What kind of research?" I ask.

"You know, the usual. More trackers. Maybe some field systems. I know the DoD is looking for ways to minimize battlefield infections. There's always interest in viruses . . ." She watches my reaction.

A cold shiver goes down my spine. This is all about Hyde. They don't care about the T-gene or anything else. While I may have baffled Figueroa with bullshit, Rosen saw right through it. She probably knows what I told the FBI, too . . . and she was talking to Veronica Woodley. *Damn it.*

Part of me wants to run out of the room. But that would be dumb and not get me what I want . . . What *is* it that I want?

Jekyll. Full stop.

He's out there and becoming a greater danger. While I'm safe in my bubble, eating Jillian's muffins and handling petty intrigues, he's killing people.

Hold on . . . stick to the plan, Theo. You came here because Figueroa ordered you to and because you wanted to find out if the DoD may have been involved with Hyde at some point.

Rosen may have just opened the door for you. Play it cool. Don't bust out with, "That sounds great!" She'll read you a mile away.

"Fine."

"Really?" Her face brightens. "I'd expected a little more hesitation from you."

"No. It's perfect timing. I actually have a side project that could go really big. This works out great."

"I'm thrilled to hear this. What project is that?" she asks.

"It's an offshoot of T-gene, actually. Virus related." I pause and shake my head. "The problem is that I'm having trouble finding prior research. I'd really rather not reinvent the wheel."

"That's an easy fix. Are you going to be in DC for a few days?"

"I can be."

"Good. I'll get you access to the Pentagon research archive. You have the clearance, and I can have a clerk help you find whatever you want. It's a mess down there, but they know where to look."

Unbelievable. Just like that, I'm actually getting access to the Ark of the Covenant.

CHAPTER FORTY-SIX
THE ABYSS

A Pentagon escort leads me down the basement hallway and to a nondescript door that has a black plastic sign next to it reading **ARCHIVE 8B**.

A soldier sitting at a brown desk that was probably requisitioned while Lyndon Johnson was in office slides a clipboard over and asks me to sign. He then picks up a phone and asks for someone named Mackenzie.

Two minutes later, a tall man in a sweater-vest greets me at the door. "Dr. Cray, let's step inside." He nods to the escort. "I'll call when he's ready to go."

The door to the archive leads down another bland hallway with occasional flourishes of faux-mahogany paneling—as if the decorator decided that the brief flourishes of faux mahogany would make the underground denizens feel like they had been transported to a magic forest glade.

I have no idea how people can work down here. As Mackenzie gives a friendly wave to a woman pushing a large cart of files, I realize that the key is getting along really well with your fellow inmates. I'm sure there's an entire subculture in this part of the Pentagon basement.

"Dr. Cray," says Mackenzie, "I hope you brought your reading glasses. We pulled a few files for you. But first, let me give you the rules." We stop at a door. "That way is the reading room, where your files await. In the event that the wonderfully talented archivists down here didn't find what you're looking for, you've been given certain privileges to search on your own."

He pushes open another door. Inside are rows and rows of metal shelves filled with filing boxes. The corridor goes on so far it almost looks like an optical illusion.

Mackenzie turns right. "This way. We're in the funding proposal section going all the way back to around 1975." We come to the end of a shelf, where a broad red line on the floor separates it from the shelves beyond. "See that line? Don't cross it. If you do, then that's a felony. They'll not only escort you out of here, they'll take you straight to wherever they take people who cross that line."

I stare at the shelves on the other side of the red line. "What's there?" I ask.

"What's where? I don't see anything beyond the line. Neither do you." He turns around and points to the stacks we just walked through. "That's your territory. Understand?"

"Yep," I reply.

Mackenzie leads me back to the corridor and through the door he said leads to the reading room. Inside is a smaller storage room filled with boxes. I walk down the narrow passage then stop when I realize that Mackenzie is still at the door.

"This way to the reading room?" I ask.

Mackenzie laughs. "Dr. Cray, my friend, this *is* the reading room."

"Where are . . . ?" I stare at the boxes piled all around me. "Oh."

He winks at me. "You ask and you shall receive. If you want bad coffee, there's a break room at the end of the hall with some vending machines. If you want the almost good kind, let me know and we'll call an escort to take you to the food court. I'll be in my office across the hall. Got it?"

"Got it."

Mackenzie gives a maniacal laugh as he shuts the door behind me. A moment later I hear the sound of a key turning in a lock, like a jailer.

I stride toward the door and turn the knob. Mackenzie is standing there checking his watch. "Need something?"

"Hilarious," I reply.

"Think of it as my chance to torture all you folks who keep sending files down here."

"Fair enough." I return to the mountain of files and contemplate a nervous breakdown, but then pass on it because I don't think I could actually find a spot on the floor large enough to collapse on.

There are at least a hundred boxes here. I'd asked them to pull any records they could on human rabies research, encephalitis-related behavior studies, and a few other areas I thought DARPA wouldn't have too much research on. Joke's on me.

I grab a box at random to see if they really did pull what I asked for instead of just throwing whatever they could into a cart.

The first file I open is titled *A Computer Model of the Impact of an Enemy-Weaponized Hantavirus.* The summary of the report makes it very clear this study is about what would happen if the Russkies decided to use hanta as a biological weapon. But reading between the lines, the research could also be applied to how *we* could use said virus. But stating it that way would violate a number of laws.

This proposal is exactly the kind of thing I asked for.

It's not what I'm looking for, but well within the parameters of my search.

Another file has a proposal for studying ways to improve the health of horses and prevent viral infections using aggressive antiviral treatment. Curiously, none of the researchers is a veterinarian, which makes me wonder if *horses* is code for *humans*, like how bodybuilders on message boards about steroid dosing talk about experimenting on their "rat"—which is really their self.

Searching through all of this would be so much easier if the files were on a computer. Unfortunately, if said computer exists, they're not going to let me anywhere near it. The Pentagon is understandably uncomfortable with private contractors having access to large swaths of data. At least they are nowadays.

I decide my only option is to settle in and start digging through the files, focusing on the ones that involve humans.

There are way too many boxes containing research into bats, horses, and other animals that don't appear directly related to Hyde.

I'm lost in a proposal that wants to fund research for a rabies vaccine that could be delivered in one shot and use time-delayed medication to release the follow-up doses—something that would make for a practical battlefield solution to be sure, but I can't understand why the Pentagon would be that concerned with bat rabies. There are maybe two or three deadly human cases a year. Is the military planning an assault on Dracula's castle?

I look around the room and realize where I am. The problem they're trying to prevent is if the enemy were to weaponize rabies. They're not worried about invading armies of feral raccoons so much as some new form of the virus that's more easily transmitted.

The research here runs the gamut from intriguing and worthwhile, in my opinion, to some crazy shit someone decided to try to get funded.

At the rate I'm going, I'll finish going through these files by the time the sun cools. Not that I would know down here.

I need to take a different approach to narrow my search. I decide to get into Jekyll's head a little. There are two kinds of research I should be looking to find him involved with. The most obvious would be the cultivation of a virus that influences violent behavior. The second would be some tangentially related study that would encounter a virus or pathogen with that violence-causing characteristic, possibly a study trying to explain something.

Now that I've had a chance to read through the language of these proposals and between the lines, I can see how the wording would be a little different than I originally anticipated. As with bodybuilders' code word *rat* or the DoD's use of the word *enemy*, I have to think of how a homicidal maniac would ask for money to find a virus that turned people into killers without actually sounding like a homicidal maniac trying to find a virus to turn people into killers.

While it's possible that Jekyll may have randomly discovered the virus, I now think that's highly unlikely. That would be like the Unabomber being randomly put in charge of nuclear weapons security.

Jekyll was looking for this virus or a pathogen like this.

So how would that start?

How did I start? Zombie ants.

I poke my head into the office across the hallway.

Mackenzie is still at his desk. He looks up from a computer. "I was about to go home. You need something?"

"Yes. *Ophiocordyceps unilateralis*. Can you find me anything on that?"

"Yeah. Once you tell me how to spell it. Come write it down."

I take a seat in front of his desk and write *Ophiocordyceps unilateralis* on a piece of scrap paper. Mackenzie takes the slip from me.

Instead of getting up and going into the archive, he starts typing into his computer.

"Wait? How can you do that?" I blurt out.

"With my fingers, thanks to Mavis Beacon, bless her heart."

"First, she's not a real person; she was a model hired to pose for the cover. Second, are the files really in the computer?"

"Yep. And in answer to your question, if you touch this keyboard or even have a squint at this screen, I'll have the marine outside shoot you. This entire system is air-gapped. It also has the benefit of being made before Wi-Fi was even a word."

"This place," I grumble.

"Tell me about it," says Mackenzie. "Here. Aisle 222, section 5. Just go into the archive. It's on the other side of the red zone."

"Excuse me?"

"Just go through the red zone and into the orange area on the other side," he explains.

"I thought I'd get arrested."

"Yes. It's a federal offense to go in there. I commit it at least five times a day when I go through there to use the bathroom. We have an official-unofficial waiver to pass through the red area."

I shake my head. "I don't understand this place."

Mackenzie opens his arms wide. "Welcome to Wonderland, Alice."

CHAPTER FORTY-SEVEN
CONGLOMERATE

I'm staring at the image of a cartoon teddy bear holding a machine gun as he sprays the air with jelly-bean bullets. A life-size model of Sergeant Grizzly Havoc, the star of the apparently wildly popular mobile game *Bearers of Arms*, is the first thing to greet you when you enter the fifth-floor lobby of West Star Games in Tysons Corner, Virginia.

A young man, barely out of his teens with a Disney Channel face, greets me from the desk. "Dr. Cray? Let me take you to meet Hailey."

He walks me through what could nominally be called an office. There are scattered standing workstations where coders type away and beanbag chairs where reclining millennials, or whatever they are now, tap and swipe away on mobile phones.

Not to sound like an old fogey, but I guess this is called working. While I like my share of whimsy—really, I do—this feels like a kindergarten with 401(k)s. But I'm not the one who had my app downloaded fifteen million times in the last six months.

I'm at West Star Games meeting with their CEO because I reached a dead end in the Pentagon basement. Or rather, I made a very exciting breakthrough that led nowhere.

My search for *Ophiocordyceps unilateralis* led me to some interesting research proposals. The most eye-catching was one titled *A Comprehensive Analysis of Potential Behavior-Altering Pathogens.*

Right there in the abstract was the mention of *Ophiocordyceps unilateralis*, followed by the question of whether or not there were similar pathogens that affected humans.

The main thrust of the study was to find out if regions of the brain that were prone to violent outbursts might be subtly influenced by certain diseases. Said diseases weren't specifically named, but from the aim of the study, it was clear that the researchers were trying to find something like a proto-Hyde.

Another study by the same group proposed *An Analysis of Neurotropic Infection: Neural Tissue Damage and Behavioral Effect.* Which sounds a lot to me like they found Hyde and wanted to infect some animals with it. The study mentions an entire zoo's worth of creatures, notably rhesus monkeys and chimpanzees.

The thought of a chimp infected with Hyde will keep me up at night for years.

All of this was promising, if not disturbing, with the exception of one major catch—there were no researchers mentioned in the proposal. All the related projects were under the aegis of the Advanced Biological Research Institute—an impressive-sounding organization if it wasn't for the fact that it brings up zero, zed, naught, nil results on Google. I've spilled coffee on my keyboard, accidentally hitting random keys, and found more results.

I'm not paranoid enough to believe that there's a secret government conspiracy between the government and Google to block those results—although they do block other things. The maps we use in my lab provided by the Pentagon have different features than the ones on Google Maps, where access roads to military bases and theme parks, among other things, are altered.

I am, however, convinced that the Advanced Biological Research Institute only existed as a funding apparatus. My own company name, Integrated Bioinformatics, was chosen in three minutes and only exists in fund requisitions and checks I sign.

I asked Rosen over email about the company last night after I left the Pentagon. I still haven't received a response.

The only clue was on one page of a proposal where a photocopied chart had an address along the bottom edge. That address is the current headquarters of West Star Games.

"Dr. Cray! I'm Hailey," squeals a pixie-faced young woman taller than me wearing a green army jacket, a ripped SpaceX T-shirt, rolled-up jeans, and striped socks last seen on the Wicked Witch of the East.

Hailey's got short-cropped hair, deeply intelligent eyes, and a smile as wide as her face. She would have been in middle school when the last Advanced Biological Research Institute report was written, so I can probably rule her out as a suspect. In fact, I'm sure ABRI was long gone before they moved their beanbags in here.

"Let's have a bounce in my office," she says, grabbing me by the hand and pulling me into a glass-walled room covered in giant versions of the stickers I used to put on my Trapper Keeper.

I have no idea what "a bounce" means until I see the large inflatable balls serving as furniture. Hailey sits on one and gestures to another across from her.

I sit down, feeling like I'm about to do a workout session.

I glance around her office. There are plenty of shelves but nothing resembling a desk. I spot a MacBook on the floor in the corner.

"I was so excited that you wanted to come and visit," says Hailey.

I emailed first thing in the morning, claiming to be a fan of the game and asking if I could visit. Hailey emailed me twenty minutes later.

"Thanks," I reply. "Of course, it's more of an accident than anything else. Not something I'm proud of."

She looks at me funny. "You're not proud of your research in bio-informatics? I listened to your lectures when I was in high school. They were amazing. My first game was a simulated ecotone of grass and snails. Your paper on using game engines to do research helped me come up with Bellyland and how it would work."

Bellyland is where Sergeant Grizzly Havoc lives. I learned this from Wikipedia.

"Oh, thanks," I reply, genuinely flattered. For a brief moment, I feel a bit of melancholy over not being able to teach anymore. What would I have learned from someone like Hailey asking me questions and pulling me into the twenty-first century?

My heart tugs at the thought of another bright young mind, not unlike Hailey's. That person was too shy to ask me questions but was more brilliant than I ever realized—until it was too late.

"We'd love to be able to work with you," she says. "On anything."

I can't tell if she's flirting with me or just schoolgirl crushing. "That would be interesting. Actually . . ." In that moment, I decide to tell her most of the truth. "I'm trying to find out about a company that was here before you, I think. Advanced Biological Research Institute. Have you heard of them?"

"Yeah. They were the previous tenants. We've got a room in back we call The Lab because it had rows of lab counters and stuff. There's still a crazy-big freezer and a huge safe. Want to see?"

She bounces into the air and grabs my hand again, pulling me along like Peter Pan.

We enter another room that looks like the first, but it also has a massive, double-paned window looking into another room filled with neon-colored walls and black lights.

Hailey leads me into that room. Her lipstick glows blue and her makeup makes her look like a video-game character.

"We were wondering what exactly they did in here," she says. "We figured maybe some secret government stuff."

"That's actually exactly what they did," I reply. "Did you ever meet the previous tenants?"

"No. They were gone months before. The curious thing was that in the rental agreement, there was some kind of government inspection certificate. I thought it was because they had to sterilize the lab."

"That's what it was." I glance around the room and suspiciously eye the air vent. "You've been here how long?"

"Four years. It flies fast."

Funny to hear that from a twenty-three-year-old who started her first company at fifteen. "It sure does. Do you know anyone who talked to the people here?"

She shakes her head. "We have the whole floor, just like they did. Some of the other offices are covert government stuff, like think tanks. They keep to themselves."

"Hmm. That's unfortunate. I'm trying to figure out who worked here."

"Is that because of your other passion?" she asks, standing a little too close to me.

"You're too smart, Hailey," I say, crossing my arms.

"Well, I can tell you who the big bosses were here. Neeve, Grehan, Hall, and Forrester."

"How do you know that?"

"Because those were the names on the four reserved parking spaces we inherited. My cofounders and I used to refer to each other by those names, pretending we were big-shot businessmen."

"What happened to them?" I ask of her cofounders, making casual conversation while containing my excitement.

"I bought the little bitches out when they couldn't take the pressure. But I bet you could. Want to give up saving the world and come play with me?"

There is something utterly fearless about her that I admire. While I've been fretting about how to put my skills to better use for humanity and almost dying or getting imprisoned in the process, here's a free spirit who's decided to let the world figure its own shit out while she has a blast making a fortune's worth of fuck-you money.

Part of me very much wants to stay in this romper room and play with Hailey, whatever that means. But it's not just my fear/respect for Jillian or my sense that I may be misinterpreting Hailey's attention that tells me I have to leave. It's the knowledge that you can run from the world, but it will eventually find you in the end.

CHAPTER FORTY-EIGHT

Collaboration

Neeve, Grehan, Hall, and Forrester. Those are my four suspects, if for no other reason than their names were painted onto parking spaces at a defunct company that the Department of Defense was funding for something that sounds suspiciously like proto-Hyde research.

It's the thinnest of thin leads, only nanometers thick, but this is how science works. You search for a causal connection—even a tenuous one is better than none at all—then you test it. Lots of causal connections don't prove a thing. Even testing a theory and reaching an expected conclusion doesn't really "prove" it in the sense that people think. It only changes the degree of certainty.

Neeve, Grehan, Hall, and Forrester are uncommon names. I find a few hundred examples of each one. LinkedIn shows me at least a dozen or more PhDs for the three oddest surnames. Thousands for Forrester.

Rather than chase them down individually, I enter "Neeve, Grehan, Hall, and Forrester" into Google and see what dark magic it reveals.

Six hundred and thirty-two results. Almost all of them references to scientific papers. I think I've found the right ones.

Sharon T. Neeve, Wayne L. Grehan, Trenton F. Hall, and Edward T. Forrester. They've collaborated on five published research papers. The first one is from 1998: *Forensic Evidence of Behavior-Altering Pathogens in Canines*. The second one was in 2000: *Paleontological Evidence for Behavior-Altering Pathogens*. The other three papers are follow-ups on those two. The last paper was published in 2004—right before they started getting funding from the Department of Defense.

The papers show an interesting evolution. In the early ones, they were looking at brain tissue of dogs to find evidence of a violence-inducing pathogen. In particular, they were examining the brains of dogs that had been put down by animal control.

This is actually a very clever way to start the search. Even though dogs have been bred for thousands of years to be obedient, sometimes they snap and display violent behavior. If you were looking for a version of Hyde contagious to humans, studying dogs would be an excellent place to start.

SIV, simian immunodeficiency virus, helped us understand HIV, and the two versions of HIV we've found today appear to be offshoots of SIVsmm and SIVcpz. While transmitting a virus from a dog to a human is harder than from one species of ape to another, there are often parallel viruses with similar factors. Dog Hyde, or the aggression-inducing pathogens they were searching for, apparently yielded positive results.

While their lab work wasn't able to isolate a specific virus, they were able to find evidence in some cases of localized tissue damage and a presence of viral antibodies similar to what you see with rabies—but none of the dogs had rabies.

Things get really crazy when they move into the next phase. This is where they start to work with archaeologists and test tissue samples from hunter-gatherers who died violently. They were able to secure samples from South America and Papua New Guinea and even some several-hundred-year-old tissue from Bulgaria.

I'm not sure if the sources were chosen by design or whatever they could find. Either way, in these studies, they appeared to find something. Again, not conclusive, but the shadow and impact of something that looked like a heretofore unknown virus.

The last study was a collaborative effort with a group of Russian researchers to look for pathogens in corpses found in Siberian permafrost.

The frightening thing is that this isn't that improbable. Scientists were able to revive a sample of *Pithovirus sibericum* after thirty thousand years. There's no real limit to how long a virus can lie dormant—frightening news for future Martian explorers and people working unprotected with ancient human tissue samples.

The Russian paper is kind of odd. They claim that they weren't able to isolate a virus and found that there was no evidence of a pathogen in the samples taken from a proto-Evens-people massacre in Siberia—while that itself isn't too weird, the photographs of the tissue samples look exactly the same as the controls from an earlier study.

Either someone screwed up, or this is scientific fraud. My guess is it's the latter. They found something, possibly dormant virus cultures, inside the frozen tissue. Then hid it.

Faced with telling the Russian scientists that they'd found a violence-causing pathogen and running the risk of it being weaponized by the Russian Federation, they chose to fake the data and say that it was a failure.

Maybe that was the plan all along. The end result is that, a year later, they're getting funded by the DoD and no longer working at their respective universities.

This deception screams Hyde virus to me. And that means that one or more of them is Jekyll . . .

Okay, time to narrow it down. Let's start in order of importance based on how their names are listed on the research papers. This order also happens to be Neeve, Grehan, Hall, and Forrester.

Sharon T. Neeve published five more papers, then stopped in 2007. Wayne L. Grehan stopped publishing in 2005, along with

Trenton F. Hall. And Edward T. Forrester's last published paper was the Russian study.

Okay . . . what happened to them next?

I put "Sharon T. Neeve" into a news database . . . and damn. She died of pneumonia complications in 2009.

All right, how about Wayne L. Grehan?

The first item that pops up in a news database is that he was murdered in Brazil during a hotel robbery . . . with Trenton F. Hall. Also in 2009.

What the hell?

Okay, how about Edward T. Forrester? Still alive. Suspiciously.

I do some Googling on the murders of Hall and Grehan.

It turns out that they were in Brazil for a conference on virology and epidemiology. A hotel guest reported seeing a man in a mask running down the hallway from their room. Inside were the bodies of Hall and Grehan. Their wallets and laptops were missing.

I'm going to cut to the chase on this and assume Forrester is my strongest suspect.

The authorities don't even take the idea of a murder pathogen seriously, so there's no way they're going to accept that or my chief suspect without an overwhelming amount of evidence.

And even if they did, in the best-case scenario, they'd send investigators around to talk to him—which would tip him off and let him permanently erase his tracks or vanish.

I need to do this alone. Again. Sigh.

Conveniently for me, he never left this part of Virginia.

His last known address is two hours away. Time to pay him a visit.

CHAPTER FORTY-NINE
MILTON DRIVE

On Google Maps, Forrester's house appears to be a bit of a compound set back behind a forest on the edge of an unincorporated township. His closest neighbors include a dog breeder, a horse farm, and a small group of houses built in the 1970s.

Forrester himself is even more interesting than I realized.

He originally majored in abnormal psychology, even going as far as interning at psych hospitals before taking a radical turn into biology and then virology.

I found a few of his papers concerning environmental factors and adolescent behavior, including some references to lead exposure.

I'm not sure what caused the change in careers, but it may have been that he started to suspect that some psychological issues had physical causes.

While his published papers don't reveal a lot, the fact that he was able to go from one prestigious school to another suggests that he must have been brilliant enough to impress the right people.

In 2002, he married an Estonian grad student named Silja Jaanaka. Birth records show that they had a son in 2005. I can't find any graduation records for Silja or anything about their son.

Like me, Forrester probably works hard to keep his family life private. I've done my best to insulate Jillian from my world, even going as far as using shell companies to pay for our house and her bakery.

I wait until an hour after full dark, then pull my car onto the side of the road that runs parallel to the property, parking under the cover of a tree line that spreads out over a wire fence. The woods around Forrester's place are made up mostly of oaks and chest-high bushes in sporadic clusters.

I climb over the fence and follow a straight path through the trees, using my mental map of his property to navigate.

About fifty feet in, I encounter a rusted chain-link fence running through the forest. Barbed wire runs along the top, discouraging visitors.

Already committed to trespassing, I use my multitool to cut through the fence. Instead of closing it back up, I leave the gash open in case I have to make a fast exit. I'll fix it later if I'm horribly wrong about my assumptions.

The woods continue for another fifty feet and then stop at an overrun lawn. Forrester's dark house sits on a small rise. It's one story but appears to have a basement. There's a large wood porch in back and a small barn at the rear of the property.

I take a step out of the tree line, and my ears twinge at the sound of a metal chain—like the sound of a dog collar.

A second later, shapes start barking and racing at me from underneath the porch.

I catch a blurry glimpse of German shepherds displaying their teeth as they fly at me with hateful fury.

Sadly, I was prepared for this. I take out the canister of pepper spray and trichloromethane that I keep in my adventure bag and spray it in the direction of the animals, keeping my own mouth shut and holding my breath.

The dogs get plastered in the snouts as they get close and veer off at the last minute to whine and rub their noses into the grass as the pepper spray burns their sensitive membranes.

The whimpers grow softer as the trichloromethane begins to kick in and they lose consciousness.

Poor guys. I really do feel bad for them.

I watch the house for ten minutes, waiting to see if a light goes on. The only thing stirring is the guard dogs twitching around at my feet.

I step past them and walk toward the front to get a view of the driveway. It's empty.

It appears that Dr. Forrester isn't home. Well, that makes things easier.

I go back around the house and step onto his porch. The back door has a Theo-size dog door. Although it's blocked with a sliding panel, I'm able to use my opposable thumbs to lift it and slide inside the kitchen.

The house is completely dark. I turn on my flashlight to the lowest setting and inspect the interior. The floors and counters appear spotless.

The Forrester family runs a tight ship.

I step into the dining room. The table is completely clear. I run my finger along, checking for dust, just in case the place had been abandoned. It comes back spotless.

I go back into the kitchen and check the fridge. There's not a lot of food in there. No milk, no eggs, and only a smattering of vegetables, but they're all fresh.

I check the cupboards and only find oatmeal, cans of soup, and a few other staples.

I guess they eat out a lot.

Past the living room lies a family room with a leather couch and a recliner. The coffee table is spartan, and the bureau below the flat-screen TV on the wall only has hardcover novels. Most of them are Stephen King—not an encouraging sight.

I poke my head into the master bedroom. The bed is empty. There's an office next to it with a desk, computer, and shelves full of medical and scientific books.

I find another room that looks like a guest room. Banker boxes fill up one wall. A scan of the titles on them suggests they're tax records. Another shelf has board games and a bunch of role-playing-game manuals.

I go down the hall to the last room on this level and push open a door to a child's room.

A small bed sits against the far wall. Transformers bed sheets are neatly made, and the rest of the room is in perfect order. I walk along the shelves, examining the toys. He's got the usual little-boy toys—*Cars*, Transformers, *Ben 10* . . .

Something is odd about the room—besides the fact that it's the most well-kept room any fourteen-year-old ever had. For starters, these toys seem a little young for a teenager, unless he has some kind of developmental disability.

The other thing that stands out is what isn't here. There are no Star Wars toys and no Marvel movie characters. Maybe the kid hates Disney . . .

I slide open a desk drawer. It's filled with the kind of junk a kid would save. Small toys, movie tickets, foreign coins, comic books. A Nintendo DS.

I'm not seeing anything later than 2009 or 2010. I go back to the master bedroom and open the closet. It contains men's shirts and suits, but no women's clothing.

I check the bathroom. No sign of any feminine products, and the one by the son's room doesn't look like it's been used in years.

Did Forrester and his wife separate? Then why keep the kid's room the same way, even if it was for visitation?

I go back to the kitchen and find the door that leads to the basement. A large industrial lock secures the entrance.

Fortunately for me, the hinges are on the outside. It takes me three minutes with my multitool to move the door out of my way.

I take the dark stairs down into the basement and flash my light around.

The hair on the back of my neck stands up as I see all the laboratory equipment and the massive freezer built into the wall.

There's even a clean room with a protective suit hanging on a hook.

I go up to the glass and shine my light inside. There are dozens of empty cages, including some suspiciously large ones.

I've found the secret lab. I've found my Dr. Jekyll.

CHAPTER FIFTY

DEBRIS

I feel a sense of unease as I realize that this was all a little too easy. Jekyll . . . Forrester didn't go to any great lengths to hide his lab or his guilt, in my opinion. If one were to suspect him and take a glance at this lab and the suspiciously large cages, they'd know that something not right was going on here.

I need to leave.

I go back up the stairs and push the door back into place, sliding the dead bolt into the slot and restoring the pins. In my haste, I push too hard and hear a cracking sound come from the frame. If Forrester looks, he'll know something is up.

No matter, as long as I'm gone by then.

I slide back through the Theo door and stand on the porch, letting my eyes adjust to the dark. Forrester's guard dogs are lying belly up where I left them. They'll have a few more hours of sleep, followed by a very bad headache.

I check around the corner of the house and freeze when I see headlights, but they pass by the end of the gated driveway and keep going. I'm across the grass and into the woods before the drowsy dogs can even muster the strength to raise their heads.

Now the question is, should I fix the hole in the fence or not? If I don't, the dogs might get loose, tipping off Forrester sooner than later that he's had a visitor.

Better not to leave it like this. I use some plastic ties to keep the fence pulled together enough that the dogs will have a hard time getting through.

I spot my car through the brush, wait to make sure there aren't any other cars on the road, then unlock it and toss my backpack into the passenger seat. I place the 9 mm pistol I've been carrying in my lap.

Now what?

My plan kind of ends here. I'm positive that Forrester is Jekyll; I even found his secret lair. The only problem is that there's no Forrester there, and I'm not so sure what I can do when and if he returns.

Calling the local police or the FBI is going to get me laughed at. I need to put Forrester onto Gallard's radar, but what will that accomplish?

There's no cause for a search warrant, let alone questioning Forrester, if Gallard's the only one on board with my suspicions. I wish this were like television, where warrants, probable cause, and case backlog aren't a reality.

Moreover, how can I prove my case without admitting to some rather illegal behavior of my own?

Besides creating my own fake serial-killer crime and committing what could be seen as several felonies to photograph Forrester, the only way I was able to connect him to Hyde—and theoretically at that—is through some top-secret government funding and the casual recollection of a parking space by Hailey.

There are so many leaps there, it'd take a dedicated prosecutor years to build a case—if at all.

Back in 2001, twenty-two people were infected with anthrax when packages containing the deadly bacteria were mailed to the media and politicians. Five people eventually died from the attack.

The investigation proved to be a very complex one.

Initially one specific scientist, a researcher with the United States Army Medical Research Institute of Infectious Diseases, was named as a person of interest.

The FBI raided his house multiple times and even ran over his foot with their car when he tried to confront them.

Ultimately, they dropped their case against him and he went on to sue, winning several millions of dollars.

The bureau then moved on to another suspect, Bruce Edwards Ivins, *another* United States Army Medical Research Institute of Infectious Diseases researcher. Ivins was never charged but died of an overdose of Tylenol and codeine when he heard that he was going to be tried in connection with the attacks.

The really crazy part of the anthrax investigation, besides the fact that they never formally charged Ivins or anyone else with the crime, was what happened early on in the case.

The FBI went to anthrax experts to try to identify the strain of the bacteria that was used in the attack. ABC News ran stories claiming that a well-placed insider had told them that bentonite was found in the samples. Bentonite was a known trace material found in Iraqi anthrax samples.

The bentonite story disappeared, and the government decided Iraqi involvement was unlikely. Later on, the source of the bentonite angle became evident, despite ABC refusing to name its sources, when it was revealed that one of the main experts the FBI went to for help on the case was none other than Bruce Edwards Ivins—the man they would go on to name as their main suspect.

In the other biggest FBI case of 2001, not related to September 11, the bureau arrested Robert Hanssen for spying for the Russians. In what was considered the worst intelligence disaster in US history, Hanssen turned out to be the intelligence leaker the FBI had been searching for for decades. The chief investigator charged with finding the mole was perfectly qualified for the hunt; the only problem was, the chief investigator was Hanssen himself.

As with Ivins, the FBI had to rely on an expert who was actually the suspect they were searching for.

None of this gives me any hope that legally connecting Forrester to Hyde is going to be easy. It's such a complicated case, from the biology to the sequence of events. I can only imagine trying to walk a conference room through this.

I glance down at the gun in my hands.

How sure am I that Forrester did it?

Confident enough to put a gun to his head and demand that he confess. While putting a bullet in his skull might be justifiable and would probably save lives, there's still an outside chance that I'm missing something.

What if he made Hyde for someone else? What if he is trying to track down the virus like I am, and isn't the one who placed it in the Pale house or infected the others?

We can't place him at the Oyo property and say for sure that he infected Marcus. I can't prove that he was anywhere other than the Butcher Creek crime scene, and it is too hard to conclude anything even from that video.

I'm in a difficult bind.

I close my eyes and think it through. Am I ready to catch him as he comes home and force a confession out of him? The last time I did that, I was prepared for it. But I suspect that Forrester won't crack that easily.

Step one is stopping him. Having the FBI or local police knock on his door might be enough to do that. I might be able to arrange that by calling the FBI, saying that I'm him, and confessing. At the very least, that will get agents to come and talk to him.

Okay, that's the plan unless I can think of a better one on the way back to the hotel. I hope I do, because it sucks.

I put the gun in my glove box, turn the ignition, and pull out of my covered spot. Once I'm clear of the trees, I turn on the headlights and pull onto the main road.

I've just begun driving down the main road when I see blue flashing lights behind me.

Seriously? Please don't tell me that the FBI had me followed. Could I be that stupid?

I pull over to the side of the road, still adjacent to Forrester's property, praying that Forrester doesn't come home now. That would be embarrassing.

I put on my best "Did I do something wrong?" smile and roll down my window.

That deep-seated animal sense that's buried in our brain is the first thing to tell me something is wrong.

The second is when I catch a glimpse of the silhouette of the man walking toward me in the headlights.

Third is the bullet that cracks through the air, shattering my car's back window.

Fourth is the sharp pain in my shoulder when I raise my right arm to try to get my gun out of the glove box.

CHAPTER FIFTY-ONE
COLLECTION

My head feels like a rag doll that's been swung around by the hair. I don't remember losing consciousness as much as fading as I tried to reach the gun. Right now, I'm seated and bouncing. My hands won't move.

Someone is pushing me in a wheelchair. I raise my head to get a better look, but sharp pain keeps me from seeing who's behind me.

"Don't worry, I patched it up," says a soothing voice behind me. "We missed the suprascapular nerve. It went right through, in fact. The bullet lodged itself in the clock. Funny thing. Wish it was analog . . . then it could have trapped the moment."

I squint my eyes, trying to understand why the hospital feels . . . outside.

Fuck . . . I'm being pushed toward the barn in the back of Forrester's property.

"Jekyll?" I say, still trying to put my world back together.

"Jekyll? No . . . Oh, is that your name for me? Oooh, clever. That would make the virus Hyde." A hand musses up the hair on top of my head. "Clever, Theo. Clever! But not clever enough."

He kneels next to me and rests his hands on my handcuffed arm and leans his chin casually on them. He's in his fifties but looks boyish. His blue eyes are piercing. He has a strange charisma.

I recognize him as one of the phantom men I captured on surveillance of Butcher Creek. He could pass for a cop, a lawyer, a doctor, a pastor. But it's the way he looks at me that makes him stand apart from his photograph. There's an intelligence there, a raging fire of curiosity.

"The barn, Theo. I was hoping you'd go to the barn. But you didn't. I sat there watching you, trying to understand why you didn't bother looking there."

I saw the barn, but I didn't want to. It reminded me of something, something that's still too painful to think about.

"Yes, your eyes just did that little dip where you visualize something. It's not the same in everyone, you know. People with exceptionally high IQs like yours do it a little bit differently. It suggests that memories aren't quite the same for you."

Forrester returns to pushing me across the grass toward the barn. "I just realized what the barn must have reminded you of. It looks a lot like the Toy Man's shed, doesn't it? I bet you still think about all the horrible things that happened there."

Forrester stops the wheelchair a few feet from the barn and walks in front of me. He's dressed like a paramedic, with the exception of a gun in a holster at his side.

He looks down at the uniform. "Like it? You were a paramedic, too, weren't you?"

I just stare at him, trying to figure out how I'm going to kill him.

"Oh, that look." Forrester gives me a broad smile. "That's something to behold, Theo. How long did it take you to become the man that would follow through on that emotion? Did it happen when Joe Vik was about to kill Jillian? Was it when you realized what Oyo Diallo really was? Is it right now?"

Forrester is not what I expected. His words sound sincere. The only way I can describe it is . . . bedside manner. He's talking to me like *I'm* the raving maniac.

I pull at my restraints. Blinding pain shoots up my right arm.

Forrester leans forward and grabs my shoulder. "Stop it or you'll tear the clot."

I say my first words to him. "What the fuck did you shoot me for?"

"You're a dangerous man, Theo. I hate violence . . . the physical kind." He reaches into his pocket and pulls out a key ring.

"Right. Did you hate it when you killed Hall and Grehan?"

Forrester pauses and stares at the keys in his hands. He makes a strange gesture, a combination of a headshake and a shrug. "I had to get drunk to do that and then blackout drunk afterward."

"Then why?"

He finds the key he's looking for and puts it in a lock on the barn. After he slides open the door, he turns to me. "Theo, my friend, that is the question."

He returns to the chair and pushes me into the dark interior. The only light is from the doorway.

Forrester shuts the door behind me, and we're in total darkness.

I start to yank at my restraints and lower my head to smash into him if he comes close.

"Theo, relax. I'm not going to kill you. I mean, I know this looks pretty bad. You're probably thinking about what Oyo did, and it's not like that. Stop thrashing. If you open the wound again, you'll bleed out and you'll miss it."

"Touch me and die," I growl.

Forrester turns on a light. He's sitting on a workbench in front of me. "Okay? Better? I'm not going to try to molest you. It's not my thing. I mean, admittedly, I have a bit of a man crush on you."

Who the hell *is* this guy?

"Right, now you're thinking, 'This guy is going to kill me. I have to get to the knife I hid in my whatever.' Listen to me: It's not going to happen. The me-killing-you part." He looks me over, up and down. "I don't think you can kill me from there, but Joe Vik made the same mistake . . . which, by the way, a couple things never added up about that. You don't have to tell me, but your girlfriend killed him, right?"

I glare at him.

"Yeah, thought so. And it was pretty obvious to anyone who cared to look that you killed Oyo before he saw you." He crosses his arms and nods. "Do you see why I'm the one who should be worried? You're getting more expedient with dispatching people. I'll be completely honest." He points to his right knee. "Tingly as all hell because I'm nervous about you."

My shoulder aches, and the more this asshole talks, the more I lose my urge to live. "What are you doing? Is this something like on television where you tell me why you did it?"

Forrester's faces suddenly gets serious. "I wish I could, Theo. I wish I could. I have theories, but nothing that makes sense. I've even looked at MRIs of my brain, trying to find some explanation." He shakes his head. "None. Hall and Grehan weren't easy. I tried to convince myself that they were going to sell the Cain pathogen to the Russians. Oh, that's my name for it, like—"

"Cain and Abel," I cut in. "I get it."

Forrester smiles. "Right. Right. Anyway, I killed them because I wanted it. More of a greed thing, I guess."

"Wanted it for what?"

He raises a hand. "I'm getting to that. I feel bad about killing them. Maybe not as bad as a normal person, but everything you see in movies about sociopaths is a lie. It's a matter of degree. Sure, some of them feel absolutely nothing, but most feel something."

"At least you know you're a sociopath, right?"

"Think, Theo. How would an outsider judge *you*? I mean, if they really knew everything you've done . . . and some of the things I suspect you've done."

"What's your point? That you and I are a lot alike?"

"No," he says almost wistfully. "We're different." He hops off the workbench. "Anyway, we don't have much time. I wanted to show you this."

He walks behind me and flips on a light, illuminating the interior of the small barn.

The shelves are filled with large glass jars, the kind you'd seen in circus freak shows containing two-headed goat fetuses. They're covered in dust, so it's hard to see inside.

Forrester pulls the one closest to him off the shelf. "Nineteen seventy-three. I'm nine years old and wake up in the middle of the night because the man across the street is yelling at his wife in the driveway. He punches her in the nose, red blood gushes over her nightgown, and he grabs her by the back of the head. He then starts smashing her head into the pavement. Over and over again. I pressed my little nose against the glass and just watched. I watched, Theo. I didn't tell my parents. I didn't call the police. I just watched."

Forrester unscrews the lid to the jar. "The next day, after the cops came and took Mr. Merrick away and Mrs. Merrick to the morgue, I went across the street and found this."

He turns the opening of the jar toward me, revealing a clump of preserved blonde hair with bloody skin attached.

"Messed up? Right? I never collected anything until then." He replaces the lid, sets the jar back on the shelf, and pulls down another. "Less than a year later, I'm walking through some woods near my house and hear a sound like someone chopping a tree. I get a closer look and see some older boys with sticks striking something on the ground. When I get closer, they startle and run away." He holds the jar up with two hands. "I won't open it because I didn't know how to preserve it, but it's a cat. They beat the stray to death. I had more nightmares over that than about Mrs. Merrick." He puts the jar back and takes down another. "When I was fifteen—"

"I don't care."

He stares at me.

"I really don't care where this is going," I say. "Is this your shitty one-man play of *Making a Murderer*? I don't fucking care how you got to where you are. You're a seriously fucked-up guy who used his talents to do some evil shit. I don't care."

Forrester tries to process this. "Theo, you're in a very vulnerable position. Why would you say that?"

"I just assume you're going to kill me. Why the hell do I have to go out watching you jerk off in front of me first?"

"Fine. Then do you want to talk about the virus? You must have questions."

"Nope. I answered them all," I reply, rolling my eyes.

"Okay, then. I thought you'd be more curious."

"Nope. I'm not."

Forrester takes the pistol from his holster and looks down at it. "The hardest thing was when Silja killed Eddie. I tried to convince myself she caught the Cain pathogen accidentally." He glances at me. "But we know that's not how it works."

"Do not care," I repeat. I seriously care, but I'm trying to get him to make physical contact with me. If he gets close enough, I might be able to kick him down and stomp on his head. It's a long shot but all I have. I just need him closer . . .

Forrester's giving me a sidelong glance. "You're a hard man."

"Why are you still talking?"

"Yes," he replies, then pulls back the slide on the pistol. "Theo thinks he has all the answers, when the fun has only just begun."

He raises the barrel, aims, and pulls the trigger.

I watch, dumbfounded, as Forrester fires the gun under his jaw and blood squirts out the side of his face, spraying the jars to his right. His body slumps sideways, hits the edge of the workbench, and falls onto the floor.

He makes a gasping gurgle. Blood trickles out of his mouth, and he starts to wheeze.

"Holy crap, you fucked up your own suicide!" I stare at his rising and lowering chest. Blood is pooling by his head, but it's not enough to be from a brain injury. Instead, the bullet went in through his jaw and exited near his sinus. He may still die, but it won't be a fast death.

Wheeze . . .

His eyes are open and looking around. He can't seem to move his arms, because he's in some kind of shock.

I shake my head in disbelief. "Seriously? I've got to go get you help now?"

Through gurgles of blood, he tells me to fuck off.

I saw a thousand different endings to this situation; this was not one of them.

I use my feet to propel my wheelchair back toward the barn door. Somehow, I'll have to make it across the grass and to the street to get help—that's if the dogs don't wake up first.

CHAPTER FIFTY-TWO
POINT-BLANK

I'm sitting in a bed in the Travis County hospital, explaining to three detectives and two FBI agents and Gallard, who drove all the way from DC, how I ended up in the middle of the highway, handcuffed to a wheelchair, while another man was bleeding out from a self-inflicted head wound.

I leave out the part about hacking up the bodies of Ukrainian hospital patients who didn't pay their bill. There's just no way to spin that.

With every breath, I wonder about the early symptoms of Hyde and how hard it would be for me to get an experimental dose of Remdesivir or Immucillin-A. Then I tell myself to relax. I'd need long-term exposure to Hyde or a massive dose that I'd feel right away.

I hope.

"And you have proof that this guy Forrester released the virus?" asks the FBI agent with the spiky gray hair. I forgot his name and simply think of him as Spike.

"It's complicated," I reply.

"We gather that. Okay. Well, he's downstairs with a ventilator. Maybe when he's ready to talk, or mumble, we can find out more. Of course, being in the state he is, we can't formally ask him anything."

One of the Travis County detectives speaks up. "I don't think we'll have a problem getting a warrant to search the premises by tomorrow. We'll send a forensics team over then. You mentioned that he was married?"

"Yes. An Estonian woman. He implied that she murdered their son after she got infected. And I think he was trying to tell me that he infected her."

"Methane probe?" asks the other detective.

"Yeah," replies the first one. "Those deaths were never reported. Good chance the bodies are still on property."

"He'll have buried them deep," I reply.

"Probably. Not like that Butcher Creek maniac."

Gallard shoots me a sidelong glance. I pretend to be oblivious.

"Anyway," continues the detective, "we'll search the premises. We've got a really good cadaver dog, too. If we get him for the murder of the wife, you FBI guys might be able to build a case on the other stuff."

"That'll be fun," says Spike. "I just don't want another Ivins situation." He turns to me. "No offense, but I want you as far away from the forensic part of this as possible."

"Understood," I reply.

Gallard is watching this without saying much. Something is clearly on his mind. I turn my head and wince to look at him. "What's up?"

"Nothing. Nothing." He shakes his head. "Every one of these is different in their own way, I guess."

"Spill it," says Spike. "You never have a problem going off on tangents in the classroom."

Gallard sighs. "I don't know. It's just . . . something isn't sitting right about Forrester."

"You think he's the wrong guy?" I ask.

"Not at all. He's guilty as sin, from where I'm standing. It's just . . . what he said to you and then how he tried to end it right there. This man sounds like an incredibly narcissistic person."

"But also a fan of mine," I reply.

"Yeah, that may well be, but Mark David Chapman was a huge John Lennon fan, too. That didn't end so well for Lennon. No offense, Theo, but I can't understand why you're alive."

"I've wondered that many times."

Gallard smiles. "Right, but I mean specifically in this case. He had you there in the chair. He had a gun and he decided to kill himself in front of you after you told him you weren't interested in his life story. It almost sounds like a jilted lover committing suicide in front of their partner. The goal is to make them live with the guilt as a form of punishment."

"I doubt I'm going to lose any sleep over this asshole," I reply. "Maybe he was too arrogant to realize that."

Gallard crosses his arms and stares up at the fluorescent lights. "Arrogance . . . that's what this is about. And you never established any connection between Forrester and the victims?"

"I assumed they'd be random. That's what I would do if I was testing the Hyde virus."

"There's a comforting thought," mumbles Spike.

"It would be the most practical way to avoid detection," I explain.

"Yes," says Gallard. "That's how Theo would do it. But Forrester is different. The fact that he tried to kill himself in front of you suggests that he sees himself as a kind of vigilante."

"Wait. What? Against who?"

"You. He probably killed his wife because she killed their son— even though it was ultimately his fault. The other victims may not all have been random. And with you, I think he expected you to find him eventually. He was clearly looking forward to monologuing to you."

"Too bad you cut him off," says the second detective.

"Are you serious?" asks the first.

"What were his last words to you?" asks Gallard.

I think for a moment. "I think he said, 'Theo thinks he has all the answers, when the fun's only just begun.'"

The first Travis detective, whom I think of as John, takes a phone call and steps out of the room. Gallard looks as if he's in deep concentration. As much as I hate to admit it, I think he's right. Forrester is an extremely intelligent man on a number of levels. This did seem kind of . . . half-assed.

John returns to the room. "Ready for this? An hour before you were found on the road, someone called 911 from Forrester's phone and confessed to being the Butcher Creek Butcher. They thought it was a crank. The best part? He identified himself as Edward Forrester. He even said he had evidence from the crime scene."

"What the hell?" I glance at Gallard.

"Well, that's a relief," says Spike. "We'll forward that on to the Kentucky office."

"Why would he . . . do such a thing?" I stop myself from saying the word *admit*. As far as I'm concerned, nobody in the room knows *I'm* the Butcher Creek Butcher. Gallard suspects it, but the others have no clue.

Is this some final trick from Forrester? But how could taking the pressure off me serve some bigger plan of his?

"This is a dick-measuring contest," says Gallard. "Pardon the expression."

"What?" asks Spike.

"Forrester might admire Theo, but he's arrogant. What do arrogant people want to do to their idols? Surpass them. Beat them. Show that they're better than they are."

"By offing yourself in front of them?" asks John.

"If that's what he was intending. Forrester may have wanted it to look like that. I don't know. But if he was suicidal and at the end of his rope, it was kind of like tying one hand behind his back, to *really* show you up."

"How?"

"Maybe by denying you the opportunity to kill him? He pointed out how it didn't turn out so well for Vik and Oyo. Maybe he assumed you were going to murder him," replies Gallard.

"While strapped to a wheelchair?"

"I don't know. He thought you were special. He said he was afraid of you. It could have been his way of getting the upper hand. That and taking Butcher Creek away from you."

"Taking Butcher Creek away?" asks Spike.

Gallard realizes his mistake. "Solving the crime before Theo could. He probably assumed Theo was on the hunt for whoever did that."

"Oh," replies Spike. "I've been hearing things don't add up about that. We caught a tissue broker who may be connected, but nothing has been announced yet. Interesting angle." He turns to me. "You have any insight on that?"

"All right," Gallard cuts in. "We can speculate later. Let's let Dr. Cray get some rest." He turns to me. "Maybe Forrester will waive his right to an attorney and tell us everything he knows."

They leave my bedside and a nurse comes in, checks on me, and turns down the lights. I respond to a good-night text from Jillian. I neglect to mention I'm in a hospital.

I try to sleep but can't. Forrester's motivations keep going through my head. Why did I shut him down like I did?

Was it because it was going to save my life? Hardly. Was I really that bored by him?

No.

Then why?

Because I wanted to show him I was superior. I shut him down because I wanted to let him know I thought he was beneath me.

I shut him up because *I* was arrogant.

What did Detective Glenn do back in Montana when he first questioned me?

He let me talk and talk.

At first it implicated me, but then he saw who I was. Glenn knew I was an intelligent man, so he did the smartest thing he could—let me tell him exactly what I was thinking.

I didn't do that with Forrester. It was as much of an ego contest for me as it was for him.

And then he shot himself? *Why?*

Because he already knew he'd won. Not the cat-and-mouse game between the two of us . . . but something else.

I bolt upright, and a thunderbolt of pain shoots through my shoulder. I focus on the pain to wake myself up.

Forrester is up to something bigger, much, much bigger. All the victims were merely lab rats for something else.

Damn it! Why didn't I let him go on? Maybe there would have been a clue there.

Maybe . . . maybe I can still find out.

I get to my feet. I'm steady as long as I don't do anything too crazy with my arm. Forrester was right, he did miss the nerve. Intentional? I can't see how, but who knows?

Nothing makes sense. But he's in the same hospital as me, and maybe I can get some answers.

CHAPTER FIFTY-THREE
Visiting Hours

Forrester's face is taped up, and his jaw appears to be wired closed. His left eye is puffy and peers out over a bandage as he watches me enter the room. He makes a sound that I can't tell is a cough or a stifled laugh as he takes in my garb: a doctor's scrubs and white coat.

While I couldn't get into a locker room without a key card, I was able to make it to the loading dock and find some dirty-laundry bags. The hardest part was pulling the shirt over my arm. I had to settle for an XXL outfit in order to avoid calling attention to myself with my screams.

The Travis County police officer waved me through the outer door when I nodded to him. His concern was Forrester escaping, not some amateur version of the *Godfather* hospital hit playing out under his watch.

I slide a chair over to Forrester's bedside so I can keep my voice low. His one working eye watches me closely as I grab the chart by his bed and start to flip through it.

"Let's see . . . we have the bullet traversing the lower palate, passing both the lower and upper molars, and exiting near the sinus cavity.

Interesting. You managed to avoid hitting any bone until the bullet exited your skull, and you missed all major arteries." I put the chart back. "They'd call that a one-in-a-million shot, but I have a feeling it wasn't." I tilt my head toward my shoulder. "Like that." I raise my right arm a few inches. "Lucky shot again."

Despite the fact that Forrester's bullet to the head did the least amount of damage I could imagine, he can't speak. I take my phone out of my waistband and open it to the Notes app, then place it in his hands.

"My guess is that it was a kind of Russian roulette. You took the shot thinking you had better-than-even odds you'd survive. Am I right?"

Forrester watches me for a long moment, then he types without even looking at the keyboard. I can tell he's working through pain, but he has amazing hand-eye coordination.

Good guess

"Yeah. Well, it worked. Now if you get tried for everything, it'll be even easier to claim you had serious mental health problems."

Can't hurt

"Well, I think it did. What I don't understand is why? Was that your plan? It seems kind of dumb. No offense."

Not dumb. Didn't want to run.

Now that makes sense. Forrester didn't want to be on the run, and he also knew that no matter how hard it would be for the FBI to build a case against him, he'd still be a person of interest and his life would never be the same.

I think he is suicidal, but the calculating part of his brain decided to play a wild card. And it worked. Sort of.

"You were telling me something, but I wouldn't listen. What was that?"

Doesn't matter now.

"It matters to me." I try to play to his ego. "I didn't listen because you had the upper hand on me and I was angry. Real angry. I should have paid more attention. Showed you more respect."

Theo. Theo. Theo. Don't insult us both with flattery. It doesn't work on me the way it does on you.

"Okay. Fine. What were you trying to tell me?"
Forrester doesn't move. He's either considering his answer or losing consciousness.
"What were you trying to tell me?"

Show. Not tell.

"Okay, what were you going to show me?"

The barn.

"You showed me the barn," I reply.

You didn't see.

"I was kind of in a hurry."
He takes his time typing out his next response.

That's your problem. You miss things. You could have caught Joe Vik much faster, but you had to do it your way. You could have found out who Oyo was if you'd talked to more parents. But you have to do your clever little tricks to show everyone how smart you are. That's your flaw. That's why people will die.

"Will die? How many more people have you infected with Hyde?"

He taps a quick response and I want to strangle him in his hospital bed.

;)

"Fuck you. This isn't a game. Did you find it funny when your wife killed your son because of your little project?"

Forrester doesn't say anything. He just glares at me with his one good eye.

"Tell me something. Give me a clue." He taps again on my phone.

"A tractor, a cow, a horse, and a house? What are you trying to say? The barn?"

I sigh. "Anything else?"

Don't be so hard on yourself when you can't save them. You never knew what you were up against.

"What do you mean?"

He lets go of my phone, and it slides down onto the bed.

His eye is glassy and stares at the ceiling, then closes.

"What does that mean?"

He ignores me.

I hear voices down the hall. If I persist here, I'll get caught and have my own cop guarding my door. I leave his room in a hurry and head for the stairs.

While I could probably catch an Uber, I might need more help, especially if I rip my stitches and pass out again.

I dial the number of the one person in Virginia I know who is crazy enough to come help me out at this time of night.

CHAPTER FIFTY-FOUR

Recollect

Right after I get out of my Uber, Hailey bounces out of her Tesla 3 and runs up to me in Forrester's driveway. "Dr. Cray! This is the craziest, coolest thing anyone has ever asked me to do. And I get some cra-zy shit asked of me."

I glance behind her. "You didn't drive through the police tape, did you?"

"No, Mylo's fixing it. Nice scrubs, by the way."

"What's a Mylo?"

"She was hanging out when you called. She was worried that you might want to murder me. I can ask her to bounce if this is about something else." She leans in and whispers, "Is it?"

"Uh, no." I take out some masks from my jacket pocket.

A young woman with Amerasian features and even shorter hair than Hailey's comes walking up the driveway dressed in ripped jeans and a "Mr. Rogers Is My Homie" T-shirt. She seems completely unbothered by the cold air.

"Mylo, this is Dr. Theo Cray," says Hailey.

"Great," I reply, cutting short introductions. "Time is important or people will die. Here, take these masks. There's a better-than-average chance that a sociopathic virus researcher sprayed everything with a pathogen that could make you want to kill anyone you meet. Got it?"

"Fuck, yes," says Hailey. "Uh, shouldn't there be cops everywhere?"

I sigh. "In the real world, they need search warrants, probable cause, and normal working hours unless it's an extenuating situation."

"This sounds pretty damn extenuating to me," she replies.

"Me too. And yet here we are, just us. From what they were saying, they'll be searching here tomorrow, but for the next few hours it's ours."

"Cool. Our own murder scene," says Mylo.

I turn to walk to the barn in the back. "This is super serious," I tell them over my shoulder. "Okay? I asked you here, Hailey, because I'm probably not seeing the whole picture. Mylo, um, are you smart?"

"When I'm not high. Which I'm not right now, thanks to you."

"Great. Anything to keep you kids off drugs."

"He called us kids," says Hailey. "That's adorable."

"Old people love doing that," replies Mylo.

"Don't call old people *old*," Hailey whispers back to her.

I spin around. "Okay, I get that this is very dramatic and exciting, but it's also real." I raise my shirt high enough to show the bandage. "I got shot earlier tonight and held captive. Right in that barn, where the man who shot me tried to put a bullet through his own head. And by the way, this is a crime scene and we're breaking the law. Understand? This is not a game. When I say people will die, I don't mean in some abstract way like if we don't recycle our bottles and cans we'll die in a horrible, far-off doomsday scenario. I mean like, there might be people right now who are about to die. And these masks probably won't work. If you get a headache or feel like you're coming down with something, tell me. We'll have to get rabies shots."

"Does our worker's comp cover that?" Mylo asks Hailey.

"Yep. You good?" she asks her friend.

"I'm good."

"Last chance." I pull open the barn door, revealing the lit-up interior. Tape covers the bench where Forrester shot himself. Everything else is exactly where it was before.

Because there wasn't a death and his wound looked clearly self-inflicted, the police didn't spend too much time securing the scene. The jars filled with horrific memorabilia apparently didn't attract their attention.

"One more thing." I take out some rubber gloves I stole from the hospital. "Wear these. Now, here's our mission. All these jars are filled with weird stuff that Jekyll . . . er, Forrester says he took from crime scenes. I don't know if any of that is true, but he really wanted me to look around here. Maybe it was so I could get infected. Maybe because he has an accomplice who is going to come back and kill me. Anything goes."

"An accomplice?" asks Mylo.

"Anything goes," I repeat. "Look at the jars. Don't open them. They could contain brain-damaging pathogens."

"Is this guy real?" Mylo says under her breath.

"Very," I reply.

We start taking jars down from the shelves, inspecting them, and then putting them back into place. Most of them contain odd things like cotton fibers or bits of bloodstained clothing. On the bottom of each one, etched into the glass, are two numbers. One is a very low digit, usually a single-digit number. The other is five digits long.

"You guys noticing the numbers?" asks Hailey.

"Yeah. Does it mean anything to you?"

"Me? No. Mylo?"

She looks up from her phone. "I can't find anything useful."

"What about in the jars?" I ask.

"Mostly clothing or fibrous material," says Hailey.

"Me too. Although I did see a letter addressed to a politician," replies Mylo.

I look up from my jar. "What was the number underneath?"

"Five and then 00389," she replies without looking.

"Was the postmark early 2001?"

"Yep."

"That's from the anthrax attacks. Five people died." I go back to the other jars. The first jar he showed me has a numeral one next to 00001.

"Okay, the smaller number is probably the number of people that were killed. The second is more than likely some kind of cataloging system." I glance around the barn. *But where are the catalogs?* "Look for anything like a journal."

We start poking behind jars and deeper into the shelves. I assume that Forrester would keep it close by; the question is how close?

"What about a book?" asks Mylo. She's holding on to a jar.

"What's inside it?"

"A Japanese edition of Isaac Asimov's *Foundation*."

"Is the number thirteen under the jar?" I ask.

She lifts it up to have a look. "Yes. How'd you know?"

"That was the Tokyo subway sarin gas attack from 1995. A cult called Aum Shinrikyo killed thirteen and almost a lot more. They were big Asimov fans."

"Hey! I like Isaac Asimov," says Hailey.

"Me too. He had a wide appeal."

"Want me to start taking photos?" asks Mylo.

"Yes. That's a great idea." And what I should have been doing from the start.

We sort through hundreds of bottles, the vast majority of them inexplicable. Most contain cloth or something else bloodstained. Others contain objects like the book.

"Think we'll find OJ's glove in here?" asks Mylo.

"Maybe, but I wouldn't be surprised if we found his ski mask," replies Hailey. "Right? He wanted something that made contact with the killer?"

"Anything is possible."

After an hour of searching through the jars and checking what everybody else looked at, I step back into the door of the barn and simply stare at the interior. We still have no sign of a cataloging system matching the jars.

"Should we look for secret panels?" asks Hailey.

"Not yet. We could try his study, but I think he wanted me to look here."

"Who cleans this up?" asks Mylo, pointing to the bloody workbench.

"They have private contractors. I wouldn't be surprised if he disguised himself as one of them to get samples from other cases."

Hailey steps over to the workbench and stares at a pool of blood that has seeped through a crack in its surface. She kneels and aims her flashlight at the floor beneath, where the blood should have pooled.

It's spotless.

"Where did all the blood go?" she asks.

CHAPTER FIFTY-FIVE
CODEX

We're sitting on the back deck of Forrester's house, reading his journals while lounging on his patio furniture. It's an odd sight. We all have on our gloves and masks. I had to chastise Mylo and Hailey several times, explaining how anthrax could be transmitted through contact with paper or even the furniture.

"So, how come they haven't quarantined this whole place off?" Mylo asked, looking around the property.

"Because I'm not exactly the most credible person to them," I replied.

"Oh, like the boy who cried wolf?"

"No," Hailey interrupted. "Like the boy who cried werewolf and Frankenstein and was right every time, but they refused to believe him when he said, 'Dracula.'"

"Er, yes. Something like that," I replied.

Most of our time has been spent calling out the different entries in the journal. They typically read like this:

5/00124

6/2/2000: Police arrested Norville Shenton for suspicion of murder. Implicated in five separate slayings of
young gay males and burying bodies in woods near workplace at 1244 Crossing Ave., Benson, AZ.

6/4/2000: Visited scene of second victim's death.
Removed bloodied rock. Entered Shenton's home, gathered biological samples. Got Shenton blood sample from
forensics.

Forrester seemed very interested in two things: collecting some
kind of trophy from the crime scenes and trying to get blood or tissue
samples from the killer, even going as far as doing on-site blood draws
dressed as a paramedic when he was close enough to make it to the scene
of the crime in time.

We've found a few vials of blood in the jars, but I don't think that's
where Forrester keeps his primary samples. More than likely he leases
freezer space from a medical services company.

We'll have to find out where that is and what's stored inside. "Any
luck finding anything about Dunhill, Marcus, or the Pale brothers?"
I ask.

"Nothing," replies Hailey. "Think he'd write up his crimes?"

"He does about visiting crime scenes," says Mylo. "Kind of
incriminating."

"Not exactly," I reply. "He could claim it's a work of fiction. If they
try to connect any of the forensic samples to those crimes, the problem
is that it opens up everything and introduces the fact that those investigations were compromised. Prosecutors would freak."

"And he said there were clues here?" asks Hailey.

"More or less. He really wanted me to see these. I'm sure it's not just because he's the most anally retentive serial-killer groupie in history."

"Whoa," says Mylo. "Check this out: We have a number forty-nine here. Gary Ridgway?"

"Green River Killer," I say. "Joe Vik's count is going to end up much higher. Oyo's, too, probably. Those numbers are what's proven. Some killers claim a lot more. Pedro López, the Monster of the Andes, probably has them all beat. Luis Garavito, *La Bestia*, had more confirmed kills, but forensics was a lot better by the time he was caught. His official number was 138."

"What's this guy's number?" asks Hailey.

"Three, I think. But if you count the murders committed by the people he infected, it's closer to twelve. Maybe higher."

Mylo looks over her notebook. "Do they count?"

"To the victims' families," I reply.

"Yeah, but how are they scored?" asks Hailey. "I mean, is there some kind of Wikipedia page for that? For being an accessory?"

"I don't know if anyone actually collects that data. It's kind of its own category."

"I'd consider him a serial killer," offers Mylo.

"Me too," says Hailey. "People are basically his guns and knives. Right?"

"I guess you could look at it that way. But it's a new thing. I'm not sure how people will wrap their heads around it."

"Damn," Mylo exclaims, looking at her phone. "I didn't realize that there were this many serial killers."

"Those are the ones we caught. The full list would be much, much longer. It has to be from a statistical point of view."

"And Ridgway is at the top for America? How come I never heard of him?"

"Because he wasn't as sensational as Bundy or Gacy. He was your run-of-the-mill kill-prostitutes kind of serial killer."

"They're called sex workers," says Mylo.

"How is that a better term?" asks Hailey.

Mylo shrugs. "So, is this asshole a first of a kind?"

"As far as I can tell. It's really hard to connect one person's actions to another person killing. I mean you could call Hitler, Mao, Stalin, Lenin, and Pol Pot the worst of the twentieth century, but only if you count other people doing what they ordered them to."

"What about FDR firebombing Tokyo or using the atomic bomb?" asks Mylo.

"First, *Truman* ordered the atomic bomb to be used. Second, civilian casualties in wartime are a harder thing to consider. Third, Hitler and the rest straight up ordered *millions* of their own people to be killed. Technically I don't think you're going to find a leader of any country that didn't give an order that led to civilian deaths. But can we focus on what's at hand? The sun is going to be up in a few hours, and we're losing time. Real lives are at stake. What am I missing here?"

"I don't see any hidden codes. Nothing that pops out," says Hailey. "The journals seem to be exactly what they are. Some psycho's version of stamp collecting."

I stand and stretch—immediately regretting it when my shoulder starts to ache. I lower it back down and walk to the middle of the lawn and stare at the barn. What was Forrester trying to tell me? He wanted me to see something.

Well, I have. I've seen his grotesque trophy collection and read through his journals. He's probably the greatest student of serial killers the world has ever seen. So, what?

What did Gallard say? This was a dick-measuring contest . . .

He's right . . . but it's not about me.

Fuck.

It's about Forrester and everyone in his evil menagerie. All the other serial killers are his real competition. Both Hailey and Mylo consider him a serial killer. Hell, the FBI will try to have him convicted as such. More importantly, that's how he sees himself . . . at least abstractly.

Forrester wasn't going to beat me by letting me live or killing himself. He planned to win by letting me watch helplessly as he did something else . . . something big.

Something enormous.

Forrester wants me to watch as he becomes the biggest serial killer in history while he sits there in his hospital bed.

But how?

Putting Hyde into air-conditioning units is unreliable, and I don't think he had the chance to scale it. Maybe he made a more virulent strain? Maybe . . . but would he be satisfied it would spread? Making something like that would be hard. Nations have tried that.

Okay, let's assume he's still working with the version of Hyde I found. How can he spread that as far as possible?

What did he say to me before shooting himself? "Theo thinks he has all the answers, when the fun has only just begun."

Just begun. As in recently . . . like *today*.

"We need to go," I yell to Hailey and Mylo. "Now!"

CHAPTER FIFTY-SIX

IMPOUND

We're racing down the highway in Hailey's Tesla. She's sitting in the driver's seat with her arms crossed while I nervously watch from the passenger side.

"You know you're not supposed to let go of the steering wheel," I tell her.

"You're not supposed to break into crime scenes and steal evidence."

"We didn't steal any evidence," I reply.

"I did," Mylo says from the back seat. "I always take a souvenir from an escape room. This one was kind of boring, to be honest. You need better puzzles."

"*What?* You know this is real, right?"

"Ignore her," says Hailey. "So where exactly are we going?"

"The hospital," I reply. "To Forrester."

"All right. And . . . ? Whatcha gonna do? Beat the information out of him?"

"In a roundabout way. I'd like to try to drug him first with something that will make him babble. Then ask him my questions."

"How long will that take?"

"Between kidnapping him out from under police supervision, breaking into the pharmacy, and getting him somewhere where we can dose him? A few hours."

"We're breaking into a pharmacy?" says Mylo.

"Maybe. Or I can just beat it out of him."

"Is this really the best plan you have?" asks Hailey.

"It would've been a horrible plan earlier today, but right now I'm out of options."

"How about hacking his computer?" suggests Mylo.

"No," Hailey and I say at the same time.

"He'll have unbeatable encryption," I tell her. "Plus, we don't know if that'll tell us anything."

"What about his phone?" asks Hailey. "That might be easier to hack. I'm sure I can find someone who has a gray box. Or we can sneak into his hospital room and use his thumbprint."

"We'd need his phone to do that. Chances are the police have it locked up in evidence."

"Why don't you go to the costume store where you got your doctor's outfit and get a cop uniform?" asks Mylo.

"I'm pretty sure that's a horrible plan. I stole this from the hospital laundry."

"Cops need to do their laundry, too," she answers back.

"I wish it was that easy. Having a uniform isn't enough . . ."

My mind follows a thread as I stare at the distant lights of a car lot. Forrester was dressed like a paramedic when he stopped me. His journals mention other disguises he's used, but I didn't see any in his closet.

Where does he keep them?

Unknown.

When does he need them?

When he goes to crime scenes—crime scenes that he tries to get to as soon as possible . . .

"Okay, change of plans. Follow my logic on this. I was shot by him in front of his house. He'd just come home. Right? Now I'm pretty sure he was expecting me to catch up with him at some point, but not so quickly. For reasons I won't get into, he just found out a day ago that he might have been identified. So that means he was in a hurry. The last place he spent a lot of time would be his car . . . in fact, he probably spends a lot of time in his car."

"Where is his car?" asks Hailey. "Did the police take it?"

"Yes," I reply. "Mylo, can you pull up the location of the Travis County Sheriff's Department's impound lot?"

"How about I do it?" Hailey presses a button and tells her car to show us how to get there, and a map appears on the center display.

Twenty minutes later, we're parked on the far side of the impound lot, which is brightly lit and heavily covered by security cameras. Any plans I had for using Hailey and Mylo to distract the guards are made irrelevant by the fact that there is nobody here to distract.

"Okay, you guys wait here." I glance up at the fence and feel my shoulder hurting. "And I'll climb this. Just watch for police."

"Why don't we pretend to change a tire or something?" asks Hailey.

"Do you know how?"

Both of them give me the look of death.

"Uh, sorry. Okay, then, would anyone care to help a wounded chauvinist over the top of the fence?"

Hailey follows me over to the darkest spot. We take her floor mats and throw them over the barbed wire at the top of the fence. I climb as high as I can, then clamp down on my jaw and throw part of my body over the fence, using the mats to keep from puncturing myself.

Hailey watches me struggle but doesn't say anything. I feel like pointing out my bullet wound but manage to keep my mouth shut.

"Just yell if someone's coming," I tell her.

"Anyone?"

"Use your judgment."

I walk through the cars until I find the black Ford Taurus that Forrester was driving. It's sitting in the middle of the lot with stickers that say "Evidence" on the windshield and driver-side door.

I check the doors. Locked. Assuming that they disabled the alarm when they towed it, I take the key chain from my pocket and use the tip of a brass key to hit the window.

It shatters into a thousand pieces. I glance around to see if anyone noticed, but the lot remains quiet.

All of this is being captured on video, of course, but I can worry about that later.

I climb into the driver's seat and start to look through the center console and the glove box. There are registrations, maps, napkins, bottles of aspirin, pens, paper clips, coins, and a hundred other random little items, but nothing that screams smoking gun—not even a gun.

Just in case, I reach under the seat and feel around. It's remarkably clean. Forrester probably has the Taurus professionally cleaned on a regular basis to remove trace evidence.

I sit back and try to think about where to look next.

Obviously the trunk, but what am I missing?

A shadow covers the passenger-side window, and I nearly have a heart attack until I recognize Hailey's grinning face.

"Let me in," she says.

I unlock the car, and she opens the passenger's door. "Whoops," she says, looking down, and throws a piece of trash back into the car, then sits down. "Well, Science Man?"

"I expect we'll find his costume collection in the trunk. Want to have a look?"

I pop the trunk, and we both get out.

Surprising neither of us, there are garment bags containing uniforms for a paramedic, security guard, postal employee, field tech, doctor, lab technician, and a half dozen others. There's also a box of ID badges to match. It's an impressive collection.

In the event that he gets randomly stopped and searched by the police, the garment bags all say, "Hollywood Motion Pictures Prop Rental."

Hailey and I lean against the trunk, arms folded. "Now what?" she asks.

"I don't know. There could be a million clues here." The sun is starting to rise in the distance. "I'm regretting not going with plan A."

"Beating the shit out of him? There's still time. He may not talk, but I'm sure it'll make you feel better," she says.

"I like your spirit." I point to the cameras. "You know they have you on tape now."

"I'm pretty sure it's not tape. But yes. I'll just tell them the world-famous Theo Cray told me I had to help him save the world. What girl could resist?"

"Good luck on that one." I stare at the asphalt, afraid Forrester has gotten the better of me.

"What could he have done in just a few hours?" asks Hailey.

"Poison a water tower. Sell it to the North Koreans. Put tampered pills on shelves."

"Okay, what would do the most amount of damage?"

"Giving it to an enemy power," I reply.

"Yeah, but he doesn't get the credit that way. He's a virologist, right? That's about vectors. The better vector, the better it'll spread?"

"Yes. In this case, Hyde is kind of weak. It takes long-term exposure or a very powerful initial dose."

"So what kind of vector could cause that?"

"You'd need some other factor. Some other means of distribution."

I go back into the car and search the floor and floor mats around the seats. "Look for anything. A receipt, a parking-garage ticket. Anything that looks new."

Hailey opens the back door and uses her phone light to search under the seats from the rear.

I shine mine under the passenger side and spot a long white strip of glossy paper. It wasn't there before—this is what fell out when Hailey got into the car.

I hold it up to the light. It's about twelve inches long.

Almost exactly. It's the backing to some sort of adhesive strip.

"From a shipping box?" asks Hailey.

"Was this inside the door?" I reply.

"Yeah. It fell out . . . it must have been tossed there."

"In a hurry. Damn."

We both start running back to the fence. I pray that Mylo didn't actually start changing a tire on the car.

CHAPTER FIFTY-SEVEN

TRANSIT

Hailey and Mylo fly across the parking lot toward the twenty-four-hour FedEx store like a couple of maniacs while I call Gallard from the car.

"Hello?" he says, sounding half-asleep.

"It's me, Theo. Listen carefully: Forrester is up to something."

"Yes. We talked about that," he replies. "Where are you calling me from?"

"I'm near Richmond. Forrester was probably trying to mail something. We're not sure how, but a box maybe a foot across. Probably a next-day-air package. I think he missed the shipping cutoff, so that means it could still be in a facility in Virginia or somewhere close by."

"Post office?" says Gallard.

"Maybe. Could be FedEx. We're trying to figure it out. Can you hold all packages at the facilities?"

"Are you kidding me? We can't even get a mail truck to pull over unless we have a federal judge tell us to. We need more than that."

"How about when the bodies start piling up? Will that be enough?" I'm shouting now. "I gotta go."

Hailey and Mylo come running back to the car with their arms full of flat boxes and envelopes.

"Everything okay?" asks Hailey. "Okay, dumb question. Here." She dumps a load of boxes into my arms.

We start comparing the size of the strip from Forrester's car to the FedEx and post office packaging.

"Close, but no," says Hailey as she tosses a box out the door. "Next."

"Nope," I reply, checking mine.

"Me neither," says Mylo. "Close, but nothing matches."

"All right, what about UPS?" I ask.

"Let me find the nearest supply center," offers Hailey.

"Hold on . . ." I get out of the car and pick up a FedEx and a USPS box, then get back inside. "What do you notice?" I hold the strip next to them.

"They're the wrong size?" says Mylo.

"What else?"

"The FedEx and postal strips have their logos on them. This is some off-brand shit," says Hailey. "Or a smaller carrier."

"A smaller carrier?" asks Mylo.

"Yes!" says Hailey. "We use a courier service at the office when it's real important stuff."

"And I use a specialty courier when I send lab samples. Damn it. Of course!"

I pull out my phone. "Look up the nearest FlowTrek center. They have special services for medical and laboratory."

"Got it," says Mylo. "Richmond International Airport. Forty-four forty-four Fox Road."

Hailey slams the Tesla into reverse and spins us around in the parking lot while I tap the address into the car's nav unit.

I realize that Gallard is calling me back. I pick up and put him on speakerphone. "Yeah?"

"Are you okay?" he asks.

"Yeah. We think we know where it's shipping from, but we're not sure. We're trying FlowTrek"—I spell it for him—"but someone should call all the local courier services. Can you do that?"

"It'll be hard."

Hailey speaks up. "Just go to their websites and pull up press releases. You'll find numbers for their PR people. Call their cell phones directly and ask them if they want to be famous for being the shipping service that helped a serial killer murder thousands of people."

"Who's that?" asks Gallard.

"Theo's accomplice," Hailey replies.

"Just do what she says," I say, then hang up.

Damn, she's clever.

We speed into the parking lot, and Hailey doesn't even bother centering the car. A light is on behind the glass door to the FlowTrek office. I burst out of the car and hurry inside.

Hailey beats me there because my shoulder screams when I try to run. She stops at the door and holds it open for me.

An older woman behind the counter peers over her computer. "Can I help you?"

"A man came in earlier. About my height. Early fifties, piercing blue eyes. Did you see him?"

"Is he single?" asks the woman.

"Uh, yeah. He murdered his wife in cold blood. Very single and could probably use a pen pal," I growl. "Did you see him?"

"What time?"

"I'm asking you!"

The woman looks at Hailey. "Is your friend always this rude?"

"It's, like, real fucking serious," she replies. "Like, people are going to die."

"Then don't you think we should call the police?"

"They're on the way," I lie, sort of. "I'm sorry, but I need to ask again: Was there a man like that here?"

"I got in at midnight," says the woman. "I'd have to call Robert. He has the evening shift."

She sits in place, unmoving.

"Well?" asks Hailey.

"Who exactly are you?"

"He's Dr. Theo Cray, world-famous serial-killer hunter."

"Oh. Never heard of you. Is that a television show?"

"Ma'am," I say, "you're going to be evening news if you don't call Robert and ask."

"I need to call the supervisor to okay this. Hey, what's she doing to my garbage?"

I turn around. Mylo has upended the garbage can and is sorting through the trash. Hailey drops to her knees and helps her.

"Call!" I shout at the woman.

"I found his *S*," says Mylo. She holds up a sliver of what appears to be a shipping-label carbon copy with an *S* at the top and part of a 2 below.

"Are you sure?" I ask.

"Yeah. I recognize that from his journals. Notice the anal way he tilts the *S* back at the top?"

I turn to the woman. "What time did the garbage go out?"

"Hell if I know."

"Okay. I notice you're not calling anyone right now, so answer me this. When did the last shipment leave?"

"Leave? Four thirty p.m."

Damn. "Wait? Is there another one?"

"Yes. But you just missed it."

"But you said four thirty was the last one."

"It left but hasn't shipped yet. Same thing. It's being loaded onto the airplane."

"Airplane? Which one?"

"The big white one. The only one being loaded."

I turn to Hailey. "Keys."

"Actually, it's a fob. What are you doing?"

"Don't ask. You're insured, right?" I toss her my phone. "Pin code is 3251914. Call Gallard. Then my lawyer."

I run outside and hop into her Tesla. I peel it around in a tight circle and race onto the main road that stops at a dead end where a fence blocks the airport runway.

In the distance, cargo's being loaded onto a 757 by an elevator lift. I back the car up as far as it can go, then press the button on the console that says "Insane Mode."

CHAPTER FIFTY-EIGHT
Hijack

Eight seconds later, I'm on the other side of the fence, dragging a section of it behind me as I speed toward the airplane.

Standard operating procedure when a maniac makes his way onto the runway is to shut down the whole airport.

After that, send the police to the problem area.

I estimate that I have about two minutes before the cops start flying like bats out of hell from wherever they're parked.

While getting the police to respond is great, their only concern will be to get me off the runway and flight operations back to normal.

At least there's a good chance that this will lead to a search of the FlowTrek plane's cargo, but because its cargo is time sensitive, there's the chance it won't. Too big of a chance to take.

I catch a glimpse of sparks being thrown into the air by the fence I'm dragging behind me. By the time I come to a squealing halt by the plane, the men loading it look baffled and somewhat afraid.

I jump out of the car, hold my hands in the air, trying to look as nonthreatening as a guy who just tore through a fence at two hundred miles per hour in a federally secured facility can, and yell, "FlowTrek! Did you load it?"

A man in an orange vest standing on the elevated lift points to the large container about to be loaded into the plane.

It would make sense that FlowTrek was last on and first off. This gives their cargo a speed advantage. Thank god it wasn't already loaded behind all the existing cargo. It would have been a long, drawn-out process. I probably would have needed hostages.

"Lower the lift!" I yell to the man at the top.

He turns to the other men on the ground near me. They're equally confused. Here I am, dressed as a doctor, acting like a lunatic . . .

I use it to my advantage. "It's a medical emergency."

A man on the ground approaches me. "What do you need?" He's the oldest one here and appears to be the supervisor.

I try to calm myself. "I need you to lower that container and open it."

"Are you threatening us?" he asks.

"Damn it." I notice there's an emergency release button on the lift. "Watch out!" I shout to the man on the platform above.

I slam the button, and the lift starts to descend. The supervisor grabs my bad shoulder.

I scream and jerk it away, spin around, and glare at him. "Touch me again and die."

The lift reaches the ground, and I notice flashing police lights and sirens in the distance.

The man backs up. "He's their problem now."

I glance down at the key ring on his belt. "Hand me those, now."

"Whatever, asshole." He drops them in front of me. "There are better ways to handle this kind of thing."

"I wish I knew what they are."

I grab the keys and flip through them until I find the one that unlocks the rolling door on the cargo container. I slide it open and reveal an interior half-filled with boxes.

The police cars come to a stop, and cops are running toward me, guns drawn. *Now what?*

Screw it. I climb inside the container, crawling over boxes to clear away from the door, then pull it shut behind me.

Let 'em come in here and get me.

It's a perfect plan until I reach for my phone to use as a light, then realize I gave it to Hailey to call Gallard.

Brilliant, Theo. Just brilliant.

CHAPTER FIFTY-NINE

VECTOR

All right, let's focus on the present.

I trapped myself inside a cargo container so I could find a roughly one-foot-by-one-foot-by-four-inch box that a deranged scientist is using to transport a murder virus.

The only problem is that I have no way to see the box because I accidentally locked myself in here with no light.

Bam! Bam! Bam! Someone pounds on the outside of the container.

"Sir, open the door and come out with your hands up!" yells a gruff voice.

"I can't do that," I shout back.

I start to sort through the boxes, trying to put my hands on anything that feels the right size. Each time I find one that comes close, I toss it to the front.

Bam! "Sir! Get out of there now!" yells the cop again.

I decide to stall. "Call Gallard at the FBI."

"Come out and we'll let you do that."

"Get ahold of him first," I shout back, still sorting through boxes. I have at least ten candidates so far.

"We can't let you continue to damage those packages. We're going to open the door!"

"Don't do that!" Actually, I could use the light. "Or . . . I'll hurt myself."

"Personally, sir, I don't care."

"Don't come in!" I desperately cast about, trying to find any more boxes.

"I'm going to open the door. Are you armed?"

"Would you stay out if I said I was?"

Damn it, I need light. I pull out the big key ring I swiped from the manager. He's got a small multitool attached to the chain. I swivel out something sharp.

I slam it into the roof of the container. It makes a *bang!* sound.

"Gun!" shouts the cop. "He's got a gun!"

Oh crap.

I lie flat, expecting a barrage of bullets to puncture the container.

Seconds go by, and I'm not dead. I still only have one bullet hole.

A few inches in front of me, a small, rough circle of light shines from the outside. Quickly, I pull packages from my pile and examine them in the tiny shaft of light. Most of them have typed addresses. I recall what Mylo said about the piece of carbon copy with Forrester's handwriting. His funky *S*. I need to find it.

"Sir? Are you okay?"

"Uh, yeah. It went off accidentally." I don't exactly say *what* went off. I need time. More time.

I make it through the last of the packages that *seemed* to be the right size. None has what looks like Forrester's handwriting.

What if I was wrong? What if he used another cargo carrier?

What if there's no package?

I have no idea how I'm going to explain my way out of this one. I might have to take a page from Forrester's book and try to fake a suicide.

Do I simply roll up the door and surrender? I can try to tell them I was under a lot of stress after getting shot . . .

Theo, you're in so stupidly deep at this point, what's the point?

You're not going to Bayesian-statistics yourself out of this one. No amount of machine learning can find the right pattern.

You screwed up. You screwed up big.

"Theo!" shouts the cop from outside. "We have your wife on the phone. She has a message for you."

Well, that's odd. I don't recall getting married.

"Uh, okay?"

"She says to call your psychologist. Do you need the number?"

Well, several things don't add up now. I don't have a phone on me. But something tells me my "wife" knows this. "What's the number again?"

"Dr. Mylo's number is 324-315-1515."

"Uh, thanks. Calling him now." I try to convince myself that I didn't just make a pretend phone with my thumb and pinkie. It's stressful in here.

Uh, 324-315-1515? What area code is that? And she knows I don't have a phone in here. Even if it's Mylo's phone number, it won't help.

Wait . . . is it a message? Wonderful, why not just send me Morse code, too, for all the good it will do. I don't have a phone or my computer.

Okay . . . 324-315-1515? How am I supposed to solve that in here?

Relax, Theo. She figured you'd get this. Start simple.

Three two four . . . What's that mean?

Well, the product of the three numbers is twenty-four. Um, not helpful. What else? The Wythoff symbol for a cube is 3|24. Okay. A cube. Like a package.

Then the number three, followed by three fifteens. Does three mean three of them? Or three dimensions? Oh, that would explain the 151515.

She's telling me to look for a cube-shaped box in the dimensions of fifteen by fifteen by fifteen!

I start sorting through packages again, this time looking for a cube. I try to make a new pile in a different part of the container—this time one that won't block the door.

A second later, I find a cube. Let's check it in the light . . . Oakline Media to STZ Digital. Typed. *Damn it.*

"Theo, we're hearing a lot of movement in there. Are you talking to your psychologist? We can't have you damaging anything."

"She put me on hold," I reply.

I keep sorting and quickly find another.

What's this one say? Oakline again. *Seriously, guys?* I reach down below my knees and find another cube.

"We're coming in, Theo. We're armed and will shoot."

"Wait!" The door starts to slide up. "Don't come in!"

I flip the box around, trying to find the label. It's cold. Unusually cold.

"I'll hurt myself!"

"You don't have a gun, Theo."

The whole container starts to move.

"What are you doing?" *Bam!* Something hits the container from the side, *like a fucking car*, and I'm thrown against the inside wall. The door flies open, and all hell breaks loose as men in tactical armor reach inside.

"It's a bomb!" I yell, clinging to the cold, cubic package. The men quickly stand back.

"Um, metaphorically speaking . . ."

I glance down at the label, heart racing, as Forrester's handwriting stares back at me.

My heart stops for a moment when I see what he's written on the label.

Oh god.

Oh dear god.

Let this be the only one.

It's undiluted flu vaccine.

There's enough in here to make one hundred thousand doses. The box has the CDC stamps and all the proper paperwork. It's addressed to the facility in New York where they prepare the dosage for the entire United States military.

Who knows what Forrester has done to make sure it would be used in the production line? I'd put nothing past him.

When the Taser hits my chest and I'm blasted with one million volts, I'm okay with it.

I can't move my arms. I'm twitching on the ground. Each pulse jerks me like a fish on a hook.

It's. Okay.

It could have been worse. Much, much worse.

CHAPTER SIXTY

AFTERMATH

My lab is quiet. Everyone else has gone home. Jillian dropped me off. It still hurts to drive. Hailey offered to buy me a Tesla to make it easier, but I declined to take her up on the offer. In part because I am not sure Jillian would quite accept that Hailey's sort of my protégée and not some younger competition.

Forrester was pissed when they told him I found his package. Real pissed. He tried to rip out his IV and had to be sedated.

I guess that means we got all of it. I pray.

If we hadn't . . .

It's not just that one hundred thousand doses of Hyde could have infected one hundred thousand soldiers . . . it's what one hundred thousand homicidal men and women in uniform could do. Most of them live at home in the United States.

It would have been an epidemic. An epidemic of murderers.

The FBI and the army are still trying to wrap their heads around it. The official story was that Forrester tried to taint the supply of flu vaccine but was stopped.

I like that story a lot better.

I flip on the lights and go into my inner lab. Hyde still has some secrets to reveal.

Figueroa knows I have samples from the crime scenes. Sooner or later, USAMRIID and the CDC are going to come collect them. But I have questions.

Forrester was trying really hard to make this thing fully airborne. Infecting one hundred thousand men and women during flu season might have led to enough mutations to make that happen.

I put on my clean-room suit and step into the negatively pressured chamber.

After checking my suit, I enter the code on the cold-storage safe and pull out the samples in the test-tube rack.

To be cautious, I place them in a sealed chamber so I can do an antibody test.

I'd ask Darnell to help me, but he's been pretty overworked since Todd left.

I'm going to try not to do so much on my own anymore. I'm going to think things through in a more commonsense manner and not just treat everything like a math problem.

Hailey and Mylo found the rest of Forrester's carbon copy of the shipping label and were able to piece together the shipment. That's how they got me the right dimensions. Hailey insists that if I hadn't driven her car through the fence and gotten airport SWAT to zap me into the next universe, the package would have gotten through.

Maybe. But I think we could have stopped it at its destination.

Live and learn, Theo. Live and learn.

Things are going to be different from now on. Figueroa sees the advantage of letting me have a little more latitude. The FBI, at least some of them, are starting to realize I can be of help.

I've also acquired a deep respect for them. Nobody is more tireless than Gallard, but a man who has to follow the law to enforce it doesn't have the same advantage as someone willing to break a few things and seek forgiveness later. The FBI's job is incredibly hard. If I ever have to sit in another conference room and explain something technical (god forbid), my first reaction when they don't understand won't be to storm out.

Things have to be different. I can only be so lucky for so long.

I pull the samples out of the rack and transfer them to the control grid. When I slide number four out, I notice that it feels lighter. Instead of containing the clear liquid the virus particles are suspended in, it's empty.

No, that's not true. There's a slip of paper inside. Did I leave filter paper *inside* the tube?

I use a pair of tweezers to pull it out. It's a folded slip. What *is* this?

My thick gloves don't make it easy, but I manage to spread the sheet apart.

There are five words written across it. As I read them, I notice the slightly acrid scent in my mask.

Try not to breathe, asshole.

;)

ABOUT THE AUTHOR

Andrew Mayne is the *Wall Street Journal* bestselling author of *The Naturalist* and *Looking Glass*, an Edgar Award nominee for *Black Fall*, and the star of A&E's *Don't Trust Andrew Mayne* and a Discovery Channel *Shark Week* special. He is also a magician who started his first world tour as an illusionist when he was a teenager and went on to work behind the scenes for Penn & Teller, David Blaine, and David Copperfield. Ranked as the fifth bestselling independent author of the year by Amazon UK, Andrew currently hosts the *Weird Things* podcast. For more on him and his work, visit www.AndrewMayne.com.